"Why didn't you ██████ what's going on?" Cole asked.

"Because I don't trust you," Tory blurted out. Her cheeks flamed the moment the words escaped. God, what if he asked her to explain what she meant by that? What the hell could she say? That she didn't trust him because he was too damned good-looking? Because he was one of the those damned Texans with an unfair share of good looks and charm? Just like—

But all he said was, "Wise woman."

Her glance flicked to his face. His eyes were shadowed, and there wasn't a trace of humor in his expression. As far as she could tell, he'd meant the words quite literally.

"I didn't mean to—"

"No, you stick to that, Victoria Flynn," he told ████ "I bring more trouble than you want to deal ██. Don't ever trust me. You'll be safer."

Dear Reader,

We're back with another fabulous month's worth of books, starting with the second of our Intimate Moments Extra titles. *Night of the Jaguar* by Merline Lovelace is the first of a new miniseries, Code Name: Danger. It's also a fabulously sexy, romantic and suspenseful tale of two people who never should have met but are clearly made for each other. And keep your eyes on two of the secondary characters, Maggie and Adam, because you're going to be seeing a lot more of them as this series continues.

Award-winner Justine Davis presents one of her irresistible tormented-but-oh-so-sexy heroes in *Out of the Dark*, another of her page-turning titles. And two miniseries continue: Kathleen Creighton's Into the Heartland, with *One Good Man*, and Beverly Bird's Wounded Warriors, with *A Man Without a Haven*. Welcome bestseller Linda Randall Wisdom back to Silhouette with her Intimate Moments debut, *No More Secrets*. And try out new-to-contemporaries author Elane Osborn, who offers *Shelter in His Arms*.

As promised, it's a great month—don't miss a single book.

Enjoy!

Leslie Wainger
Senior Editor and Editorial Coordinator

Please address questions and book requests to:
Silhouette Reader Service
U.S.: 3010 Walden Ave., P.O. Box 1325, Buffalo, NY 14269
Canadian: P.O. Box 609, Fort Erie, Ont. L2A 5X3

OUT OF THE DARK

JUSTINE DAVIS

Silhouette®
INTIMATE™ MOMENTS®
Published by Silhouette Books
America's Publisher of Contemporary Romance

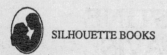 SILHOUETTE BOOKS

ISBN 0-373-07638-X

OUT OF THE DARK

Copyright © 1995 by Janice Davis Smith

Printed in U.S.A.

Books by Justine Davis

Silhouette Intimate Moments

Hunter's Way #371
Loose Ends #391
Stevie's Chase #402
Suspicion's Gate #423
Cool Under Fire #444
Race Against Time #474
To Hold an Eagle #497
Target of Opportunity #506
One Last Chance #517
Wicked Secrets #555
Left at the Altar #596
Out of the Dark #638

Silhouette Desire

Angel for Hire #680
Upon the Storm #712
Found Father #772
Private Reasons #833

Silhouette Books

Silhouette Summer Sizzlers 1994
"The Raider"

JUSTINE DAVIS

lives in San Clemente, California. Her interests outside of writing are sailing, doing needlework, horseback riding and driving her restored 1967 Corvette roadster—top down, of course.

A policewoman, Justine says that years ago, a young man she worked with encouraged her to try for a promotion to a position that was, at that time, occupied only by men. "I succeeded, became wrapped up in my new job, and that man moved away, never, I thought, to be heard from again. Ten years later he appeared out of the woods of Washington State, saying he'd never forgotten me and would I please marry him. With that history, how could I write anything but romance?"

To TSO—
Thanks for not giving up.
DWK

Chapter 1

Oh, great.

Tory Flynn watched the big, broad-shouldered man envelop the laughing woman in a bear hug. *Just what I need,* she thought, *a guy who can't keep his hands to himself even in the office. A guy who is so busy with his office squeeze that he doesn't even notice a prospective client standing in the doorway.*

Not, she observed wryly, that the woman seemed to mind. Most wouldn't, Tory admitted grudgingly. That six-foot-four inches of prime, dark-haired, steel-blue-eyed male on the hoof—or in this case, oddly scarred snakeskin boots—would have most women wishing for the kind of treatment that woman was getting. But most women decidedly did not include Tory Flynn. And unfortunately, it was Tory Flynn who needed Cole Bannister's help.

With Hobie's letter and the piece of paper she'd written the Sanders Protection address on both crinkling in her jacket pocket, she leaned against the doorjamb and crossed her arms, determined to wait out Bannister's heavy-handed flirtation. She wasn't above hoping he'd be embarrassed when he realized he was being watched by a total stranger and potential client. She couldn't believe this galoot was really a friend of Uncle Hobie's. She'd driven all the way to L.A. for this?

He released the woman at last, only to plant a loud, smacking kiss on her forehead.

Forehead? Tory's brow creased. That didn't seem particularly romantic. Not that she was an expert, by any means. But then, she had learned long ago that romantic gestures weren't worth a flyspeck. All the window dressing in the world didn't change the view.

"Damn, that's great news, Kyra!"

Lord, his voice sounded like two miles of gravel road. Rough and low and rumbling, sending a shiver down Tory's spine. She shook off the odd sensation.

Kyra, he'd said. Pretty name. But she wasn't a pretty woman. Unexpected combination, Tory thought, the gorgeous man and the not-so-gorgeous woman. She would have thought a man who looked like this would have been surrounded with nothing less than twelves on the proverbial ten scale.

But this woman *was* striking, Tory amended silently. Very striking. And tall. She looked nearly six feet. She carried it well, with a grace and style that made her rather ordinary looks unimportant. And she had beautiful eyes, Tory realized, a lovely blue-gray, and right now, they were glowing with so much happiness it nearly made Tory smile, even as it filled her with an odd emptiness she couldn't explain, and so ignored.

"When?" That voice again. "Do you know what it is yet? Are you all right? What does—"

"Whoa," the woman said, laughing. "In reverse order, I'm fine, we decided we don't want to know, and February."

The man grinned, widely. It was genuine, there was no doubting that, Tory thought, but the grin didn't quite reach his eyes. There was a darkness there in the steel blue, a shadow. As if, she thought suddenly, he felt that same odd, nameless emptiness she had.

"Damn," he repeated with a wondering shake of his head. "A baby. How about that."

Tory backed up a step, hastily revising all her estimations. She felt suddenly like the worst kind of eavesdropper, the judgmental kind. The man had the right to hug his wife didn't he, especially if she's just told him she's pregnant? If there had been a way to exit without being caught, she would have done it immediately.

"What does Cash think?" Bannister asked.

"He's torn between being elated and terrified."

"Have you gone public, yet?"

Kyra wrinkled her nose, making Bannister grin. "Not yet," she said.

"Can't hide it forever, darlin'," he said, grinning again. The hint of a Texas drawl that crept into his voice only added to his considerable charm. Except to Tory. "The first Riordan baby—you guys are headline news."

Riordan. Tory blinked. My God, this was Kyra Riordan. Even as out of touch as she was most of the time, Tory had heard of the fairy-tale romance of Cash Riordan and his lady bodyguard. But she hadn't realized this was the same agency the woman had worked for.

"Oops." The woman had spotted Tory. The tall, lanky brunette gave Tory a rather shy smile. "Sorry. I didn't know Cole had a client waiting."

"Neither did Cole," the man said.

God, that gravel voice did crazy things to her nerve endings. It's not fair, Tory grumbled silently, that he has the voice to go with those looks.

"Excuse us," Kyra said, blushing. And suddenly Tory thought she'd been totally wrong in her assessment of the woman's looks; she was beautiful. "I just had...some good news for Cole."

"I'm afraid I heard. Congratulations." Surprisingly, she found that she meant it. It was hard not to, when faced with the kind of joy that was glowing in Kyra's eyes. "And I promise not to run to the tabloids."

A trace of pained annoyance flashed in the brunette's eyes, and Tory knew she'd struck a nerve.

"I promise," she repeated. "I don't even wrap my trash in them."

Kyra smiled at her then, a sweet, genuine smile. "Thanks. I'm a bit touchy about that."

"I can imagine," Tory said fervently.

Kyra smiled again, and Tory wondered that she'd ever thought her plain.

"I'll leave you two to your business," Kyra said. As she left, Tory thought, unexpectedly and rather wistfully, that this was a woman she could grow to like. But she had no time now for friendships of any kind in her life. If it weren't for Hobie she'd have no one to talk to at all, except the horses.

The horses. They were the reason she was here, and she'd best remember that. She turned back to Cole Bannister, who was looking at her and frowning. And frowning, the big man was an intimidating sight. But Tory refused to be cowed. If a sixteen-and-a-half hand, green-broke stallion couldn't do it, this man certainly couldn't, either. Even if she found herself thinking there were probably more similarities between them than differences.

"You wanted to see me?" he asked after a moment.

"If you're Cole Bannister."

"Since you seem to have eavesdropped on everything else, I'm sure you heard that, as well."

Tory's chin came up. The charm he'd shown the tall brunette obviously did not extend to her, not that she wanted it to. But she would not let this man intimidate her, even if he was a foot taller than she was.

"I wasn't eavesdropping. I was standing right here in the doorway, all you had to do was look. Besides, the receptionist *told* you I was coming back here."

He stared at her, then let out a long, slow breath. He lifted a hand and shoved his thick, dark hair back with spread fingers. Another breath, short and compressed this time, and then, at last, he spoke.

"My apologies, Ms. . . . Flynn, was it? That was uncalled for, and rude. Usually I know better than to take out my moods on innocent bystanders."

As an apology, it was utterly disarming. Tory nodded shortly, accepting. But she didn't speak. She couldn't. A stunning realization had just come to her, a gut instinct she guessed was in reaction to some flickering look of resignation in his eyes.

He might have sincerely congratulated the woman, but inside he was quietly mourning. He loved her, Tory thought, the realization denting her assessment of him slightly. She would never have guessed a man who looked like this could care for a woman less perfect than he. But he loved Kyra Riordan. Or had. Because she saw that as well, that he was resigned to the fact that it would never be returned, not that way.

For a moment she almost felt sorry for him. As sorry as she could, that is, for a man who so blatantly had all the tools necessary to fly through life without a care; looks, charm, and a smile that could light up Houston—if it ever reached his eyes.

"Will you sit down?"

He gestured toward a chair in front of the huge desk. She took it, sinking down onto cushions more comfortable than she would have expected in an office chair. Hobie's letter rustled in her pocket, and she reached in to smooth it, wondering if she should give it to him now, or wait.

From a seated position, the desk before her seemed even larger—a broad, high expanse of heavy, dark wood. It and the huge leather chair behind it were the only truly expensive-looking pieces in the Spartan office, except for the computer that took up a corner of the desk top.

She realized as he sat down that the desk and chair were not an affectation; with his long legs he needed the size of both. Still, the heavy wood and the dark leather seemed more in keeping with the other offices she'd glimpsed on her way down the hall to this high-tech corner of the Sanders Protection offices. This part of the business was ultramodern, cluttered with computers, printers, faxes and other pieces of equipment whose purpose she could only guess at, but assumed were necessary to fulfill the promise made by the plaque on the outer door that said simply Research.

But then, this man seemed out of place here, too. She supposed she was succumbing to a stereotype to have expected a more studious-looking person to be in charge of all this high-tech equipment, but indeed, this tall, powerful man didn't look at all the type to spend his day at the keyboard that sat at his right elbow. He did, however, look like the rodeo rider Hobie had told her he once was. And determined—or stubborn, as Hobie put it—enough to insist on riding bulls when he was far bigger than most bull riders.

"What can I do for you, Ms. Flynn?"

Those words, in that voice, sent racing through her brain a couple of suggestions that shocked her. Where had those come from, those sudden startling images, images of strong, broad hands touching her, of steel blue eyes looking at her with warmth? Forgetting the letter, she blurted out the first words she could coherently form.

"My horses are dying."

He blinked. "What?"

Taking a deep breath, she shoved those disturbing images into the never-never land where they belonged. She'd been out on the ranch too long, she thought ruefully. When she spoke again, she was her usual businesslike self.

"I train horses, Mr. Bannister. Stock horses. And roping and cutting horses. With my uncle. We have a small ranch in the eastern foothills of the coastal range, near Summer Springs, inland from Santa Barbara. We've had three good horses die in the last two months. In this business, a good reputation is everything. We'll lose ours if this keeps up."

"Die of what?"

He'd leaned forward, dark brows furrowed, more than ever looking like he belonged in the other end of this office instead of this maze of electronic equipment. That stereotype again, she told herself.

"Two of colic." The old fury rose in her again. Her words became clipped, short. "Contaminated feed, they said. But that's impossible."

"Who's 'they'? The police?"

"No." She grimaced. "We're trying to keep them out of this. The last thing we need is this splashed through the headlines. There are rumors flying already, and that's bad enough." Her mouth twisted. "Besides, right now there's no evidence that would bring them in."

"Expensive horses?"

"Two," she said grimly. "One not so expensive, but still insured."

He looked thoughtful. "Insurance investigators, then?"

She nodded. "One from each company." She frowned. "They've been over the ranch with tweezers."

"I imagine so. They probably get a cut of whatever they save for the company. Each horse had a different owner?"

She nodded. "And a different insurer."

"They've collected?"

She nodded again. "John Lennox and Harry Crain have." She had to stop to steady her voice. "They owned the two they said were colic. The insurance people had autopsies done. They said they found evidence of bad feed in one horse's stomach." Her chin came up. "If they did, the feed wasn't from us," she repeated adamantly. "Every ounce of hay and grain is checked top to bottom. Regularly and personally, by either my uncle or me."

"What about the other colic case?"

"There was nothing unusual in his stomach, but the signs were similar, they said."

"And the third?"

She clenched her jaw, trying to rein in the rage that still threatened to overwhelm her every time she thought about it. She felt her hands curl into fists. She shoved them into her jacket pockets to hide the betraying evidence of her anger; the letter crinkled again. Hobie's letter. She took a deep breath. For Hobie's sake, she had to stay calm and convince this man to help them.

"A third had to be put down. Just last week," she said, her voice flat with her effort to keep it even. "He broke a leg. Shattered it. He was a gelding, and the owner didn't feel it was worth the cost to try and save him."

"How?"

"They—the third insurance company—said he slipped in a puddle left after a waterline running to the main pasture broke."

"And your version?"

She stiffened. Her eyes narrowed as she stared at his face, searching for the sarcasm she was sure had been intended in his words, if not his tone. She found only an expression to match the unreadable look in his eyes. And she thought inanely that her earlier characterization of those eyes as steel blue had been more appropriate than she'd realized at the time.

"That waterline was new. It had just been laid last year." Her voice was tight, strained.

"So you think... what? Somebody broke his leg, then broke the waterline to cover it up?"

"That horse didn't have a speck of mud on him, except his feet." She knew she sounded defensive, but when he stated what had been her theory, it sounded awfully far-fetched.

"And their explanation for that?"

God, she couldn't read this man. Was he buying any of her story, or laughing at her behind that cool gaze? She sighed and went on.

"They said he slipped and hit the bottom fence rail, but never went completely down."

"But you don't believe that."

"That horse," she said flatly, "*hated* water. He wouldn't even cross the tiny creek we have running along the north boundary. Freaked if you even pointed him at it. If it wasn't in a waterer or a trough, you couldn't get him near it. He would never have gone near that puddle, let alone run through it fast enough to slip.''

"And they didn't believe that?"

She shrugged. "They're insurance people, not horse people."

"And that explains it all."

There wasn't a trace of laughter in his voice, but Tory felt herself bristling anyway.

"Look, I came here for help. I need someone to come to the ranch, to find out what's going on. That is what you do, isn't it?"

He leaned back in his chair. His expression never changed, but Tory thought she saw the shadow in his eyes darken.

"No."

She blinked. "What?"

"No, that's not what I do."

Instinctively she glanced around once more, at the office that suited him, and the rest of the outer room that didn't.

"Yes, Ms. Flynn. What I do is research, just like the sign on the door says. Not fieldwork. Not ever."

The tone of his voice left no room for argument. Whatever this man had once been, this was what he was now. There was no help for them here.

"I'm sorry," he persisted, "but Sheila must have made a mistake. She shouldn't have sent you to see me."

"She didn't—" Tory stopped herself from admitting that she'd asked for him by name. She didn't trust this—or any other—too-handsome man, even if he was Hobie's friend. And if he was, and she brought Hobie into this now, she might not be able to get out gracefully.

"She didn't what?"

"Er, know what I wanted." That much was true, she hadn't told the receptionist what it was about, but Bannister's eyes narrowed as if he knew she was being evasive. Hastily, she went on. "Maybe I should talk to someone else."

He seemed about to ask something, then shrugged. "I'll be happy to find out who's available, Ms. Flynn."

Maybe that would be the best thing, she thought. Hobie must have been mistaken; he'd told her Cole Bannister was one of the best investigators around. Obviously Hobie hadn't talked to his old friend lately. Or maybe he had, and the ex-rodeo rider hadn't told him he was a desk jockey now. She wondered what had made Bannister change. He'd certainly seemed vehement about it.

"Someone who knows horses," she said when she realized he was waiting for a response.

He lifted one dark brow. "Now that could be a little tricky. Not a lot of call for that here in metropolitan L.A. Kyra did some work for a racing stable a couple of years ago, but that's about it."

That would be nice, Tory thought suddenly. Another woman around to talk to. Heck, anyone else to talk to. Not that she didn't love Hobie dearly, but she'd been working so hard to keep things going with just the two of them and some part-time help, she felt totally isolated from the world. She liked the idea of a woman. She liked even more the idea of not having to deal with this too-charming cowboy.

"Ms. Flynn?"

Reality shattered the pleasant if farfetched notion of finding a friend in Kyra Riordan. "I . . . er, how much does she charge?"

"She gets the going rate here. Three hundred dollars a day plus expenses for routine investigative work. But now that she's pregnant . . ."

Tory understood, not that it mattered. She didn't know whether to laugh or groan. That price was so far out of their reach right now it might as well have been a million an hour. They'd leased some new land last year, so they could run a few head of their own livestock for training purposes, and the cost of the land and the cattle had them so strapped they barely made expenses each month. It would pay off eventually, but she knew it was going to be in the long, long run.

She got to her feet. Bannister rose, too, whether from innate good manners or a desire to hasten her departure, she didn't know. She jammed her hands into her jacket pockets. The letter buckled beneath her fingers, and she barely resisted the urge to crumple it. This had been a wasted trip, a pointless effort. She was about to say a rather inept goodbye when a question, spoken in that low, gravelly voice, stopped her.

"If Sheila didn't know what you wanted, why did she send you to me?"

"I..." She couldn't see any way out of it. "I asked for you."

That dark brow lifted again, not in surprise but more as if he'd had a suspicion confirmed.

"I...heard your name somewhere, and that you knew about horses, from when you were rodeoing," she said quickly, giving him enough of the truth to hope that he'd let it drop. She turned to go. She heard an odd sound, half sigh, half groan. Then he stopped her dead for the second time.

"How is Hobie?"

She whirled, startled, her eyes wide. Bannister merely shrugged, but the shadow in his eyes had been replaced with something infinitely softer. To his credit, he didn't dissemble.

"I thought of him the minute I heard your name," he said quietly. "And I knew the minute I saw your eyes. You're Victoria."

It wasn't a question, and she didn't bother to answer—he obviously already knew he was right. She sank slowly back down into the chair. Her eyes had given her away to this man, those eyes that were that odd shade of blue-green, and the only feature she was proud of, no doubt because they looked exactly like her beloved uncle's.

Bannister was just looking at her, as if waiting for her to speak. She couldn't find any words. There was no point in keeping Hobie's letter from him any longer. She pulled it out, grabbing the piece of notepaper as it came out, too. She wadded it up with one hand as she held the letter in the

other. She still couldn't bring herself to give the envelope to
him.

"You were really going to leave without telling me,
weren't you?"

A little numbly, she nodded. Her fingers curled around
the letter.

"Why?"

She didn't think she could even begin to explain.

"Why, Ms. Flynn? You're Hobie's niece. He must have
sent you here, must have told you about me."

He didn't tell me what you looked like, she wanted to ex
claim. He didn't tell me you were one of those damned
Texans with an unfair share of good looks and oozing with
charm. Just like my father.

She shivered slightly and told herself it was because, even
with the big desk in between them, he seemed to be tower
ing over her. He never moved, but she felt pressured, any
way. It made her angry and, with a sharp movement, she
tossed the wadded up note into the big wastebasket, al
ready half-full of a discarded computer printout.

"Why weren't you going to tell me?" he repeated even
more insistently for a third time.

"Because I don't trust you," she blurted out. Her cheek
flamed the moment the words escaped.

He stared at her for a moment. She lowered her gaze,
horribly embarrassed. God, what if he, as any man would,
asked her to explain what the hell she meant by that? What
could she say? That she didn't trust him because he was too
damned good-looking?

He sat down once more in the big desk chair.

"Wise woman," he said.

Startled anew, her glance flicked to his face. His eyes were
shadowed once more, darker even than before. And there
wasn't a trace of humor in his expression. As far as she
could tell, he'd meant the words quite literally.

"I didn't mean to—"

"I bring more trouble than you want to deal with, so you stick to that, Victoria Flynn. Don't ever trust me. You'll be safer."

Chapter 2

Tory stared at him, and somewhere beneath her discomfiture stirred the knowledge that she had never seen so much loathing in anyone's eyes. And that it was directed entirely at himself.

"I'm Tory," she said suddenly, unable to bear that look any longer.

He blinked, the hardened expression wavering for an instant. "What?"

"Tory. No one calls me Victoria." Not anymore, she added silently. Yet another way she had cut all ties to the past, and the man who had always called her by her full name.

"Oh."

He seemed taken aback by her sudden softening. He let out a breath, a long, drawn out exhalation. And Tory, in spite of her decision not to, found herself wanting to ask again for his help. Would he react differently now, now that he knew who she was?

"We really do need help, Mr. Bannister. Uncle Hobie said you're the best. He wouldn't—"

"No."

That cold, masklike expression was back, looking even more impenetrable than before. Tory just looked at him for a long, silent moment. There wasn't a trace of pain in his voice or in his face, so she didn't know where she was getting the idea that beneath that mask was a man in agony. It was ridiculous anyway, that idea. Charming cowboys like this never felt anything that strongly. Her father certainly hadn't. And he'd been the most charming of all. And he'd also taught her the painful lesson that the more charm on the surface, the less substance there was underneath.

He seemed to think better of his peremptory response, and elaborated once more.

"I'm sorry, Ms. Flynn. I realize Hobie didn't know I'd...changed my line of work. I'm sorry I can't help you. But someone else—"

"No," she interrupted hastily, images of their already-drained checkbook forming in her head, "that's not necessary. We'll think of something."

His dark brows lowered. "You came all this way, you clearly need help—"

"It's all right," she said, cutting him off again. She tried desperately to think of something else to say. She could hardly tell him they'd hoped he would help for nothing, because of his old friendship with Hobie. Or if not that, out of a sense of obligation to Hobie. In fact, Hobie had been sure of it.

"He never had much in the way of family," Hobie had said. "So I kinda adopted him when he was a kid on the circuit. You just give him this to read, honey, and he'll come. He's a man who understands about friends in need."

But Hobie was wrong. People changed, and he hadn't seen this man in too long a time. One look at Cole Bannister now told her he didn't understand a thing about people in need. She'd never met a cooler, more self-possessed man in her life. Except maybe her father. But where her father had never turned off the charm—except with his family—

Bannister was apparently selective in whom he chose to turn it on for. She didn't know which was worse.

"I'm sure we can find somebody to look into this for you." Then, in an odd tone that made Tory feel like he was testing her somehow, he added, "I'll make sure you get the corporate rate. It's a bit lower."

"Not low enough," she muttered.

His eyes narrowed, making him look again like a man who had just had what he'd already suspected confirmed. Whatever that test had been, she thought, she'd apparently failed. His gaze shifted to her hand, where the letter was now crushed beneath her fingers.

"Why don't you quit torturing that letter and give it to me?"

Her breath caught, her eyes widened.

"It's from Hobie, isn't it?"

"I... How did you know?"

"You've been fiddling with it like a set of worry beads. And I know Hobie wouldn't send you here alone without ammunition."

Bannister's voice had taken on a wry tone that told her volumes about how well this man knew her uncle. She smothered a sigh and smoothed out the creases her fingers had put in the letter. Then she held it out to him.

For a moment she thought he wasn't going to take it. When he did at last, he made no move to open it. He stared at the writing on the envelope. Then he shifted his unreadable gaze back to her face.

"Why didn't he come himself?"

"He's... been sick."

Something flickered in that steady gaze, then, something sharp and tense. Worry, she realized suddenly. He was worried about Hobie. She felt a flood of relief; he *was* Hobie's friend, and she'd been right to give him the letter.

"He's going to get well," she said quickly, positively. "It's just that he had a bad case of pneumonia about six months ago, and he hasn't gotten his strength back, yet."

He seemed to relax, and returned his gaze to the envelope. But he didn't open it.

"Do you want me to leave?" He looked up sharply, as if startled. She nodded at the letter. "So you can read it in private?"

His forehead creased. "You don't know what it says?"

She shook her head. "Uncle Hobie just told me to give it to you."

He turned the envelope over and studied the back. When he realized what he was doing, she felt like he'd reached out and slapped her.

"You don't need to check the flap," she snapped out. "I don't read other people's mail, Mr. Bannister."

He looked up. To her amazement, a tinge of color stained his chiseled cheekbones.

"Sorry," he muttered. "Force of habit."

He lowered his gaze to the envelope, stared at it for a long moment, then finally moved to open it. His fingers were long, Tory noticed as he unfolded the letter, tapered yet strongly masculine, and his nails were neatly, bluntly trimmed. Yet his hands were used—scarred here, calloused here. Like Hobie's hands, marked from years of ropes, reins and hard work. An odd thing to notice, she supposed—

She heard an odd sound, that half sigh, half groan again. Her gaze shot to his face. His eyes were closed, and for a split second she saw such pain in his expression that she found herself holding her breath. But then it was gone, so swiftly she thought she must have misinterpreted the look— no one could turn off such pain so quickly. It was just a false impression she couldn't shake, this idea that he was in such misery.

"I—" His voice sounded oddly taut, and he broke off abruptly, then coughed, as if her perception wasn't so far wrong after all. But again, when he went on, it seemed as if she'd imagined it; his voice was cool and even.

"I'm sorry I can't help you, Ms. Flynn. But I don't do what you need done, anymore."

So Hobie really had been wrong. Whoever or whatever this man had once been to him, he wasn't any longer. She sighed inwardly; she hated the thought of Hobie being let down. He had been disappointed too often in life.

"I'll...help you, though. I'll find someone who can handle this, and I'll take care of the cost—"

"No, thank you." Her uncle might call in a favor, but he would never take charity. "Hobie would never... He wouldn't want that."

"No, I don't suppose he would." Bannister's voice was flat, inflectionless.

"I'm sorry to have bothered you." She stood up. "Thank you for seeing me," she said politely. She held out her hand, and after a long, silent moment, he took it. Although it lacked the used, rough skin of Hobie's, his hand was strong. And warm. And surprisingly gentle. None of which explained the odd little sensation that raced along her skin as his fingers grasped hers.

She almost jerked her hand back, barely managing to make the movement merely quick instead of panicked. Her gaze flicked to his face, hoping he hadn't noticed. For a split second he looked as startled as she had felt. And then, as solidly as if it had been a physical thing, a wall seemed to come down between them.

"I'm sorry your trip was wasted," he said stiffly. "Good afternoon, Ms. Flynn."

She nodded and turned away. She was at the door when she heard the sound of paper being crumpled. She didn't look back. If Cole Bannister was throwing Hobie's letter away, she didn't want to see it. She closed the door behind her, and wondered how she was going to tell her uncle that his old friend wasn't the man he'd thought he was, at all.

The room was quiet and dark, although it was nearly dawn. Cole sat on his battered sofa, his sock-clad feet up on the corner of the old trunk that served as a coffee table in his small rented half of a duplex, his eyes gazing fixedly at nothing. It was a technique he'd perfected long ago—this floating, this drifting in the dark, thinking about nothing.

But tonight he was having trouble. Not the usual trouble, it wasn't the old, painfully familiar images that threatened his calm tonight, no ghosts, no visions of blood and echoes of screams. Tonight it was simply the memory of a pair of blue-green eyes that flitted around the edges of his consciousness, tapping gently but persistently, not demanding entry but wearing him down like the wind wore stone down to desert sands.

Hobie Flynn's eyes. All the old jokes, come to life in the face of his niece. How often had they teased the man about his woman-beautiful eyes—that deep, startling turquoise color, and the thick, soft lashes, so unexpected in the weathered, scarred face? They'd been merciless, that rowdy bunch of young rodeo tramps. And Hobie had merely grinned, saying the good Lord had simply been making up for the odd arrangement of the rest of his features. That had generally shut them all up. They all knew that Hobie Flynn's face and wiry body bore scars that carried every one of their names. There were few of them who didn't owe him. Some more than others.

Well, there was nothing odd about the arrangement of Tory Flynn's features. Her chin was a little stubborn looking, and her nose had a sassy tilt to it, but her lips were soft and full, her jaw delicate and feminine in line. He didn't know where the streaky, sandy hair had come from—he'd never met Hobie's brother, the girl's father, and Hobie's was a bland brown—but those eyes were Hobie's, and as striking in a female face as they had always told Hobie they would be.

Not to mention the rest of her, even clad as she was. She clearly hadn't dressed up for this meeting. Or maybe she had, he amended, remembering her tension about money. Maybe the clean but well-worn jeans and the battered boots were the best she had. The shirt had been newer, a bright turquoise-and-white Western pattern that had made those

eyes even more vivid, and had hugged feminine curves as
sweetly as the jeans had.

Girl, he thought suddenly, was not the word. Victoria
Flynn was all woman.

You're a real class act, Bannister, he thought grimly. She's
Hobie's niece, for God's sake. For that alone she deserves
a hell of a lot better than having you assess her body parts
like she was a prize filly you're looking to buy, or some bar
pickup you're planning to take home. Especially you. And
for more reasons than what you owe Hobie.

Not to mention that she looked exhausted, physically and
emotionally. Those dark circles and weary eyes were not
simply the product of the lack of sleep that went with a long
drive. She'd been under a strain for a long time now, and it
showed. He recognized the signs, he'd confronted them too
often in his own mirror not to.

And that, he told himself, was proof that it was a damn
good thing he was strictly flying a desk now. It would be a
major mistake to make an exception, even for Hobie. This
case had all the earmarks of another Bannister disaster—a
woman, a man she loved, and, if she was right, somebody
else who was playing very dirty. All the elements he had such
a knack for juggling into tragedy.

He heard a faint scrabbling, the distinctive sound of claws
tugging on fabric. A rangy gray shape, looking like a lighter
piece of the darkness, moved toward him soundlessly across
the cushions of the couch.

There was that, too, he thought. If he left, who would
feed Rocky?

He nearly laughed out loud.

God, you've reached a pretty pass, he told himself scathingly, when you start using this mangy, raggedy-eared cat
that's not even yours for an excuse.

The pale, smoky-colored cat stopped at his own invisible
boundary; the next sofa cushion was close enough, sharing
the same cushion was entirely too intimate for his inde-
pendent nature. He'd been on Cole's doorstep one night, as
if waiting for his arrival, with an air of regal condescen-

sion. Cole's dislike for cats in general had been muted by the animal's ripped, bloody ear, and he'd left it alone instead of chasing it off as he usually would have done. For a couple of weeks it hung around, never begging, or intruding, but just there. One day he had surrendered to an impulse he'd regretted ever since; while stopping in at a local convenience store for a newspaper and a cup of coffee, he'd bought a can of cat food. And when he'd arrived home, he had been treated to a condescending look of congratulations that he had finally figured it out.

"You got along just fine on your own before, you can damn well do it again," he muttered to the cat as he leaned over and switched on a lamp. Rocky blinked once, unimpressed. And apparently unfrightened by the threat.

"Go find somebody else's snakeskin boots to claw on," he said, still disgusted that he'd actually taken to pulling the boots off before he ever got into the house because of the silent—and sneaky—animal's damaging aversion to the expensive footwear. He'd finally stopped clawing at them while Cole was in them, but abandoned they were fair game.

"Fine thing when a man can't even wear his own boots into his own house."

The cat yawned widely.

"I keep telling you, I don't even *like* cats."

The tip of the raccoonlike tail, that went so perfectly with the bandit-masked face, twitched.

"Why the hell did you pick here, anyway? Couldn't you go hang around Mrs. Waldon's or something?"

The cat made a tiny, expressive, sniffing sound. And Cole had to admit, the idea of battered, rough-and-tumble Rocky cavorting with his landlady's disdainful, temperamental Siamese made for an unlikely picture. And it almost made him smile.

Almost. There was something a little too unnerving about the steady stare of those pale blue feline eyes. Thinking of this pair of blue eyes reminded him yet again of another pair, tinged with green, rimmed with soft, thick lashes.

And he was back to square one, wrestling with the problem that had driven him to this sleepless night of staring into the darkness.

"Damn."

It came out sharply. It echoed in the empty room, mocking him. Rocky's head tilted as the cat looked at him steadily, unblinkingly. Cole glared back.

"What are you staring at? Worst thing you've got to worry about is being a hot lunch for some urban coyote."

Abruptly, as if expressing his opinion of that statement, the cat turned his back on Cole and plopped down to go easily to sleep.

"Damn, I hate cats," Cole muttered. All this one was was a half-welcome distraction from a problem he had no answer to.

It should be so simple. He didn't do that kind of work anymore. Period. End of explanation.

But it wasn't that simple. Nothing ever was, not when you were talking about debts the size of life and death. So add it up, he told himself. Balance the record, Bannister. Three people dead, because it took you so damned long to catch on. Three ghosts, who will haunt you to the end of your days. Stack it against the debt you owe Hobie Flynn. Against the promise you made him, that some day you'd pay him back.

The bottom line added up to zero.

It always did.

He wasn't going anywhere. The best way he could repay Hobie was to stay the hell out of his life. And that was that.

Maybe he should just send someone else, over her and Hobie's protests, and foot the bill. He hadn't spent much in the past five years, he could certainly afford it. But who? Kyra was the only one with any experience dealing with horses, and even if the Flynns would let her stay, he certainly wasn't about to ask her, not when she'd just discovered she was pregnant.

So, somebody else. You can find someone. Someone who will understand that this job is different, that . . . that what?

That you owe a personal debt, the greatest of personal debts, but you want somebody else to pay it? You want to buy your way out of the biggest obligation a man can have?

God, he couldn't deal with this anymore. He'd made the decision. It was over.

He'd fix a cup of coffee, he thought. Or maybe catch a few winks on the sofa, even though it was six inches too short to accommodate him comfortably—provided he could move the damn cat. But there was no point in going to bed, not now, at—he glanced at his watch—after four in the morning.

He yawned, then stretched expansively as he considered the risks of physically moving a sleeping cat who was more used to alley fights than civilized reactions to sudden moves.

The sound of paper crinkling in his shirt pocket stopped him before he made what could have been a fateful decision, and spurred him into making what surely was. He reached in and tugged out Hobie's letter. And the second piece of paper he'd retrieved from his wastebasket just as the janitor had been about to empty it. He sat staring at them for a very long time.

Tory yawned as she stood before the motel room mirror. She should have gone back home last night instead of waiting until dawn, she thought as she neatly twisted her long mass of hair into a knot at the back of her neck. There was nothing left to accomplish here after her futile meeting with Bannister. She hadn't slept, anyway. And it would have saved the cost of this small room, an economy she should have taken advantage of after recklessly splurging and buying that new hat for Hobie. She'd been so terrified when he'd gotten sick this winter that she hadn't been able to resist treating him. It would have been rough, driving both ways in a day, but she should have done it. Never mind that she wouldn't have pulled in until midnight; at least she would have been home.

And she would have behind her the unpleasant task of telling uncle Hobie that his trusted friend had let him down.

Sighing at the thought, she grimaced at her image, then retreated to the bathroom to wipe away a fleck of mascara from beneath her right eye. She rarely bothered with makeup at the ranch, so was unused to it when she did apply it. The horses never cared what she looked like, and her daily work wasn't conducive to anything except sweat and dirt.

There was nothing she could do about the dark circles beneath her eyes. She never slept well away from home, and yesterday's frustration had only added to her restlessness. She frowned at her reflection, then grimaced again and turned away. Her looks were nothing to write home about anyway, not with her snub nose and too-wide mouth, so what did dark circles matter?

She went back to the bed and folded her shirt—the one dressy shirt she owned, her wardrobe consisting mainly of work clothes and a few leftovers from another life—and tucked it into one side of her saddlebags. The bags, given to her by Hobie in a flush rodeo year long ago, were the closest things she had to any kind of luggage. They served well enough, and she treasured them because they were from Hobie. She put her hairbrush and toothbrush in the other side, then slung the bags over her shoulder and headed for the door. She'd paid for the room in advance, since she had wanted to get an early start back without the bother of checking out.

She tossed the bags onto the front seat of the white Jeep wagon, then paused for a last stretch before she climbed into the cab for the long ride. She would push as hard as she could; she wanted to get home. She only hoped that when she got there, there wouldn't be more bad news, another disaster to deal with.

She had her foot in the Jeep's cab, ready to clamber in, when she sensed the movement behind her. She whirled, muscles tensing—this was, at least to her, the big city, and awful things happened here.

In this case, the awful thing was, unexpectedly, Cole Bannister.

She felt the tension drain out of her as she recognized him. Then, as she looked at his face, she wondered if she hadn't been a bit premature. He looked like a man who had, as Hobie was wont to say, been rode hard and put away wet. And he looked like he'd gotten no more sleep than she had.

"What are you doing here?" she asked, only hearing the abruptness in her voice after she'd spoken. Something about this man truly unsettled her.

"I was looking for you."

God, his voice was even rougher this early in the morning. Kind of sleepy. Sexy, like a man still in bed among rumpled sheets. With a woman he'd pleasured thoroughly.

As if she knew what a man would sound like then, she snapped inwardly, furiously embarrassed at the turn her thoughts had taken.

"Well, you found me," she said, snapping at him almost as vehemently as she had at herself. Then, embarrassed yet again by her rudeness, she asked hastily, "How *did* you find me?"

He shrugged. "That note you tossed in my wastebasket."

She blinked, then remembered she'd written the address of the Sanders office on the notepad with the motel's name and address on it.

"And they told you what room I was in?" Maybe she didn't do this often, but she didn't think that was usual.

His mouth quirked, softening his usually harsh expression. He nodded at the Jeep. "You weren't exactly hard to find."

She felt color tinge her cheeks—in reaction to her foolishness, she was sure, not at the little frisson that had raced up her spine when he'd almost smiled. The logo of the ranch decorated both doors, proclaiming her presence.

"Oh." She tried to smile. "Guess that's why you're the detective."

His expression again turned chilly. "Was, Ms. Flynn. I'm very...rusty. I've been out of the field for a long time."

"You don't have to explain." She wished he would finish, so she could be on her way. "It's all right, Mr. Bannister. I understand."

She put her foot on the running board again.

"But Hobie won't."

She looked back at him. She was tired, she wanted to go home and she didn't have the energy to lie.

"No," she agreed, "he won't."

No, Hobie wouldn't understand a man who let down a friend, she thought. He never would do it himself. Hobie just wasn't that way. Besides horses, he'd told her often enough, friends were all you had in this life. Your family was stuck with you. Friends were there because they wanted to be.

And Bannister was looking at her as if she'd said everything she'd just been thinking. But she was too weary to care about his feelings, if indeed the man had any. From her experience, men who looked as he did rarely had the time—or the need—for such things.

She pulled herself up onto the cab floor and stood there. For a moment she savored looking down at him instead of craning her neck to look up. But then she realized, by the sudden narrowing of his eyes, that she'd put her breasts at his eye level, and much too close. Flushing, she sat down on the edge of the driver's seat.

To her surprise, he averted his gaze, as if he'd sensed her embarrassment. She'd have thought he'd be pleased, knowing the little country girl was flustered. Instead, he seemed to intently study the painted logo on the door as he leaned against it.

"I owe Hobie my life, you know," he said softly, unexpectedly.

"No. No, I didn't know."

He nodded toward the door. "'The Flying Clown Ranch,'" he read, almost under his breath.

"Yes."

Hobie had laughingly said that he'd named it after the way he'd spent most of his life. He'd been joking, but Tory had thought it more than a fitting tribute to the rodeo clown who had saved the lives of countless rodeo cowboys, at great cost to himself. Apparently one of those cowboys had been Cole Bannister.

Bannister straightened up. "I'm rusty," he repeated, "and out of practice."

"Mr. Bannister—"

He kept on, with the determination of a man who was saying something distasteful but had no choice. "It's only fair to warn you. I'm not what I used to be, what Hobie remembers. I've lost...my edge. But I have no choice. I owe Hobie. More than I can repay. If you're willing to take the chance, I'll try."

"That's all Hobie ever asks of anyone," she said softly. Then, as his expression abruptly returned to stony remoteness, she added rather grimly, "And we have no choice, either."

Chapter 3

Rocky yowled in protest as the pickup hit another deep chuckhole.

"Shut up," Cole told him unsympathetically. "Coming along was your idea. You and that kid maneuvered this, now live with it. You go crazy on me, and you're out the door."

He still couldn't quite believe how he'd been manipulated. Bobby Waldon, the twelve-year-old nephew of Cole's landlady, who was spending the summer with his aunt—and who had named the battle-scarred cat in the first place—had shown up early that morning as Cole had been trying to load up the truck, while Rocky kept climbing into the cab and Cole kept taking him out.

"Going away?" the boy had asked, eyeing the large duffel, the case for his notebook computer, the small binoculars he usually kept in the glove box and the old, worn straw cowboy hat he'd tossed on the dash.

Brilliant deduction, Cole nearly said, but managed not to snap at the boy in his aggravation at the annoying cat.

"Yes."

"For how long?"

"Don't know," he said shortly as he lifted the cat once more off the seat, set him outside, and replaced him with a cooler full of cold sodas. The air-conditioning in the old truck was questionable, and he hadn't gotten around to fixing it yet. He'd hung on to the truck for several years because it was the only thing he'd found comfortable for his height, and things were starting to go wrong with it. But it perfectly fit his meager cover as an itinerant ranch hand, hired to help out at the Flying Clown Ranch while Hobie was recuperating.

"Want me to feed your cat while you're gone?"

Cole jerked upright, whapping the back of his head on the truck's roof. He bit back a curse. "It's *not* my cat," he growled.

"Sure he is. He picked you, didn't he?"

Cole rubbed the back of his head as he gave the boy a warning look. Bobby merely shrugged.

"Aunt Marge says cats decide who they belong to."

"You mean who has the privilege of being the designated feeder," Cole retorted sourly as Rocky scrambled back into the truck. He took up a position atop the cooler, seemingly pleased with the better view this afforded.

"Same thing, to a cat, I think." Bobby grinned as Cole again scooped the cat up and set him on the ground. One corner of Cole's mouth twitched slightly. A wry chuckle escaped, and Bobby's grin widened as the cat evaded Cole's grasp and clambered back into the truck.

"Damn," Cole muttered under his breath. "I thought cats didn't like cars."

"Guess you'll be taking him with you, huh?"

"No." Cole picked up the cat, set him down outside and this time shut the truck's door.

Bobby's brow furrowed. "Then you do want me to feed him?"

Cole had his mouth open to repeat that the cat had gotten along fine before he'd foolishly succumbed to the lure of that can of cat food, and it could no doubt do so again, but as he looked at the boy's face, he couldn't quite say the words. Nor did he feel up to explaining how he'd planned to simply drive away, and let the cat worry about himself. Cats were supposed to be good at that, weren't they?

Bobby's expression cleared suddenly. "I think he's decided he's going along," he said, pointing.

Cole turned to see Rocky sitting once more atop the cooler, an expression that could only be described as smug on his bewhiskered, masked face, the open window in the passenger door explaining his presence.

"Cats are like that, Aunt Marge says. They choose somebody, and that's it."

And so here he was, Cole thought now, cruising along in the midday heat of an inland California summer day, out of cold drinks, with an air conditioner that didn't work and a worse-for-wear street feline who'd made the sad mistake of adopting someone who hated cats. And all because he'd been too soft in the head to just leave it, and too embarrassed to ask a twelve-year-old to feed the pesky animal, because it was too close to saying that the cat was his. He'd known from the first that this whole trip was a mistake; so far nothing had happened to change that assessment.

When he finally pulled up in front of the drive that led onto The Flying Clown Ranch, he stopped for a minute, a little startled. He'd done some checking in the two days before he'd left, in between winding up or reassigning the things on his desk. He had a few contacts left from his rodeo days, and they'd put him in touch with some people who dealt in the stock-, roping- and cutting-horse business. A business that was booming, flush with new money as more and more wealthy and celebrated people took an interest in the sport of cutting. These days, one old-time trainer told him wryly, there were more Hollywood and show business types at cutting futurities than at movie premieres. It was, the grizzled veteran told him disgruntledly, getting to where pretty soon only big syndicates would be able to afford the game, like in horse racing.

And while the people he'd talked to had universally spoken of the Flying Clown Ranch with respect, and genuine liking for the Flynns—with only a scant mention of a bit of trouble they'd been having—nothing they'd said had prepared him for the spread before him. He'd somehow pictured, perhaps because of Tory's obvious money concerns, and the fact that she and Hobie were virtually running it alone, a more shoestring kind of place.

But the Flying Clown, although small, was the picture of prosperity, at least on the outside. He pushed his battered straw hat with the rodeo-creased crown—even more battered from being shoved in the back of a closet for longer than he cared to remember—back on his head as he studied the layout before him.

Everything looked recently painted, even the long stretch of white board fence that lined the drive, not an easy feat in the sometimes blistering California sun, which took its toll on paint rather quickly. The barn looked in good repair, as did the long, low house that sat off to one side in the shade of a stand of towering eucalyptus trees that looked out of place among the scattered scrub oaks.

The Jeep Tory had driven was fairly new, too, he realized, now that he thought about it. And now that he thought about it, it all made sense. You didn't draw the kind of people who had the money to spend on horseflesh that could run into seven figures with a shabby, run-down operation, and Hobie Flynn was shrewd enough to know that. And the smallness only gave a sense of exclusivity; another thing Hobie was shrewd enough to realize and cash in on.

One corner of Cole's mouth lifted in tribute to his old friend. *You did it, Hobie. Everything you always said you were going to do, thinking about the future when all the rest of us fools were only thinking about our next entry fee.*

And nowhere was there a sign that disaster loomed. That death had already struck three times.

Sobered, he put the truck back in gear, fighting off misgivings once again. He knew he could function marginally as an investigator by virtue of the intimidation factor of his size alone; people generally thought twice about cross-

ing him. He would just have to hope, he thought grimly,
that for this case, sheer size would be enough.

He drove slowly up the drive, glancing around. In the
distance, on the flat, and on the hills far behind the house,
he could see a few head of white-faced cattle. In the pad-
dock next to the barn stood two well-muscled horses, a
rangy sorrel and a close-coupled buckskin who looked like
he could stop on a penny and give you change.

As he got closer, he found himself breathing deeper, rel-
ishing the rich scent of the air. It was an inimitable smell—
a combination of cut alfalfa, sweet feed, fresh air, sun-
baked earth and the living, breathing scent of horses. Some
fastidious types, or those who preferred the aroma of car
exhaust or industrial smoke found it offensive. Cole felt like
he was coming home.

He pulled to a stop in front of the house. There was no
sign of anyone, but he'd made good time and was a bit early,
despite a small contretemps when Rocky had decided that a
cool, shady roadside rest was a good place to while away an
hour or so. Only when Cole had started the truck and begun to pull away did the cat believe his bellowed "Now or
never, cat!" and make a run for the still-open passenger
window. Cole seriously considered not slowing down, but
figured the damn cat would probably just take off after him,
and he'd look pretty silly driving along with a raccoonlike
cat chasing him. Rocky made it in a scrabbling, clawing
leap, then settled into his spot atop the cooler, grooming
himself placidly, as if he'd planned it that way. And he
probably had, Cole had thought then, rather acidly.

And now Rocky was sitting up, looking around with interest. Cole could see his whiskers move as his oddly pink
nose twitched at the new scents.

"When the cat food runs out, you're on your own," he
warned. "Time to get back to your roots, cat. Probably lots
of mice around here. You'd better hope so, anyway."

Rocky let out a tiny yowl. Cole wasn't sure what it meant,
and decided he was probably better off not knowing. He

opened the truck door, and just then heard the sound of a door sliding open from the direction of the barn.

Tory was there in the shadowed doorway, untangling the trailing reins of a bridle. She wore a bright-red sleeveless T-shirt tucked into black jeans, faded from wear, Cole guessed, not some manufacturer's process. A pair of slim, shotgun chaps encased her legs, and he was suddenly struck with the notion, after all those youthful years of seeing them and wearing them, that chaps were sexy. Not so much because they delineated the long, slender line of her legs, but because of the way they stopped short of her tautly curved, jeans-clad hips and backside.

She looked up as if she'd felt his intense gaze. She waved, hung the bridle up just inside the door, then started walking toward him. He'd never seen her in full sunlight, only in the office and the gray light of dawn. The hair that had seemed a sort of sandy brown with lighter streaks, in the sun turned into a glorious meld of gold and amber and a flaxen shade that reminded him of the mane of a little sorrel mare he'd had as a kid.

Horse had had the same sassy look to her, too. She'd been the sweetest, most giving—and trusting—horse he'd ever known. And she'd died trying to jump an arroyo for him. It was the first time Cole had ever cursed himself, as he crouched there beside her broken body, a fourteen year old face-to-face with the results of his own bad judgment for the first time. And it was the first time someone else had paid for it. But not the last.

The memory stirred in his mind like a warning. He watched Tory walk toward him, with a lithe, leggy stride that was absolutely devoid of feminine artifice—and far too rife with feminine appeal for his peace of mind.

She's Hobie's niece, he reminded himself sternly. And off-limits, even if you were interested, even if you weren't on a case. Besides, she's too damned young for the likes of you. No matter how old she is.

She came to a halt in front of him. Before he could stop himself, the ridiculous words popped out.

"How old are you?"

Tory blinked. "What?"

Damn, Cole swore inwardly. "Er, never mind. I was just trying to remember how old Hobie is."

"Oh," she said, accepting his explanation. Trusting, Cole thought. "Hobie was fifty-four this year."

Fifty-four. Lord, had it really been fourteen years since Hobie had quit the rodeo-clown business? Interrupting his own last round on the circuit, Cole had gone to see him up at Pendleton, Oregon, that last year. It was a young man's game, Hobie had said, and his forty-year-old body wasn't up to it anymore. He'd taken too many hits, had had too many broken bones, too many concussions. And once, Cole knew, although Hobie never mentioned it, he'd been trampled nearly to death.

Fifty-four. Hobie had said that last time that he wanted to get back to Texas in time for Victoria's—he'd been calling her that then—thirteenth birthday. So that made her at least twenty-seven. The number hit him with a shock; he would have guessed she was much younger. She certainly had an air of innocence about her. But if she'd been hidden away on this ranch since she was twenty-two, as Hobie had once written him, then—

"Something wrong, Mr. Bannister?"

"I...no."

"I see you found us, all right."

"Yes. Your directions were fine."

She studied him for a moment, as if puzzled. "I'm glad you changed your mind," she said at last.

"Don't be," he returned, sounding short in spite of his efforts not to. "You may be sorry, yet."

She looked startled at his tone, but recovered smoothly. "Maybe. But at least I didn't have to try and explain to Hobie that you weren't coming."

Cole winced inwardly. Perhaps she wasn't so young after all. She'd certainly cut to the heart of things quickly enough.

"He...doesn't know, then?"

"That you weren't going to come? No. I didn't see any reason to..."

"Disillusion him?" His tone was biting, because he knew it was what she'd meant, and the truth of it stung.

"Yes," she said, not denying it. "Look, Mr. Bannister—"

"Cole." His mouth twisted wryly at her look. "I'm the hired help, remember? Better get into the habit now, so you don't slip up when someone's around."

She seemed about to say something else, then merely nodded. "Hobie asked to see you as soon as you got here." She nodded at the house. "He's resting, albeit grudgingly. He wanted to be able to show you around."

Cole frowned. "He's that sick?"

"No. Just weak. And he won't rest enough to get his strength back. We've got some temporary help for the summer, a couple of kids from the local high school who come out in the afternoons, but he still won't slow down."

"He always was stubborn," Cole said.

"Funny," Tory replied, looking up at him through lashes he only now noticed were tipped with gold that matched the golden strands of her hair. "That's what he said about you. Something about a bull named Stomper?"

Cole nearly groaned aloud. He pulled off his hat and ran a hand through his hair. "He would go spreading that around."

"So, how many times did you ride him?"

"Five." And he remembered every jarring, tooth-breaking jump, every brain-scrambling spin. "He's the one who finally taught me I was too damned big to ride bulls, which everybody else already knew. And before you ask," he added ruefully, "the final score was three to two. And not in my favor."

She grinned at him, an open, good-hearted grin that reminded him of Hobie. Which didn't explain why his breath seemed to catch in his throat.

"Stubborn." She mimicked the tone he'd used about Hobie.

One corner of his mouth twisted wryly. "I broke five bones when I was riding the circuit. Stomper broke four of them. That doesn't count the three times he broke my nose. Or the muscles and ligaments he pulled. I lost track of those. After a while, I started to take it real personally."

"So the last time you waved off the pickup rider and rode him on past the buzzer."

Cole flushed. That had been a piece of pride-driven preening he would just as soon forget. "He was a tough competitor. He deserved better than to be shown up like that."

She looked startled, then thoughtful, but only said, "Come on inside. Hobie's— Well, hello. Where did you come from?"

Cole stifled another groan. Rocky had obviously grown tired of waiting to be properly introduced, so in his usual manner had taken care of it himself. He stropped himself across her legs once, which was his limit, then retreated to a circumspect two feet away, sat and waited regally to be acknowledged.

"He, er, sort of came with me."

She looked at him, brows raised. "He's your cat?"

"No!" It came out a little too fervently, and he felt a tinge of heat in his face. "He just . . . sort of stowed away."

Tory looked at Cole, then at the cat, then back at Cole.

"Look," he said, "if it's a problem—"

"No. Not at all."

Damn it, Cole thought, she looked like she was about ready to laugh. He was sure she was. Who wouldn't, at the thought of a man like him and a cat?

"Does your . . . er, the stowaway have a name?"

He hesitated, then figured things couldn't get much worse. "Rocky."

She smiled then, and he knew the laughter was about to break loose.

"A neighbor kid named him," he said, denying responsibility. "After the movies."

"He does look like he's been through a fight or two. But I thought it was because of the raccoon resemblance."

"That, too." He thought he should warn her, so he added, "He's kind of ... weird. Standoffish."

"I imagine he's had to be. It doesn't look like he's had an easy life."

"No."

"And he certainly doesn't look like a lap cat, does he? Definitely a tough guy." She was smiling again, and he wondered if she meant something by that. "But he's not yours?" she asked.

"No," Cole said definitely. "I hate cats."

She turned away then, kneeling before the cat, and Cole just knew she'd done it to hide her mirth. He slammed his hat back on his head.

"Well, Rocky," she was saying lightly, "welcome to the Flying Clown. Lots of fun stuff here for a cat. We haven't ever had one around before, but I'm sure we can adapt. You'll teach us, won't you?"

Rocky cocked his head, then out came a noise that sounded eerily like one of assent. Tory laughed, and Cole's muscles flexed involuntarily against the shiver that ran down his spine at the light, musical sound of it.

"Well, have at it, Rocky." She moved her hand in a sweeping gesture encompassing the ranch as she stood up. "It's all yours."

Again, eerily as if he'd understood, Rocky darted away, a low, gray streak heading for the barn. And again Tory laughed.

"I'm glad you found him so entertaining," he said, knowing he sounded disgruntled, but unable to help it when that crazy feeling tensed him up again at her laugh.

"I did," she agreed, but her expression was somber now as she faced him. "There hasn't been much to laugh about around here lately."

She turned then, and walked up the steps and into the house.

* * *

Tory smiled when Hobie lit up at the sight of his old friend. His eyes twinkled as the rather stiff handshake became the kind of shoulder-pounding greeting men seemed to be prone to.

Then Hobie tugged on his thick gray mustache as he looked Bannister up and down. "Damn, you're still bigger'n a quarter horse stud, aren't you?"

To Tory's amazement, Bannister flushed. "And you've still got a wise mouth on you."

"Wiser than you might think," Hobie said rather cryptically. "You been through some hard times, my friend."

Bannister went very still. "What makes you think that?"

"It's in your eyes, son. There's not much left of that cocky kid who didn't care about anything but that all-around title."

Bannister smiled, but once more Tory saw it didn't reach his eyes. "No," he said. "The last of that kid disappeared a long time ago."

"About five years ago? That was the last letter I got."

Tory knew she wasn't imagining the big man's sudden rigidity. The silence lasted for a long, strained moment, Hobie looking at Bannister as if merely curious, Bannister staring back in a way that made Tory feel compelled to break the sudden intensity.

"I'll leave you two to catch up." The words sounded forced, but she couldn't help it; the tension radiating from Bannister was making her edgy. "I know you have a lot to talk about. You can see the ranch later, Mr. Ba—" at his lifted brow she caught herself "—Cole."

"I'll show him around," Hobie said determinedly. "I'm not that feeble. We can catch up as we go."

Bannister nodded, the tension vanishing as quickly as it had risen.

"Good," Tory said, meaning it. Despite the comfortable familiarity of Bannister's faded jeans, boots, Western shirt with pearl snaps and obviously well-worn hat, she was on edge every time she got too close to him. The man had only been here twenty minutes, and already she wanted a break. Just like his size, the very atmosphere around Bannister was larger than life, somehow more intense. Cole, she amended silently. If she was going to call him that, she'd better start thinking it, too.

The two men were talking easily as she left the room to retreat to the kitchen. It was obvious that despite the twenty-year difference in their ages, the two had found much in common. Or perhaps it was as Hobie had said, and Cole was just another of the kids Hobie had sort of adopted over the years, to take the place of the kids he'd never had.

After all, hadn't he done that with her, taken her in when she'd at last fled from her father's kind of life? When at last the charm had oozed too much, threatening to drown her in its false sweetness? Only Hobie, who had grown up in the shadow of his charismatic, oh-so-attractive older brother, truly understood why she'd had to leave what seemed, at least to others, the perfect life.

Putting aside the thoughts that were too worn now to be truly painful, Tory turned her attention to an evening meal. She hadn't really thought this part through. She and Hobie usually traded off cooking chores, with Hobie bearing the brunt of it since his illness because she'd had to pick up the slack with the horses, but neither of them could be considered anything more than adequate cooks. In her father's household, there had always been a cook on the staff. She had memories of her mother overseeing the work in the kitchen, but they were the kind that provided only the vague longing and sorrow and remorse she associated with thoughts of her mother, not any concrete help in the area of actual food preparation.

She heard the ranch Jeep start up, and glanced out to see Cole climbing in for the tour Hobie had planned. Lord, what did you feed a man the size of Cole Bannister? What would it take to fill up a man with shoulders as wide as the Texas panhandle? A side of beef and a couple of loaves of bread?

Spaghetti, she thought. A huge pot of it, and a gallon of sauce. It was easy, virtually foolproof, and the one thing she made that she knew tasted better than merely edible. With enough garlic bread, it should fill up even a six-foot-four ex-rodeo rider. And she wouldn't have to start it for another two or three hours, giving her enough time to work with John's colt.

Quickly she set out the fixings for the meal so she wouldn't have to later, then headed back out to the barn. She felt a certain obligation to John Lennox, or, at least to his horse. The man had stuck with her, even though his other horse had been the first animal felled by the supposed attack of colic. And he'd been so nice about it, despite the fact that he'd lost a proven—and very expensive—prize winner, and been left with only an unpolished three year old.

And when Firefly, the second horse, had died, John had been even more concerned; odd, because the animal wasn't his. But he'd been very supportive and helpful, dropping in every time he was in Santa Barbara for a meeting with the heads of a small company he'd bought last year, and she'd been grateful. And embarrassed when he'd at last told her his concern was for her, that he hated to see her so upset. The more upset she got, the more tender and concerned he became, although it did more to make her edgy than ease her pain. She wasn't sure why.

But she owed him, even if he did disconcert her with the casual flirting she knew was only teasing. A man of the financial stature of John Lennox would hardly waste his time with a mere horse trainer. Especially one who didn't have the kind of looks—or wardrobe—to travel in his circles.

"Hi, there, Mac," she said as she reached the colt's stall. A trim, intelligent-looking head popped over the bottom of the Dutch door, ears pricked forward, liquid brown eyes watching her with interest. Tory patted the sleek neck, admiring yet again the glossy coat that was that odd and striking shade between red and dark brown that was known as liver chestnut.

"How are you, ol' Macaroni?" she crooned, rubbing the velvety nose. The horse nickered softly. "Ready to play, hmm?"

Mac snorted and bobbed his head. Tory laughed. She loved a horse with personality, and Mac had it to spare. She patted him again, then reached for the halter and lead rope that hung beside the stall. Then she swung open the door to step inside.

When he saw the halter, Mac amenably lowered his head. As she slipped it over his head and fastened it, Tory felt a twinge of remorse. She'd always liked Mac, whom she had affectionately dubbed Macaroni rather than using his fancier registered name, better than the horse who had died. John Lennox, had, in fact, bought this colt on her recommendation. Although the other horse had taken several prizes in national cutting-horse competitions, and been valued—and insured, thank God—at a figure that staggered her, she'd always felt he lacked something, that indefinable quality that set a horse apart for her. Hobie called it "bottom," that sense that a horse would run himself into the ground for you, if you asked it of him. That horse hadn't had it. Mac did.

And just thinking it made her feel guilty. John's Prize— a name that had always made her waver between mild amusement and an uneasy curiosity about the kind of man who changed an animal's name to hang his own on it—had been an impressive creature. With near-perfect conformation and lots of grace and flash, he'd shown beautifully. But he'd also been a bit short on heart, and deep down Tory had thought that, good as he was, he never would have made it all the way to the top.

But he'd still been a good horse. And it had still torn a piece out of her when he'd died. Especially like that. She was grateful she hadn't had to watch it happen, but hated that he had died alone and in pain. As had Firefly, the little bay mare who had been so willing, even if she had lacked any great talent. And then there was Arthur, the lovable, clownish Appy with the water phobia....

Tears stung her eyes, then spilled over before she could stop them. She wiped quickly at her eyes as Mac nudged her gently, as if in commiseration. She had to stop thinking about it, she told herself. She couldn't function if she did; dwelling on it was too painful.

She should feel better, she thought, now that Cole Bannister was here, hopefully to do something about the disasters that had overtaken them. But somehow, thinking about him wasn't at all comforting. And she couldn't help remembering the flat, dead look in his eyes when he'd warned her never to trust him.

Chapter 4

Nothing in that afternoon's workout changed her assessment of John's remaining horse. The colt was willing, intelligent and marvelously coordinated. He had it all—drive, instinct and as much heart as any horse she'd ever ridden. Even this early in his training, she could see it, could feel it: this horse was something special. When he reached his full growth, and had muscled out, he was going to be spectacular. In a couple of years, she'd really like to see the cow that thought it could get past this guy.

Even when Cole's cat—she grinned to herself at the memory of his fervent denial of ownership—had dashed out unexpectedly from the barn, the colt had merely danced sideways a couple of steps and snorted at the unfamiliar creature, and when she had reassuringly patted him, had settled down immediately.

When they were done, and she was bathing Mac in the washrack, laughing as he playfully tried to catch the stream of water from the hose with his teeth, she thought how lucky she was to be able to make a living—although a sparse one at the moment—doing this work she loved with the animals she loved.

And how easy it would be to lose it all.

Mac gave a short whinny as his head came up, ears swiveling forward. Tory looked around and saw Hobie and Cole heading her way. Her uncle looked almost fragile beside Cole's height and breadth, although she knew when he was healthy his wiry strength and quickness was a match even for men who towered over him.

And at their heels was Rocky, who suddenly dashed ahead, startling Mac.

"Hi, honey," Hobie said, grinning as the horse's quick movement ricocheted a spray of water that drenched her already spattered T-shirt. It felt wonderfully cool.

"Hi," she said, an odd feeling flooding her as Cole looked at her. When she realized she was feeling self-conscious about her bedraggled appearance, she averted her eyes, confused at her own reaction.

She had long ago given up worrying about her appearance while she was working. Horses and tidiness did not mix, not if you were really doing the work yourself. Only those women who picked up their horses already clean and saddled, and turned them back over to grooms when they were done, managed to always look chic and polished while riding.

But something about Cole's eyes on her made her aware of how she must look. She turned away, busying herself with shutting off the water and neatly coiling the hose to be hung out of the way, and only then realizing just how wet she was—and that her nipples had tightened against the chill of the wet shirt. She was grateful her back was turned as heat flared in her cheeks; she knew she must be the color of her red shirt.

"This is the one I was telling you about," Hobie was saying. "He's only three, but he's coming along like a house on fire. All the way back to Poco Bueno and Three Bars, top and bottom. He's going to be a plum good horse, someday."

Feeling less flushed now, Tory looked at her uncle. "He's already good," she corrected. "Someday he's going to be great."

Hobie's grin widened beneath the bushy mustache. "You'll have to forgive her, Cole. She's a little head over heels about this young fella. Has been since the first day he got here."

"Yes, I am," Tory admitted, Hobie's gentle teasing erasing the last of her discomfiture and bringing a smile to her face. But the embarrassment came rushing back as Cole eyed her once more, one dark brow lifted.

"Do you always fall in love so easily?"

For a split second it seemed to her that he might have intended the obvious double meaning. But his expression was, as it so often seemed to her, unreadable, and she was certain she must have been wrong. So she answered the question as if it had been innocently asked.

"Only with horses like this one."

She patted the colt's shoulder, then began to use a long strip of smooth, hard rubber to squeegee the water out of his coat. She felt Cole watching her, but she didn't look at him. She wasn't a chatterer by nature, but for some reason she felt compelled to talk now.

"Usually, when we get a horse, it becomes obvious pretty quickly what they're best suited for," she said. "Dancers, real athletic horses who are great at balance and quick on their feet, take well to cutting, if they've got the instinct for working cattle."

Cole nodded. "Nothing quite like a good cutting horse. Great to watch, and a challenge to stay aboard. 'Dancer' is a good description."

There was nothing critical in Cole's tone, but Tory felt the heat rising in her cheeks again anyway. She paused in her work and looked at him. "Sorry. I didn't mean to... sound like a lecturer. I forgot you probably already know all this."

He looked surprised for an instant, but then it was gone. "Don't apologize. It's been a long time since I've been this close to a horse, let alone astride one."

"Well, now," Hobie drawled, "I reckon we can do something about that. You could do me a favor, and take my old buckskin out for some work."

"That the one I saw in the pasture next to the barn coming in?" Cole asked.

"Yep. Ol' Buck, he's been gettin' fat and lazy since I been laid up with this damn new-monia." Hobie rolled the syllables off his tongue in disgust.

"Fat and sassy, no doubt," Cole said dryly. "You trying to set me up, old buddy? Give the horse a nice long rest and plenty of feed so he'll buck down the first dumb cowboy you can talk into climbing into the saddle?"

Hobie grinned. "Why, I'd never do such an unkind thing."

"Yeah?" Cole gave Hobie a sideways grin. "Tell it to Charlie Horn, why don't you? He bought it once."

"Now, it wasn't my fault that horse took a notion to go sideways," Hobie protested, but his laughter detracted greatly from his struggle to maintain an innocent look. "Besides, he oughta have known you always check your gear before you get on a strange horse."

"I'll bet he never forgot to check it again, after that saddle let go on him," Cole said with a laugh.

Tory stared at him. It was only a laugh, and a slightly rusty sounding laugh at that. So there was no reason for the odd sensation that seized her, making her want to smile and have to blink back moisture at the same time. The sound of it just made it seem like Cole Bannister hadn't laughed much in a very long time.

Like she hadn't, not since the troubles had started. Until today. Perhaps, she thought as she untied Mac and backed him out of the washrack, Cole hadn't had much in his life to laugh about, either.

"Good food, honey," Hobie said as he finished off the last of his third piece of garlic toast. "I haven't eaten that much in ages."

"I know."

Tory's voice was as soft as the expression in her eyes as she looked at her uncle. Cole felt something twist painfully inside him at the pure love that glowed in her face. He didn't want to be responsible for this, didn't want to be the one they pinned their hopes on. Old, ugly memories rose up to haunt him. He squashed them with an effort.

Then he wished he hadn't. At least those old memories had displaced the image his mind couldn't seem to let go of—Tory, her eyes alight as she played with a clever young horse. Her soft lips curved in a happy, loving smile . . . and her breasts clearly outlined by the clinging, wet cloth of her shirt . . . wet cloth that had urged her nipples to a jutting tightness that had caused a similar sensation in his groin.

It had been a long time since he'd reacted this way. In fact, he wasn't sure he ever had, not so hotly, or so fast. He'd longed for Kyra, but it had been more for the pure goodness of her than this sharp, instant, physical reaction. And with Kyra, not for the first time he had cursed this chance arrangement of features that drew flashy—and shallow—women to him and scared the real ones off.

Not that he had any intention of pursuing this unexpected feeling now. Not only because she was Hobie's niece, but because he'd finally figured out that it was best that he stick to the flashy women, the ones who played the game for its own sake. He only hurt the others. In one way or another, he always hurt them.

He yanked his thoughts out of the well-worn groove as automatically as he had earlier squashed the ugly memories. He turned his attention to Hobie.

He looked like he hadn't been eating, Cole thought. Hobie had always been thin and quick and wiry, it was what had made him such an effective bullfighter. But he looked almost fragile now. And by the time he'd finished showing Cole around the ranch, pointing out the new cattle and introducing him to Kurt and Eric—the two boys who'd been helping out—Hobie had been visibly tired.

He tried to hide it. Hobie had put on a good front when they'd walked around to the washrack where Tory had been bathing that young but impressive-looking colt. He had been teasingly cheerful, but Cole guessed his niece's sharp eyes hadn't missed the signs of strain around her uncle's eyes. She'd quickly finished with the horse and ushered them inside to sit down and finish their talking. Cole had taken the hint and pled the necessity of unpacking, and when he'd returned to the living room Hobie had been asleep in his recliner. Cole had retreated quietly, to look around a bit more himself. And, reluctantly, to make sure Rocky wasn't out there causing trouble.

"Your cat seems to have made himself right at home," Tory said, as if she'd read his thoughts. She sipped the last of her glass of the wine Hobie had insisted on opening, to celebrate Cole's arrival, he'd said. The smooth, deep taste of the cabernet belied Hobie's insistence that he didn't hold much with those "fancy, cork-smellin' libations."

"He's *not*—"

"—your cat," she said, finishing for him with a grin. "So you said. He may not be yours, but judging from the mice he brought you, I'd say you're his."

"Damn cat," Cole muttered.

The first time Rocky had laid his dead offering ceremoniously at Cole's feet, so pleased with himself that he didn't take even a token swipe at the hated snakeskin boots, Cole had been startled. The second time, right before dinner, he'd just been annoyed. It had been Tory, walking past the tack room where he'd been standing in time to see the second presentation, who had laughingly explained that it was a token of high esteem, a great gift, at least in cat protocol. He wasn't impressed.

"I'll need a list of all your clients, past and present," he said abruptly, changing the subject without dissembling.

Hobie merely nodded, but Tory looked as if he'd tossed a glass of ice water in her face, which, in essence, he supposed he had. For the moment at least, perhaps in her happiness at seeing Hobie's appetite returning, she seemed to have put the Flying Clown's problems out of her mind. Until he'd forced them back in her face.

"But...they would never...I know they wouldn't ever..." Tory's protesting words trailed away and she lowered her eyes to her empty wineglass.

"You asked me here to do this, remember?"

Cole knew he sounded irritated. He knew he *was* irritated. What he didn't know was why. A client's reluctance to admit that the source of their problem might be someone they knew and liked was something he'd encountered before. He was usually able to deal with it easily, figuring they were going to learn the lesson of not taking everyone at face value sooner or later, anyway.

But somehow forcing Tory to face the possibilities wasn't coming easily at all. He turned his gaze back to Hobie. Hobie understood; he'd seen all kinds in his years on the rodeo circuit. And he'd never been fooled by much of anything.

"I'll need anything else you know about them, too," Cole said. "Their primary business or income source, where they live, names of family, banks—"

"We don't ask them to fill out an application," Tory said a little sharply, still fiddling with her glass.

Cole shifted his gaze back to her. "Maybe you should," he returned flatly. Her head came up and her eyes narrowed as she met his look steadily.

"They're hiring us, remember?"

Cole knew the phrasing, echoing his own, was deliberate. And she had a point. A good one. She also obviously had more than a touch of Hobie's grit and sass—she wasn't the least bit intimidated by him. In fact, he got the distinct impression that she, unlike most women he met, wasn't impressed with him at all. It wasn't conceit, just a knowledge born of the wearying fact that women tended to get either tongue-tied or outrageous around him.

"Good point," he conceded mildly. She looked surprised, as if she hadn't expected him to agree. "Just tell me what you know. Or can find in your records, like what bank their checks were drawn on. Or what they might have mentioned in passing. Business problems, family problems, that kind of thing.''

''You think somebody's after insurance money?'' Hobie asked.

''When three expensive and insured horses die, insurance fraud is the first thing that comes to mind. Yes. You have copies of the autopsy reports? I'll need to read those.''

Hobie nodded, but Tory shook her head slowly. ''I just can't believe it. These people are horse people. None of them would actually—'' she grimaced, obviously repulsed at the idea ''—*kill* their horses for money.''

''Be honest, honey,'' Hobie said gently. ''You can't imagine anyone ever intentionally hurting a horse. Your mind just doesn't work that way.''

She looked at her uncle, her expression troubled. Then she glanced at Cole. He didn't think anything showed in his face, but she suddenly crumpled her napkin in her fist until her knuckles were white.

''All right,'' she said, her voice tight. ''I'm a naive little fool, then. I'll leave you two to plan this war, since I'm obviously no help.''

''Tory,'' Hobie began as she stood up and threw her wadded napkin on the table.

''And since I cooked, you can clean up while you're doing it.''

She turned sharply on her heel and walked to the screen door that led out to the yard. She yanked it open and was down the steps before it closed behind her. Cole silently watched her go.

''She's just upset,'' Hobie said after a moment. ''She hates seeing animals hurt, and those three horses going like that really got to her.''

Cole only nodded. Hobie wasn't telling him anything he hadn't already guessed.

''Arthur especially,'' Hobie elaborated. ''He was special to her. That Appy was such a clown. We didn't think he had it in him to make any kind of a stock horse, but Tory stuck with him, and he turned out to be one of the best roping horses I've ever ridden.''

"Which one was he?" Cole asked, still looking through the fine mesh of the door at the slender figure who had stopped mid angry stride to stoop and pet Rocky, who had appeared from behind the barn. Surprisingly, the aloof cat allowed it, although after two strokes he was back on his hunt.

"The one we had to put down. Foreleg was shattered."

"The water-phobe?"

Hobie nodded. "Tory was the one who insisted he had talent in him somewhere, we just had to find it. I would have given up on him long ago. But when she got through with him he handled a rope and a calf as well as any horse I've ever seen."

Cole nodded absently as he watched Tory disappear into the barn. It was to the horses, obviously, that she went for solace. He felt a pang that he apparently had sent her there, but he couldn't be sorry that he'd made her face the facts; too often in cases like this, the cause was very close to home. She might not like it, but it was the truth.

"I'm just glad nothing's happened to Mac. I don't know if she could deal with that."

Cole turned his attention back to Hobie to find the old cowboy watching him thoughtfully, with an expression Cole couldn't define. And he found himself hurrying to fill the silence.

"How many horses do you have now?"

"Five, plus Buck." Hobie said. "As of now, anyway. The story's gettin' around. I'm surprised no one's pulled out, with all this happening. One of the owners has talked about it, but he hasn't done anything, yet. Tory doesn't know that."

"Protecting her?"

"Somebody has to," Hobie said gruffly. "She sure won't take care of herself." Then his mouth twisted in disgust. "We were at our maximum number, doing real well, but then I got sick and we had to cut back. Tory tried to keep it all going, but she was wearing herself out."

"I know," Cole said softly. "She looks . . . drained."

"She'd run herself into the ground if I'd let her. She loves this place as much as I do."

"She loves you." Cole's voice was quiet, and even he heard the touch of wistfulness in it. Hobie's expression became even more thoughtful, but he went on without commenting on it.

"It was bad enough that I went and got sick right after we made the deal on that extra acreage I showed you. But to have this start on top of already being strapped . . ." Hobie's eyes, so much like those of the woman who'd just left them, were sad and troubled now. "Let's just say I'm damn glad you're here. I told Tory if anybody could get to the bottom of this, you could."

Cole bit back the gut-level, instantaneous protest his mind screamed out. He should leave right now. Just walk out. He wasn't up to this. He'd been a fool to come here at all. He'd known better, and he'd come anyway. But when he looked at Hobie, when he remembered that weathered face, pale and waxen from internal loss of blood after he'd put himself between the dazed Cole and the bull who wanted him dead, he knew he couldn't walk out. But he couldn't—wouldn't—make any promises, either.

"Maybe," he muttered. Then, as Hobie's brows lowered at his tone, he quickly changed the subject. "Any theories of your own?"

Hobie leaned back in his chair and reached up to tug at his mustache in a gesture that, although it had been over five years since Cole had seen it, still seemed comfortably familiar.

"Well, now, there's my problem," he drawled.

"What?"

"Too many theories."

Cole lifted a brow. "Such as?"

"A psycho, maybe. Lord knows there's enough of 'em running around these days. Or it might be somebody wantin' revenge, or—"

"Revenge?" Cole glanced at the door once more, although Tory was no longer in sight. He couldn't believe she'd ever made anybody that angry at her. "For what?"

"Oh, not Tory," Hobie said, reading him easily. "That girl could never hurt anybody that bad. Sometimes that's what gets her hurt."

Cole's head snapped back around. Had that been a warning? Or was he reading too much into Hobie's words, because of his own suddenly wayward imagination? But Hobie was merely looking at him with that same thoughtful expression again.

"Revenge on who, then?" Cole finally asked. "And for what?"

"Me."

Cole blinked. "You?"

"Yep."

"Hobie, you've saved more lives than most doctors, my own miserable one included. What would anyone have against you?"

"I've lost a few over the years, too," Hobie said. "Times when I wasn't quick enough, or that old bull just wouldn't change targets."

"Hell, nobody can blame you for that—"

"George Wheeler does."

"George... You mean Marvin's kid?"

Hobie nodded. Cole's brows lowered. He'd been there that day, at the Pendleton Roundup fifteen years ago. He'd made his ride, barely hanging on for the buzzer, and was still dusting himself off from a dismount that had left a bit to be desired for style and grace, when Marvin Wheeler had begun his ride. He hadn't seen it, but he'd heard the shocked gasps and then the ominous silence as the cowboy had gone down under the deadly hooves and horns of a vicious Brahma, dying in front of the horrified eyes of the crowd—and his ten-year-old son.

"Nobody could have turned that bull. He went crazy. That's why they pulled him from the circuit after that. He didn't want to buck, he wanted to kill."

Hobie shrugged. "George don't see it that way."

"But he was just a kid—"

"He's twenty-five now. But he remembers like it was yesterday. Kids do, I guess."

"But to blame you..."

"I saw him at a stock auction a couple of years ago." Hobie rubbed at his jaw. "He slugged me. Damn near broke my jaw. And he wanted more. If a couple of guys hadn't pulled him off me..."

Cole shook his head in astonishment. "That's crazy."

Hobie shrugged. "Then there's Bart Brock."

Cole's eyes widened. "Bart Brock? His hand got hung up in his rigging! How the hell is that your fault?"

"When you're looking at the rest of your life sittin' in a wheelchair, I reckon logic don't count for much. He calls now and again, just to remind me he holds me responsible for not distracting that bull 'til he could get loose."

Cole shook his head again. "Are they nuts? You put your life on the line for us every time you went out there. All of us knew that. I can't believe they'd really blame you."

Hobie lifted a bushy gray brow at him. "Hmm. You sound like somebody else who was just here."

Cole drew back, eyes widening. Then his brows lowered once more. And then, at last, his mouth curved ruefully.

"Damn you, Hobie, you always did have a way of twisting things sideways until we saw it your way."

Hobie shrugged. "Just pointing out the obvious."

"You mean that we all have our blind spots?"

"Something like that."

Cole let out a long breath. His glance flicked to the screen door, then back to Hobie. "I suppose I owe someone an apology."

"That's up to you," Hobie said. Then, with a grin as Cole got to his feet, "I'll tell you, though, she's mighty quick to forgive, unless you've hurt someone she loves. Makes it a lot less painful.''

He didn't answer, couldn't think of anything to say in response to that. Grabbing his hat from the rack just inside the door—which also held two brightly colored baseball caps, Hobie's sweat-stained old Stetson and a new straw one that looked like it hadn't even been worn, yet—Cole stepped into the fading evening light, Hobie's words echoing in his mind.

Unless you've hurt someone she loves.

If she only knew, he thought grimly, what a track record he had in that arena, she never would have asked for his help. Because when a woman came to him for help because a man she loved was in trouble, that man usually wound up dead.

Chapter 5

The minute he walked into the tack room, Cole found himself under an aerial attack. He swore, then glared at the raccoon-marked cat who had apparently launched himself from a shelf to Cole's shoulder, and was now maintaining his precarious balance with an attention-getting set of claws.

"Damn it, cat!"

Reflexively his hand came up to swipe the offending animal off its perch, but halted midswing when he realized just how far it was to the floor. He'd heard cats always landed on their feet, but he didn't want this to be the exception that proved the rule. With his luck, Rocky's scars weren't from fighting but from being a klutz, and he'd have a broken cat to explain.

The claws dug in deeper—he'd be bleeding in a minute, he knew—and Rocky made a low, odd sound. Seconds later Cole heard footsteps approaching. They were light and quick, and somehow he knew it was Tory. When she appeared in the doorway a moment later, he felt no sense of satisfaction at the accuracy of his guess, just a growing tension low down in his belly.

She looked startled to see him there, and even more startled when she spotted Rocky on his shoulder. A smile began to curve her lips, then, as her glance flicked to his face, it faded away. Good for you, Bannister, he thought glumly. The cat rates a smile, and you rate—

He cut himself off with a sharp internal reprimand. What he rated didn't matter. Tory Flynn had already demonstrated she wasn't bowled over by his looks. In fact, he got the distinct impression his appearance was part of the reason she hadn't trusted him from the beginning, and that only his connection with Hobie had made her accept him at all.

Oddly, he wasn't sure if he didn't prefer that reaction to the blatantly ingratiatory approach of women who took one look at him and decided he'd make a great scalp for their belt. Or bedpost.

He saw her take a quick breath, and then, unexpectedly, she said, "I'm sorry."

His brows furrowed. "What?"

"I know you're here to help. And I suppose from your point of view, our clients are the first place to start looking. I shouldn't have . . . reacted like that."

He felt like a horse who'd just run off a cliff, as if suddenly he had no solid ground beneath him. "I . . . er, I'm sorry, too," he finally managed to say, wincing as Rocky dug in once more. "I shouldn't have snapped at you like that. I know it's tough to think that somebody you know could be so . . ."

"Sick?" she said, when he didn't finish. "Vicious? Evil?"

"All of those."

She turned away from him suddenly, to face the wall that held several bridles on wide, rounded racks. He saw the tension in her slender shoulders, and instinctively knew she was fighting not to cry.

"No one has the right to do that to an innocent, living creature." Her voice was so choked up he could barely understand her words.

"No."

He didn't know what else to say, so he left it at that. After a moment her shoulders came back and her head came up. Yes, Tory Flynn had gotten her share of her uncle's grit, he repeated silently. She turned to face him again.

"I won't let it happen again." Her voice was fierce now, determined.

"*We* won't," he said, before he could stop himself. Idiot, he thought. Haven't you learned not to make those kind of promises?

Tory hesitated, then nodded. She lifted a bridle down from a rack and busied herself with adjusting it. Her trembling fingers made a mess of the job, and Cole could see the effort she was making at regaining control. He said nothing, sensing she needed a minute to manage it.

He reached up and scooped Rocky off his shoulder. The cat yowled a protest, but quieted as Cole set him down with more gentleness than he had originally intended. He straightened up, righting the hat the animal had knocked askew. The cat gave him a baleful look, walked over and stropped himself once on Tory's legs, then strolled regally away, tail high. Again a slight smile curved Tory's mouth. The cat, it seemed, succeeded easily where he failed.

But he was grateful the animal had distracted her from her anguish over the dead horses. She was calm now, even amused at Rocky's demeanor.

"He's quite a character," she said.

Cole's mouth quirked. "He's a nuisance."

Her smile widened. "But he's your nuisance."

Cole gave an exasperated sigh. "He's not my—"

He stopped when her smile became a grin. "I don't think you get a choice. With a cat, they do the choosing."

"So I've been told," he muttered.

"Do you need a dish? To feed him?"

"Let him eat mice."

A laugh broke from her—light, teasing and totally at odds with the crazy shiver that ran up his spine.

"I begin to see why he picked you. You have a lot in common. Starting with that royal arrogance."

Cole blinked. Had she actually called him arrogant? He'd been called many things by women before, but arrogant wasn't usually one of them. And the women weren't usually laughing when they did it.

"Be careful, though." She was really grinning now. "The last royal who talked like that lost her head."

The corners of his mouth twitched. He fought it, but her grin was too infectious. At last a rueful chuckle broke from him. "He's tried that a time or two already."

"And lived? Brave cat."

"Stupid cat. With considerably fewer than nine lives left."

She started to smile, but the expression faded. "At least cats are supposed to have nine lives. Horses aren't."

Lowering her eyes, she bit her lip, worrying at the soft flesh in a way that made Cole remind himself that she was Hobie's niece, and that this was hardly the time to be thinking the kind of thoughts he was thinking—like doing a little nibbling of his own. And she was hardly the person to be thinking it about. He reined in his suddenly too-responsive senses with an effort.

"So what's your theory?"

Her head came up sharply, as if searching for evidence of a taunt in his face. He hadn't—this time—meant it that way, so he hastened to soften what he realized had sounded pretty chilly.

"Hobie told me his ideas, I was just wondering what yours were."

"Oh." She appeared mollified, and answered him. "I think somebody's after the ranch."

He kept his expression even. She was touchy enough about this, especially, it seemed, where he was concerned. "The ranch? Then why kill the horses?"

"Because it's common knowledge we'd never sell out. This place is Hobie's dream. The only way to get this land would be to put us out of business. And the easiest way to do that is to ruin our reputation." She bit her lip once more before adding, "In the horse world, your reputation is your business. Lose that, and it's all over. People will never trust you with their horses again. Not at this level.''

"So they try to prove you're...what? Careless? Incompetent to take care of expensive animals?''

She nodded. "And it doesn't take much to destroy even a reputation like Hobie's. Smaller things might be overlooked, but dead horses? No way.''

Again she bit her lip, but Cole guessed this time it wasn't in worry but in an effort to keep from crying once more. He resisted the urge to reach up and gently smooth the harried flesh.

"Why? Why would somebody want this ranch that badly?''

She hesitated, and when she finally spoke, Cole was reasonably certain it wasn't what she'd been going to say. He was rusty, but he hadn't lost every instinct he'd once had.

"We're in a prime location here," she explained. "Good water, and direct access to the main road to the coast. There are big operations on two sides of us. The Crains, and then Charlie Lee. They both had their eye on this place when Hobie bought it. They wanted the land we just leased, too, but Glen Porter wouldn't sell. It made them mad when he leased it to us, because that put it off the market for five years.''

"So you think one of them is behind this? Or both?''

Her delicate brows lowered. "I don't want to think that, even though they were really upset. Besides, the second horse that died was Harry Crain's. What would he have to gain by killing his own horse?''

"Besides the insurance? Who knows. But if not them, then who?'' She looked at him warily. "Who?'' he prompted again. "What were you going to say, before?''

She wavered, then appeared to decide. "I was out on our west boundary one day, about a month ago. There's a draw up there, with a little spring. The cattle congregate there because it's cool and shady. I was up there on Mac, because we're starting to get him used to the stock.''

He merely nodded, afraid she'd stop if he said anything.

"I saw somebody up in the foothills. On our land. Like he was camped out, with all sorts of gear."

"Gear?"

"I couldn't see what all it was. Looked like maybe a sleeping bag, and a lantern. And I'm pretty sure I saw a pick. Or maybe it was just an ax. But I couldn't get up there to check right then, without scattering the stock. By the time I did, he was gone."

"And?"

"There's an old story that's been going around here for at least a hundred years, about a gold mine up in the foothills. Supposedly the old man who worked it died on his way down to register the claim. He had a full poke of gold dust on him, and a couple of sizable nuggets."

"You think this guy was a ... prospector? And that he wants the ranch because of that ... story?"

She grimaced. "I know it sounds farfetched—"

"But a lot easier—and more pleasant—to believe than that one of your neighbors, or one of your friends is responsible."

He'd carefully kept any censure out of his voice, but she answered defensively, anyway.

"I said I knew it sounded crazy. But the legend's for real. There are records of it in old newspapers, and in a history of the area that somebody wrote around the turn of the century. And every once in a while, every couple of years, somebody'll turn up, hunting. And if this guy found something—" She broke off, shaking her head as she looked at him. "Never mind. I knew you'd think—"

"I'll check it out."

She blinked. "What?"

"I said I'll check it out. I'll have my office get a copy of the last geological survey maps, for starters. And the satellite surveys."

"You will?"

"It's worth checking out."

"It is?"

He shook his head, a chuckle escaping him at her surprise. "Everything's worth checking out at this early stage. We'll narrow it down as we go."

"Oh." A touch of color pinkened her cheeks. "I thought you'd think I was...being naive again."

"Naive doesn't necessarily mean wrong."

She studied him for a moment, then said wryly, "Somehow I don't think that was a compliment."

"Were you looking for one?"

Her color deepened suddenly, and an expression that almost seemed like chagrin flickered in her eyes. He didn't want to dwell on the possible reasons for that. Just like he didn't want to dwell on the weird sensations she seemed to rouse in him. It was time to get this relationship back where it belonged. Employer to employee. Hobie's old friend to his niece. Any safe niche would do.

He made sure the mocking note in his voice was obvious when he went on.

"How about 'You look pretty when you blush?'"

His tone, as he'd intended, seemed to help her gather her composure, and she gave him a rather scoffing look.

"That's right up there with 'You're beautiful when you're angry.'"

"One of my favorites," he drawled.

"And I suppose it works for you?"

"Sometimes."

"Stupid women," she muttered.

"Exactly," he agreed mildly. "It's how I weed them out."

"What?"

"If they're stupid enough to fall for that, then I know I'd be bored to death in five minutes."

She stared at him, as if unsure whether to laugh or not.

"Of course," he said easily, "if they're really pretty enough...."

"Then a little stupidity can be forgiven?"

The sudden sourness in her words was unmistakable, and Cole congratulated himself on achieving his goal. The fact that he didn't feel particularly good about it was something he would learn to live with.

"A nice little equation, is that it?" she said, each word bitten off a little more sharply than the last. "The amount of stupidity that can be tolerated is in direct ratio to the quality of the looks?"

He was a little taken aback at her growing vehemence. "It was a joke, okay? I—"

"It's always a joke to men like you, isn't it? 'She's thick as a brick, but with that body, who cares?' 'Sure she's an airhead, but she's a great-looking one.'"

Cole stared at her. There was something much bigger going on here than a little needling, far too much to have been brought on by what had been, obviously, he'd thought, simple teasing.

"Look—"

"Are you married, Mr. Bannister?"

He blinked. Under other circumstances, he might have welcomed that inquiry. "No. What's that got to do—"

"Too bad. You've missed out on the chance to dump her for the newer, better, younger, prettier trophy wife, or maybe simply a mistress, if you like to really twist the knife."

"Apparently I've missed the entire point of this."

"Of course you have," she growled.

Before he could answer—not that he had a clue about what he was going to say—she had stalked out of the tack room. In two long strides he was at the door, but shut his mouth on what he'd been about to say when he saw her already talking to the two high school boys Hobie had introduced him to earlier. The boys were helping out temporarily—for a respectable wage, yet another reason they were strapped, Cole guessed—while Hobie was recuperating. He backed up until he was out of their sight, and watched.

Kurt, tall, thin and gangly, with blond hair that was shaved on the sides and longer on top, was tugging on the gold cross that hung from his left ear, while Eric, the shorter, more muscular boy, with brown hair that constantly fell in front of his eyes, talked to Tory about their chores for tomorrow. He'd thought this afternoon the boys were unusually quiet and respectful for their ages—they didn't look more than sixteen—and now was no exception. They listened quietly, nodding, accepting. And not once meeting Tory's eyes.

They looked uneasy, Cole thought. Almost wary. Which made him uneasy. Here was a possibility that hadn't been mentioned, yet.

When the boys had gone, driving off at a surprisingly sedate pace in an old, battered gray compact that seemed held together by the countless decals and stickers on it, he stepped outside.

"What do you know about them?" he asked, still watching as the gray car hit the main road and took off westbound at a much faster pace. After a moment, as if it were an afterthought, the headlights came on in the gathering dusk.

"Kurt and Eric?" she asked, looking at him in surprise, for the moment, apparently forgetting her earlier anger. "They go to the local high school. They're both sixteen, sophomores. I put a request in at the school office, where they post part-time work for the kids. They were the most willing to do what we needed. And they do help, a lot."

The gray car was out of sight now, and he turned back to look at her. "When did they start working here?"

"A couple of months ago. At the beginning of summer. They—" She broke off, eyes widening as she stared at him. "You don't think they had anything to do with this?"

"Let's just say I find the timing interesting."

"But they're just kids!"

"You want a list of the sixteen year olds that have killed a whole string of people, let alone horses?"

For a long, silent moment, she just looked at him. Then, so softly he could barely hear it, she said, "God, what an awful way to live. Suspecting everyone of everything."

After the way she'd just been chewing on him, he was startled by the genuine distress in her tone. "It...has it's moments."

"Is that why you quit?"

He drew back, as if she'd threatened him somehow. Stupid, he muttered to himself, fighting to keep his expression even.

"No," he said flatly.

She looked about to say more, then, as his brows lowered in warning, took the hint and stayed silent. He quickly changed the subject.

"I'll want to look around some more tomorrow. But I'll need to look like I'm working, unless you want the world to know why I'm here. Any suggestions?"

She looked at him wryly. "A million. But they all involve really working."

He shrugged. "I didn't figure I was here for a free ride."

She lifted one arched brow, but said only, "What do you want to look at?"

"Where you saw that guy up in the hills, for starters."

"Oh." She thought for a minute. "Well, some of the stock is up in that area. I wasn't planning on bringing them down until Friday, but I suppose we could do it tomorrow. On the way we could ride up to where I saw him."

"Ride?"

She gave him a sideways look. "There's still no better way to move cattle over short distances on rough ground, you know. And you can't get to where I saw that man in a car, not even in the Jeep."

"Oh."

"Don't tell me the cowboy doesn't ride."

Cole winced inwardly at her tone. "He does. It's just been awhile."

"We'll find you a nice, gentle horse."

"And shove a burr under his saddle?" He leaned against the side of the barn, crossing his arms across his chest. "You don't like me much, do you?"

She colored, but held his gaze. Nerve, he thought again. "I don't trust you much," she corrected.

He knew she was right not to, he'd even warned her never to trust him, but somehow it stung, hearing it like this. "You haven't accepted much else I've said. Why that?"

Her chin came up. "I don't trust you," she said, "because I know your type. That Texas charm is as thick and sweet as honey, and you turn it on and off like it came from a faucet. And you're too darn pretty for anybody's good."

Cole blinked. He'd been called charming before. And, on occasion, usually by a man irritated by the way his wife or girlfriend had been looking at him, he'd been called pretty. But never had there been so much fervency in the words. And never had he been so sure that the emotion beneath the words was pain.

"Why do I get the feeling we're not talking about me anymore?" he asked softly.

The color abruptly fled her face, leaving her looking pale and making the weary circles beneath her eyes stand out.

"I'm sorry." She let out a tiny breath. "I keep having to say that, don't I? I don't know why I—" She broke off, then went on. "You're Hobie's friend, and I had no business saying those things. Now or... before."

"But I hit a nerve, didn't I?"

Her eyes narrowed. "You're also very observant, aren't you?"

He shrugged. "Comes with the territory."

"I guess... I'm tired," she admitted at last, lifting her hands to rub at her eyes. "Trying to keep this place going, and Hobie not getting well and then... then the horses."

"You're allowed, Tory."

He'd meant it merely as a kindness, but it came out something closer to a caress. Especially her name. He never would have guessed it would feel so good, just to say it.

She was staring at him as if it had felt that way to her, too. Instinctively he moved to back up a step, as if distance would ease the feeling, but came up against the barn wall. At almost the same instant, Tory did back up a step.

"I... If you want to ride up there, we'll need to leave early, or we'll end up eating dust during the hottest part of the day."

He nodded.

"There's no alarm in your room—"

"I'll be up."

She nodded in turn, edging away as if she were afraid of him. Cole stifled a sigh as he watched her go. Sometimes he wished that Stomper had caved in his face instead of his ribs. Maybe then women—the real ones, at least, the ones with depth and more facets than just their own looks—would quit reacting like this, thinking that because of the way he was put together, he was automatically someone to be wary of.

Kyra had been that way, too, at first. He'd finally understood, once he'd learned about the way her too-perfect husband had treated her. It had taken a great deal of time and patience to get Kyra to trust him—and then she'd fallen for Cash Riordan, a man who, despite his spectacular screen success, was not what the world considered drop-dead handsome. Not, he thought sourly, like Cole Bannister.

But weren't they right, he thought, those women who didn't trust him? Hadn't he proved it? He had no right even thinking about a woman who was involved in a case, not with his grimly dismal record. Any woman who would trust him was a fool. And hadn't he told Tory exactly that? So what right did he have to complain because she believed him?

And what the hell was he worried about it for, anyway? She was Hobie's niece, and he should be treating her that way. Like the precious niece of a dear friend. Someone to be protected, not... not whatever it was he was feeling like doing—not kissed to within an inch of her life, not tasted from head to toe, not—

"Damn!"

His fist hit the side of the barn, and he heard a startled snort from the next stall. A dark chestnut head popped out, and a pair of wise, liquid eyes looked at him. Under their gaze, he felt amazingly like a kid who'd lost control of his hormones.

"Temporarily," he muttered. He'd have it back under control soon. Mac whickered softly, and Cole's mouth twisted up at one corner. "She's all yours, Mac, ol' buddy. She's crazy about you, you know."

The horse bobbed his head as if in agreement. Cole chuckled wryly. He reached over and patted the sleek, muscled neck. This truly was a beautiful animal.

"She's right, you've got the look. And you'll never let her down, will you?"

At least he never would if the jinx doesn't extend to horses, Cole amended silently. If I can manage to keep him alive.

Chapter 6

The first pink streaks of dawn were just beginning to appear when Cole finally gave up. Twice he'd actually gone to sleep, lulled, no doubt, by the quiet peace of this place, so unlike the constant hum of background noise he was used to in the city. But the peace hadn't extended to his sleeping mind, and the dreams had come as usual to churn up his night.

What hadn't been usual were the dreams themselves. He was, as much as he could be, used to the other images, to the dying eyes, the accusing faces. But in his mind this time the dying eyes were Hobie's, and the look of accusation, of blame, came from Tory. He'd awakened in a sweat, feeling her stare as palpably as if she were in the room.

And, hours later, when he'd surrendered reluctantly to sleep the second time, a new dream slipped in to haunt him. An impossible, tempting dream that was both searingly sweet and hotly erotic at the same time. And at the center of it, enticing him with her shy unawareness of her own beauty, with her innate and unstudied goodness, her quick, fierce loyalty and passion—that he could too easily imagine translating into passion of a different sort—was Tory. The sweat he woke up in that time was of an entirely different sort.

He sat up now, fighting a shiver of reaction to the memory of that sensuous dream as he swung his feet over the edge of the double bed he'd wound up sleeping on diagonally, since it was too short for him to be comfortable.

Tory had apologized for the small room, but Hobie had temporarily moved into the downstairs guest room, since the stairs had been a little difficult for him while he'd been ill, and Hobie's own room upstairs had only a narrow bunk that would be even more cramped for someone Cole's size.

Cole had told her it was fine, but he'd been thinking if she was going to apologize for something, it should be for putting him right across the hall from her own room. Because Tory Flynn unsettled him in a way he wasn't at all sure he knew how to deal with. And repeatedly telling himself she was Hobie's niece didn't seem to be helping much.

He stood up, stretched wearily, pondering what he'd let himself in for today, wondering how much of the plan was really for the job at hand, and how much was just to feel like he was doing something. Anything. So far, all he'd done was call in the list of names Tory and Hobie had given him, and the map coordinates of the ranch. The office was already fielding the results of the inquiries he'd made among the horse people he still knew before he'd left. And that had turned up the depressing news that word of the Flynn's troubles was spreading. He kept that to himself.

It could be days before the Research department had a set of files compiled. At least going up to the spot Tory had seen this guy would feel like doing something. Even if he didn't really think it had anything to do with the attacks.

He let out a long breath, rubbing at the chronically stiff spot on his back. The scars were a familiar pattern beneath his fingers, snaking ridges of hardened tissue that were the only reminder of the day that had taken him one step closer to the end of his career.

Well, not the only reminder. There were the dreams.

And you're feeling damn sorry for yourself this morning, aren't you? he thought caustically.

With short, sharp movements, he grabbed his jeans from across the foot of the bed and yanked them on, then headed down the hall to the bathroom and a shower. A cold shower, he amended as he pulled the door shut behind him. A very cold shower.

Just to wake himself up, he told himself firmly, nothing else. He didn't need it for anything else; the taut heaviness of his body would abate. And it wouldn't come back, because he was going to put that completely inappropriate—and utterly arousing—dream out of his head. For good. If for no other reason than that she was Hobie's beloved niece, and Hobie was one of the few people left in the world who thought, for now at least, that Cole Bannister was worth the powder it would take to blow him to Hades.

Tory heard the sound of running water, and decided to give up her fruitless pursuit of sleep. She rubbed at gritty eyes, knowing it was going to be a long, hard day, and for more reasons than just because she hadn't had enough rest.

And she could only blame part of it on Hobie. Yes, she'd gone down several times to linger in the doorway of the guest room and listened to her uncle's improved but still slightly raspy breathing, but she'd been awake anyway. Awake and thinking, her mind seeming to run in restless circles. And at the center of those circles was the man who was right now in the shower a bare twenty feet away.

That realization gave rise to some thoughts that made heat flood through her. To images of that tall, broad body, naked and powerful, with streams of water tracing their lucky way over swells and hollows of muscle. To visions of the sinewy strength and rough-hewn grace that had once let him conquer over a ton of powerhouse horse or bull bent solely on bucking him loose, bared to her gaze.

"Stop it!"

She instantly felt silly at issuing orders to herself out loud, but she was afraid nothing else would have worked to erase the vivid pictures her mind kept tantalizing her with. And it *was* silly, really, she told herself firmly. Her experience was so limited, she had no idea what a man built like Cole would look like . . . like that.

But her imagination was more than up to the task of filling in the blanks, she thought as she slipped out of bed and pulled a pair of jeans and a pale yellow T-shirt out of a drawer.

A good blast of cold water in the face is what you need. And a way to stop these ridiculous thoughts of yours.

It wasn't until she was out of her own shower, dried and dressed, her still damp hair pulled into a loose, haphazard knot atop her head, that she thought of the guaranteed cure.

She went back to the dresser and pulled open the bottom drawer. She reached inside, far to the back, probing until her searching fingers found the long-hidden but still familiar oblong shape. She pulled it out, cradling the heavy silver frame in her hands, face down. She drew in a long, deep breath, and turned it over.

Her father looked back at her from the photo in the sterling frame. A strikingly handsome man, with perfect features, golden hair, twinkling brown eyes, straight, chiseled nose, dimpled cheeks and a sensuous mouth that seemed on the verge of laughter even in the stillness of the frozen image. The touches of gray at his temples only added to his overall attractiveness.

Remember what he taught you.

The old refrain, the words she hadn't had to summon up in years, came back to her as if she'd been chanting them every day of every one of those years.

It hadn't all been bad. She'd spent her childhood loving him with the pure intensity of a daddy's girl. He'd said she was beautiful, and she'd believed him. He'd taught her to ride. He'd taught her to dance. He'd taught her to sing.

And in the end, he'd taught her to cry.

But she wasn't crying now. She had let slip her last tear over this man long ago. She felt nothing but anger, looking down at the perfect image he'd used so well, so effectively, to charm anyone and everyone to his way of thinking and doing.

She hugged her anger to her like a protective cloak as she shoved the photograph back in the drawer and slammed it shut. She was armed now, she told herself. Immune to whatever charm the equally handsome Cole Bannister chose to exert.

She pulled on her socks and trotted down the stairs to pull on her boots and check on Hobie.

He'd forgotten, Cole thought.

He'd forgotten how good it felt to be out like this. He was away from the bustle of the city, breathing fresh air scented with sage and the heat of the rising summer sun, riding across land dotted here and there with the last of the season's golden poppies, atop a smooth-moving horse who was so finely attuned to his rider that it seemed all he had to do was think about turning and the animal was already doing it. Yes, Hobie's buckskin was quite a horse.

"You look... contented."

He looked at Tory in surprise. She'd said so little this morning, he thought she'd sworn off talking to him at all, as if that moment of unexpected intensity last night had scared her. Lord knew it had rattled him. And he hadn't even touched her. That fact rattled him even more.

So he had almost welcomed her silence. Their only communication had involved Hobie—who had still, to her relief, been sleeping quietly when they'd left—the tack for the buckskin, and the fact that Rocky, in between frenetic hunts for more mice and wreaking havoc in the tack room as he learned to walk across the racks, had taken to sunning himself lazily on the porch railing.

"Hell of a life," Cole had said as he looked at the dozing cat. He felt a little irritated at himself for sneaking down to the kitchen late last night for a plate for one of the cans of cat food he had stuck in the truck at the last minute, when he'd realized the stubborn cat was not going to be left behind.

"It looks like he's earned it," Tory had said, reaching out to tickle the darker gray, ragged ear. Rocky didn't respond, there was no purring approval from him, but he hadn't dodged her touch, either. Nor had he made his usual meow of protest at the audacity of this human for daring to touch him without being asked.

Mellowing with the easy life, Cole had thought then. But now he wondered if it just wasn't being here, because he was starting to feel the same way. And, judging from Tory's words just now, it showed. He didn't try to deny it. "Contented is probably a good word for it." He tugged off his sheepskin-lined denim jacket, much too warm now, and twisted around to tie it behind his saddle. "It's been a long time. I didn't realize that I ... missed this."

"I couldn't live any other way." Her voice was solemn, and he almost smiled.

"I don't blame you. Who was it who said that about the outside of a horse being good for the inside of a man?"

She smiled, much too small a thing to cause the little tumble his stomach seemed to take, even after a morning of steadfast silence. "Winston Churchill, I think."

"Well, he was right."

She lifted a brow at him. "Even this horse? After this morning?"

Cole couldn't help grinning. "He was just feeling his oats. Hobie said he hadn't been ridden in a while. Any horse with some spirit is going to let his feelings be known. And he got over it pretty fast."

In fact, he'd been expecting the explosion since he'd saddled the stocky buckskin and felt the hump in his back at the feel of the long-absent weight. The spunky horse hadn't disappointed him—it had been a wild, bucking ride for a minute or two.

"It didn't take him long to realize you weren't going anywhere." The acknowledgment in her tone was quiet, but there. "You settled him down pretty quick, for a guy who hasn't ridden for a long time."

"And I'll be feeling it longer than he will," Cole said dryly, although he was absurdly pleased by her compliment. He was in decent shape, but he'd been long departed from that kind of furious activity, and he knew he was going to be dealing with the aftereffects.

Her smile widened at his self-deprecating words, and he felt a ridiculous warming from somewhere low and deep. And right now, riding along beside her in the morning sun, he couldn't dredge up the desire to squash that feeling. He smiled back at her, for no better reason than he thought she looked adorable with that baseball cap on, and her hair tugged through the opening in the back into a jaunty ponytail.

As long as he remembered, he told himself, as long as he knew it was only for today, as long as he never forgot that she was a woman he was trying to help for the sake of a man she loved, which usually meant disaster—and that someone else always paid the price—he could relax, couldn't he? Just for one day? He felt like he was stealing back one of the golden days of his childhood, and he couldn't bring himself to reject the unexpected gift, whether he thought he deserved it or not.

"Now that little pony of yours, there," he said, nodding at Mac, "is a keeper."

He'd thought her expression lovely before, but the way she lit up at his praise of the liver chestnut made him wonder if she ever had, or would, look at a man that way.

"He's wonderful," she agreed fervently. "All heart and give, with talent to spare. He could go to the top. If he were mine, I'd never sell him."

"If you feel that strongly, why don't you buy him?"

"Buy him?" She gave him a look that was half amused, half resigned. "Right now I couldn't afford what John paid for him as a two year old, let alone what he's worth now."

"Too bad," Cole commiserated. "He should belong to someone who really appreciates him."

"Oh, John does appreciate him. But he... It's just that he likes to win, and he had his hopes pinned on John's Prize. And he—"

"On what?"

"His other horse." She lowered her gaze. "The one who died."

Cole's mouth quirked. "Did he name it after himself? Or the goal?"

Her head came up then, and she shrugged ruefully. "Both, I suppose. But he's not like that, not really. And he's stuck with us, even after..."

She trailed off, and Cole saw the pain flicker in her eyes. Already he'd come to know Tory Flynn well enough to realize that the death of any animal would hurt her, and the death of one she'd known and worked with would strike her very hard.

He saw her reach down to stroke Mac's neck, and wondered if she was even aware of what she was doing, or what she was revealing by doing it.

He wanted to tell her not to worry. He wanted to tell her he'd make sure nothing happened to Mac. But he couldn't. He'd given up making promises. He hadn't broken many. Just the biggest ones. The ones like "I'll keep him safe," or "He'll be all right," or "We'll find him in time."

He turned away, staring out at the foothills they were beginning to ride into, wishing he could regain that comfortable feeling, that feeling of relaxing in a way he hadn't been able to for years. They rode on in silence, and after a while he began to feel it creeping back in, slowly, like the growing heat of the sun as it warmed him.

"I saw him up there," Tory said at last, gesturing upward and slightly to her right. Cole nodded in answer, and they headed that way. There wasn't any kind of a trail, but Tory seemed certain of where she was going, so he just held the buckskin back and let her lead the way over the rocky ground.

The liver chestnut took to the uneven terrain without hesitation, and Tory let him go, only using an occasional tug on the reins or a nudge with her legs to guide him. She'd told Cole this morning when they'd been saddling up that she'd only recently changed from the gentler hackamore to a bridle on the young horse. Cole never would have guessed he was new to the bit, for the colt handled like a trained reining horse, even out on the trail like this. It was clear Mac had complete faith in Tory, accepting with equanimity even the strange piece of metal in his mouth in place of the hackamore that would have used only pressure on his nose for control.

He'd known she had to be good. Hobie would have taught her, and Hobie was one of the best horsemen he'd ever seen. But until now, when he watched her ride a green horse, new to the bridle, through terrain treacherous enough to trip up even a trained trail horse, he hadn't realized how good. She anticipated every hazard, and with gentle encouragement guided Mac through, past or over it.

And she talked to him. The gentle, loving words floated back to Cole as if on the breeze, and once again he caught himself wondering what it would be like if she ever turned that soft, crooning, coaxing voice on a man.

He'd ride right off the nearest cliff, if that's what she wanted, he thought grimly. And if you don't stop thinking about things like that, you might as well find that cliff yourself.

"Over there," she said, pulling Mac to a halt and pointing upward to a group of small trees, barely more than shrubs, that seemed clustered around a small level spot between two large rocks, just above his eye level from atop the buckskin.

A good spot, Cole thought, pulling up beside her. For a lot of things. Situated above the sketchy trail, it was hidden unless you knew it was there. Protected from view on three sides by the rocks and the trees. Shady in a place where there wasn't much shade. And, he thought as he swung down from the saddle, with maybe one advantage more important than all the others.

He pulled the reins over the buckskin's head. For a second he contemplated asking Tory if the horse would ground tie, but then realized that any horse Hobie rode would be trained to do everything but dance—and maybe that, too, he thought with a stifled grin as he remembered a little pinto Hobie had once danced through a barroom outside Cheyenne on the last night of the Frontier Days Rodeo.

As he'd expected, the stocky horse stood docilely, reins trailing on the ground as he settled in to await his rider's return. Cole studied the hillside for a moment, looking for the most logical way up to the spot that, now that he was on the ground, was more than head high even for him. He wasn't much for rock climbing, especially in slick-soled boots. If he could get a grip somewhere, he could pull himself up, but the edge looked far too rounded and smooth from here.

"I didn't see a horse," Tory said, "or any sign of one when I came back later to look around, but I suppose he could have packed all that stuff in."

"Where's the nearest road or track that doesn't cross the ranch?" he asked, moving to his left, where a small boulder lay up against a larger one.

"There's a county road that comes off the main road just east of us. It winds back in the hills a ways." A new note came into her voice. "And it goes on past the end of the paved part almost another mile or so, up to the fire break. I hadn't thought of that."

He looked back over his shoulder at her. "How far from here, if you came up the back?"

"Less than a half mile, if you had a four-wheel drive that could take you up to the very end of the track. It'd be steep, but short."

Cole only nodded, then took a step up on top of the smaller boulder. From there he found it easy to wedge one foot in a split in the bigger rock, and after a quick scramble he was up. And when he turned around, he found what he'd guessed at to be true: there was a straight shot, an unbroken view of the ranch buildings in the distance. With a good pair of high-powered binoculars—or a good rifle scope, he thought grimly—you could see everything that went on outside the buildings themselves.

"What?" Tory asked, sounding concerned, and he realized his grim thoughts must have been reflected in his face. He squelched that gut reaction. There had been no indication that anyone other than the horses had been or would be the target of whoever was behind this.

"Somebody's been here, all right." He crouched down and ran a finger over a slightly darker spot of dirt, then lifted his hand to his nose. "Kerosene. That would fit with the lantern you saw."

"City guy."

"What?"

"Kerosene lanterns are heavy. So's kerosene. I wouldn't lug the stuff on foot. But city folk have to have big lights."

Cole stifled a grin. "Am I supposed to feel insulted?"

She looked startled. "I didn't mean— I mean, you aren't..." She shrugged, then added rather sheepishly, "You seem to fit, out here. I forgot you live in L.A."

"I'm flattered." He said it jokingly, but he meant it. "And that's a good point. I wouldn't lug one of those things up here, either, unless I was going to be here awhile."

She looked pleased at his agreement, but then her expression turned troubled. "Do you think he's still around, then? I've checked up here a few times, and never saw any sign of him again."

"Tell me something," he said casually as he walked back to the edge of the outcropping that formed the floor of the little natural alcove, "do you always go charging off after trespassers by yourself?"

"I didn't. I told you, he was already gone."

"But if he hadn't been, or if you'd found him somewhere else—or he'd found you—what would you have done?"

She flushed. "I know you think I'm—"

"I don't think you have the slightest idea what I think of you," he muttered, then jumped down from the outcropping before she could react to the words he hadn't meant to say. "I want to look around a little more. Do you want to wait, or start back down?"

She looked about to protest his abrupt change of subject, but after a moment merely let out a compressed breath. "I'll wait. If you'll tell me what you're looking for, I'll help."

"I don't know," he said as he started walking farther up the hill, "but I'll—"

"Know it when you see it?"

He looked over his shoulder at her, half expecting her to be laughing. She wasn't, she was just looking at him, quietly, intently. "Yeah, something like that."

He had turned back around when she spoke again. "Tell *me* something . . . Cole. Why did you quit?"

He went very still, his back to her. He'd never experienced a succession of feelings quite like the one that swept through him then—a spurt of that electric warmth when she said his name, then the icy chill brought on by her question.

"Too many people died," he said flatly, without looking around.

Then he started up the hill again.

Chapter 7

By the time they had rounded up the steers that had congregated around the tiny spring up in the draw between two of the smaller foothills, and had pushed them unhurriedly down to the flat, Cole was seriously wondering if he'd be able to walk tomorrow. He'd gone a long time without using the muscles that staying atop a horse took, and the longer they rode, the more glum his prognosis for mobility tomorrow looked.

They'd managed to return to that pleasant, companionable atmosphere. It was hard not to when they found, as they moved the small herd, that they worked very well together. Some of the younger steers weren't used to being herded, and more than once Cole, riding the more experienced Buck, had been the one who had to head off an escapee. Meanwhile Tory and Mac—who appeared utterly fascinated with these strange beasts—spent their time chivying along stragglers. Despite the short distance of the move, it took them the better part of the morning to get it done.

"And they'll only stay here awhile," Tory said as Cole pulled the buckskin to a halt beside her. "They like that draw, for the springwater and the sense of protection, and eventually they'll wander back. But we try to bring them down now and then, at least for a few days, so we can check them over."

He twisted in the saddle to look around. "Is there enough graze here for them?"

"We have to supplement it a little with hay, but not too much. We're not raising them for beef, so putting weight on them isn't the goal."

"You want 'em lean and quick, hmm?"

"Exactly." He should be used to it by now, he thought. There was no excuse for this crazy inner free-fall every time she smiled. "That way we learn real fast if a horse has what it takes."

"Hobie says this one—" he gestured at Mac "—has it."

It had been true, Hobie had said it, but Cole had only repeated it to watch her eyes light up again. She didn't disappoint him.

"Yes, he does. Hobie calls it savvy. He says you can't train a horse to have it, he either does or doesn't. And if he does, like Mac here, you can always count on him. He'll do right when things get rough, and save you more often than not."

Cole nodded, only vaguely listening to the words, so intent was he on the innocent enthusiasm in her voice, and the delighted sparkle in her eyes. The man who could inspire that kind of ardor in this woman would have his hands full, he thought. And his heart.

And he was turning into a soft-headed idiot, he observed in silent self-mockery. First a cat you let move in and take over, and now a woman—a client, yet—you let turn your gut inside out with a smile.

Damn, you're a slow learner, Bannister.

They rode sedately back to the barn, giving the horses a chance to begin to cool down. Once there, they dismounted, and the minute his feet hit the ground Cole felt the first harbinger of the misery he was in for tomorrow. His legs nearly buckled.

"A little sore?" Tory asked sympathetically.

"Nothing compared to how sore I'm going to be."

"Maybe I'd better get the liniment now," she said teasingly. "You may need a rubdown."

A sudden image assailed him, born of her joking words, an image of Tory's hands running over him, massaging every aching muscle, sliding over his bare skin. The image was followed almost instantly by a fierce rush of heat and sensation as his mind pushed the vision over the edge into pure eroticism—Tory's hands caressing his body while he did the same to her, and then their mouths following the trails their hands had traced.

"Cole?"

Her use of his name intensified his gut-level response; only the sudden breathlessness of her voice reminded him that he was treading on very dangerous ground.

"I'll cool out the horses," he said, hating the tight, tension-laden sound of his voice.

"But I—"

If she didn't go in the next second, he wasn't sure he could stop himself from grabbing her and starting in on making that image a reality.

"Why don't you go check on Hobie?" he suggested, seizing on the one thing he knew would distract her.

He felt a burst of relief when she at last nodded and started toward the house. But it wasn't until she was almost there that he remembered to breathe again. And when he did, a long, low groan escaped him. He leaned forward, resting his head against Mac's muscled shoulder.

It was a long time before, loaded down with both saddles and bridles and his jacket, he made it to the tack room. He hung the bridles up neatly. He placed the saddles on the racks with care. He picked up his jacket, and folded it over his arm. None of his careful actions did anything to relieve the lingering tightness of his body. He flung his jacket into a corner in disgust.

* * *

That afternoon, after working two of the other horses and helping Eric and Kurt—who were acting oddly quiet, and refusing to look at her—finish cleaning stalls, Tory at last returned to the house, knowing she was too weary to accomplish any more today. She was selfishly grateful when she found Hobie had dinner ready to go into the oven. It was a meat loaf she was certain would be liberally laced with her uncle's special blend of peppers and spices that made it both mouth-watering and eye-watering. She hugged him fiercely.

"I'm glad you're feeling better," she said.

"Hmm. A bit." He studied her for a moment, then turned back to the stove.

Tory's eyes narrowed. "What is it?"

"Nothing. Dinner in an hour."

"Hobie—"

"Don't be late or I'll throw it out."

She stepped over beside him and stood there until he looked at her. "What is it?" she repeated.

Hobie sighed. "Ralph Hudson was here this morning."

She fought off a sudden hollow feeling. "He pulled Starwalker?"

Hobie nodded.

They'd been expecting this. She'd thought she was prepared for it, this first sign that maybe things really weren't going to be all right. But she wasn't, though she couldn't let Hobie see that.

"Well," she said, "we knew it was coming."

"Guess we couldn't keep it a secret forever. News travels too damned fast in this business."

"We'll be all right," she said, wishing she could believe it.

"Where's Cole?"

"I don't know. I'm going to go take a shower," she said, changing the subject abruptly and retreating to her room.

She didn't know where Cole was. Didn't want to know. She'd spent the afternoon trying not to know. She couldn't

bear to face him, not until she'd dealt—mentally at least—
with what had happened between them this morning.

She'd never seen a man with the look that had flared in his
eyes in the moment after she'd jokingly mentioned giving
him a rubdown. But she'd known immediately what it was.
She'd seen stallions with that kind of fire in their eyes, the
stark, ravenous heat of aroused male.

She sank down on the edge of her bed, clasping her trembling hands tightly between her knees. Her one college experience with sex had been painfully dismal, her one
experience since hadn't been much better, and she'd never
gone in much for fantasizing. So why was she now fighting
off a flood of heated, wildly erotic fantasies, that started
with her massaging Cole's naked back and legs, and pro-
gressed rapidly on to stroking every massive, powerful inch
of him. *Every* inch. And doing it with more than just her
hands.

She drew up her knees and lay back on the bed in a fetal
curl. What was wrong with her? Was she that desperate, had
she been that isolated, that the first eligible man that came
along—

No, there were other men around. She just chose not to
see them. She liked it that way. At least that's what she'd
told herself for the past five years. So what had happened?
After years of treating too-handsome men as pariahs, had
she suddenly forgotten why? Had she forgotten the anguish
and humiliation her mother had lived with, forgotten her
own blissful ignorance, which had no doubt caused her
mother even more pain? Was she going to throw her hard-
learned caution to the winds just because one of those too-
handsome men deigned to notice her? Because he seemed to
touch places in her she'd never known were there? Because
of those rare moments when something flashed in the depths
of a pair of steel blue eyes and she caught herself wondering if it hinted at a man who felt, and felt deeply?

Was she going to make a fool of herself because of the
way a man, climbing a rock face with careless, controlled
grace, had taken her breath away? Because, when that sud-

den fire had flared in his eyes, she'd felt the shocking urge
to let it consume her?

With a shiver, she drew up into a tighter curl on the bed.
Only when the tempting odor drifting upstairs from the
kitchen made it obvious that dinner was almost ready did
she rise. She took a swift shower, left her damp hair loose,
then dressed in a long, dark green knit dress she sometimes
wore in the evenings because it was soft, comfortable and a
change from the jeans she seemed to live in. For a moment,
after she'd slipped it on, she wondered if she had subcon-
sciously picked it tonight because Cole was here. She re-
belled at the idea, and left her face devoid of any makeup to
prove that wasn't the reason at all.

It was after the meal, and after Hobie had glumly re-
layed to Cole the loss of Starwalker—a promising cutting
prospect—that Hobie's expression changed, giving Tory
some slight warning.

"Your dad called this afternoon."

She felt that familiar knot tighten in her stomach. "Oh,"
she merely said, her voice even as she continued to stack the
dinner plates.

Hobie nodded. "I told him you were out rounding up
stock. Didn't figure you'd changed your mind about talking to him."

She let out a breath. "No."

"You know he still wants you to come home."

"I *am* home."

Hobie smiled, not hiding his pleasure at her words. Then,
with a note of concern, "He sounded…pretty adamant this
time. Angry. And nasty. Accused me of keeping you from
talking to him."

The knot in Tory's stomach tightened another notch.
"I'm sorry he said that."

Hobie shrugged. "I'm used to it."

"He shouldn't keep taking it out on you, because I left.
After five years, he should believe I meant what I said." She
bit her lip. "I…I'm sorry you had to lie for me."

Hobie shrugged. "I could lie from now 'til doomsday, and still not catch up with Jack."

Her gaze lifted to her uncle's face. He wore an expression of gentle understanding. Both of them had long ago lost any remaining illusions about Jack Flynn. She glanced at Cole; his expression was unreadable. She felt as if she'd been sent a reminder, a sign that she was headed for trouble if she let herself fall for a man who seemed the same kind of man as her father.

God, was this how my mother felt, helplessly drawn to a man whose flame would sear her beyond repair? Hastily she gathered up the rest of the dishes and carried them to the kitchen counter. It caught up with her there, that sinking, sick feeling that rose in her every time she remembered her mother's face—waxen, pale and at last at peace in death.

Without looking back, she set down the stack of plates and silverware and walked hastily out through the screen door into the fading afternoon sun.

It was nearly dark when Cole found her sitting on the porch swing, her arms wrapped around knees pulled up in front of her. Her hair was loose and falling over her shoulders. The long dress swirled around her, and draped nearly down to the porch. And he couldn't get out of his mind how the color of it turned her eyes an astonishing sea green.

He leaned a hip against the porch railing in front of her, then bent one knee and swung his foot up to rest flat on the rail as he leaned back against the upright post.

"Want to talk about it?" he asked after a moment.

He sensed her sudden stiffness. "No." Then, sounding a little forced. "It's nothing to do with you."

Interesting, he thought. He hadn't suggested that it was. "Isn't it?"

Her eyes flicked to his face. "What's that supposed to mean?"

He shrugged. "Just that I'm still wondering who we were really talking about last night."

Suspicion narrowed her gaze. "Has Hobie been talking to you?"

"A little," he admitted. "Only because I asked. I always wondered why he never talked about his brother. I didn't even know he had one for years."

"So," she said, bitterness tinging her voice, "did he tell you that my father is as charming as a politician running for reelection? That women come after him like lemmings going over a cliff, and he picks a new one every week? That he's been on that magazine list of the fifty most beautiful people in the country *twice?* That he's rich enough to buy half of Texas? Or anything—or anyone—else he wants?"

He saw her arms tighten, drawing her knees up even closer. She laid her cheek on her knees, facing away from him.

"No," he said softly, then hesitated. He wasn't even sure why he was pursuing this, only that it seemed very important somehow. "Hobie told me that his brother expected all the adulation as his due. And that he hurt a lot of people."

"Yes. Yes he did."

"And that he really wants you to come home."

She let out a sharp little breath of disgust. "Oh, he does. He's been after me for months now. Lord knows why."

"Couldn't he just want you home because he loves you?"

Her head came up sharply, and she faced him once more. "My father doesn't love anyone, except himself. If he wants me home, he's got a reason. Some private agenda. He always has a motive."

He paused again, knowing she would be naturally protective of her own pain. But his years in the field had taught him that if you could get someone talking about something else first, then talking about the real subject sometimes came easier. And he knew where at least one weak spot of Tory's was.

"I got the feeling," he said slowly, "that one of those people he hurt was Hobie."

Her head came swiftly up. "Yes," she said, a little fiercely. "He did hurt Hobie. Often. Called him useless, a failure, a loser. Said being a clown was what he'd been born for, since he'd been a joke most of his life."

And that hurt you, too, Cole guessed. Probably more than it had hurt Hobie. "And you fought with him over it?"

She made a tiny, choking sound. She sprang to her feet, sending the porch swing swaying violently. She looked about to run, then stopped, her hands going out to grip the porch railing a couple of feet from Cole's boot.

"No," she said at last, her voice heavy with remorse. "He was my father. My daddy. And I was daddy's girl. The worst kind of daddy's girl. I thought that man hung the moon. So I..."

Cole could practically feel the tightness in her throat as she took in a quick little breath.

"I believed him. For years Hobie was just my crazy uncle, the family clown. Literally. My mother told me I was wrong, that Hobie was a good, fine man. And the few times I saw him, I thought she was right. He was funny. He made me laugh. And he was good to me. But he never stayed."

"How could he?" Cole hadn't meant to say it, but the thought of Hobie going through such humiliation made him furious.

"Of course he couldn't. I should have seen that. Just like I should have seen the truth. But I had to believe my father. Because I was daddy's little girl, and that's what daddys' girls do."

Cole shifted uncomfortably, something about the pain in her voice was digging at him in a way he wasn't used to. Guilt, he thought. She felt guilty about this. He recognized the feeling all too well.

"It wasn't your fault—" he began.

She whirled on him. "No? Maybe not when I was five, or six or seven. But I kept on believing him. Even after my mother died, I believed him. I never even realized that she'd been hanging on, hoping I'd see the truth. When I reached sixteen and still worshipped Jack Flynn, she gave up. She just gave up and died."

The way she talked about him, using his full name as if he were some species too deadly for familiarity, told Cole a lot about the way she'd reacted to him. God, first Kyra, who'd been burned by her husband, and now Tory. Was he going to pay the price for his unasked-for-looks, a price driven up by men he'd never even met, forever?

"And Hobie," Tory persisted, her voice shaky. "All those years, wasted. Years I can never get back. Years he spent thinking I was laughing at him just like my father. Because I didn't have the courage to stop believing in the god, and the little fantasy world he created."

She turned back to grip the porch railing once more, so tightly her knuckles gleamed white even in the gradually fading light.

"Then I went away to school. For the first time, daddy wasn't there to charm me into believing his version of the truth. I started to see things differently." She laughed harshly. "I started to see things, period. People would show me newspaper pictures of my father and the flavor-of-the-week bimbette. Girls would laugh at me, saying it must be weird to have my father dating all those women who were my age. That's when I found out it had been going on for years. Long before Mom died."

She stopped and took a shuddering breath. "And guys . . . admired him. He got things done, they said. And using people, either charming them or seducing them, was just a way to get the job done. To them, it was something to be proud of."

Another shaky breath. "And they seemed to think . . . like father like daughter. After a while I got tired of fighting them off, and I didn't go out at all. Even the one man who . . . seemed to understand, only had his eye on my father's money."

"Tory, stop. I'm sorry. I shouldn't have pried." He meant it. The anguish in her voice was drowning him, making it hard for him to breathe, causing the kind of pain he'd worked so hard to become immune to.

"I hate him." It broke from her as if forced out under impossible pressure. "I know you're not supposed to say things like that about your own parents, but I hate him. I hate Jack Flynn."

"Or anyone who reminds you of him?"

Cole didn't know if he'd finally asked it because he wanted to know, or because he was desperate to stop the flow of her words. She turned on him again, and he could feel her eyes on him as if they were projecting the heat he heard in her voice.

"Yes," she snapped. "Anyone who oozes that charm, or has looks enough to stop a stampede. I've had a lifetime of a man who used what God gave him as a weapon, a tool, to get whatever he wanted whenever he wanted it. And to hell with anyone who got hurt in the process. In his business, or in his family."

"And if I went and got myself caught in that stampede, Tory? Would you trust me then, if I looked like I'd been trampled into the dust? Even though I'd be the same man I am now?"

This was crazy, Cole thought as she stared at him. He didn't want her to trust him. He didn't want to get any closer than he already—dangerously—had. But he couldn't seem to stop himself.

"But you wouldn't be the same," she insisted. "Not after living for a while like the rest of us, not able to get by on your looks—"

Cole's boots hit the porch with a sharp thud. "My looks," he growled, "didn't matter a hoot to any of the horses or bulls I rode. Or to my DI's in the Army, except to make them want to push me even harder, because they thought I was 'too darn pretty,' as you put it. And my looks sure as hell didn't stop that bomb from—"

He broke off, appalled at what he'd almost said. He never talked about that. Never. To anyone. He went on before she could speak, before she could probe, before she could say whatever her shocked gaze told him she was working up to.

"Maybe before you start talking about other people's looks, you should look in a mirror, Victoria Flynn."

He swung over the porch rail, dropped to the ground and walked away without looking back. She made a faint sound, but he kept going. He heard a car out on the main road, but didn't look. He saw Rocky darting around the side of the barn, but didn't react.

"Cole, wait."

He lowered his head and kept moving; he didn't want to hear this. He wasn't sure where he was going, just that he needed to put some distance between himself and this woman who was jeopardizing his self-control.

"Please."

It was soft, entreating and a little breathless. It stopped him in his tracks.

"I didn't mean..." She trailed off as she came up beside him. "I don't know why all that came out like that. I never...talk about him. Not like that, and especially not to...a stranger."

A stranger. That's what he was, all right, Cole thought. And if he wanted to keep it that way, he'd better back away from this woman in a hurry.

"Forget it."

"But—"

"What you think of me doesn't matter. What matters is that I find out who's killing your horses. And why. Then I'll get the hell out of here, and you can go on with your life."

"I'm sorry!" she exclaimed. "You're Hobie's friend and I've been inexcusably rude to you. I know he would never have asked you here if he didn't trust you. It's just..."

"Just what?"

She lowered her eyes. Her feet shifted, and Cole saw they were bare. He hadn't noticed before. He'd been too stunned by the dress, flowing over her slender body, softly caressing each gentle curve and turning her eyes to green fire. But he should have realized—she didn't even come up to his chin.

"I...You scare me," she whispered.

Cole's breath caught. "I...what?"

Her head came up. "You scare me. I feel...strange around you, and I don't want to, but I can't seem to help it. And I'm afraid that means I'm like her. She couldn't help it, either, and... Oh, God, I'm not making any sense."

She might not be making sense, but she was making mincemeat out of him. When she looked up at him and he saw the sheen of moisture in her eyes, he almost lost it. How many times had he made a woman cry? Never meaning to, but doing it, anyway?

And then, without even thinking about it—reacting from some gut-level instinct buried so deep he'd thought it didn't exist any longer—he pulled her into his arms. She stiffened. And he, too, shivered at the feel of the little quivers that went through her.

"Shh," he whispered. "It's okay."

It wasn't, things were getting more mixed up by the minute. And this was only going to make matters worse—much worse—but he couldn't let her go, not now, not when it felt so damn good to hold her like this.... God, he wasn't making any more sense than she'd made.

"I can't explain it," she said, her voice catching on a little gulp.

"You don't have to," he said, sounding a little grim even to his own ears. "I understand."

He understood, all right. Because she scared the hell out of him, too. And that was a feeling he thought he'd put behind him, the day he'd pulled himself from the field and taken over a desk.

The sudden flare of a car's headlights made them both jump—Cole with a smothered oath, because he'd been so intent on Tory that he hadn't realized the car he'd heard earlier had turned onto the ranch drive. He was worse than rusty, he was stupid. More so because, whereas Tory's response had been to quickly pull away from him, his had been to pull her closer. And as he reluctantly let her go, he had an edgy feeling in his gut that the reaction had nothing to do with any protective instinct.

"Well, well. I'm so glad I dropped in on my way back to L.A."

The sound of a masculine voice, laced with a rather mocking undertone and punctuated by the slamming of a car door, came at them from behind the glare of light. Cole felt a little too much like a pinned deer, and backed out of the probing high beams.

"Too bad the clients don't get the same treatment as the new hired help," the voice said, still mocking.

Already, without even seeing the man, Cole didn't like him. Nor did he like the way Tory had gone so very still.

"You want to kill those lights, whoever the hell you are?" he snapped.

"Cole," Tory said warningly, in a voice low enough to be heard only by him. "It's John."

"Lennox?" Cole asked as the shadowy man laughed and reopened the car door obligingly. "He of the prize winning ego?"

She stiffened. "Yes, Mr. Ex-rodeo cowboy. Any other kettles you'd like to call black?"

She didn't miss a trick, Cole thought wryly. Or mince any words. "Touché," he said softly. "Sorry."

The lights went out. The man—a tall, lean man dressed in an expensive, Western-cut suit, Cole could see now—straightened up.

"There. Is that better, Mr....?" The voice was smooth, urbane and polished. It didn't make Cole like him any better. So, childishly perhaps, he didn't answer.

"Well, if you're not feeling sociable, perhaps Tory will introduce us."

"I... Of course, John. This is—"

Before she could get the words out, a low, gray shape appeared out of nowhere at a dead run. With a yowl that was eerily like the roar of his bigger cousins, Rocky latched onto the new arrival's pant leg and gave a furious, claws-extended swipe at his polished boots.

"What the hell?" Lennox jumped and swore, but Rocky clung tenaciously.

Cole could have sworn he heard Tory stifle a giggle before she went on with her interrupted introduction.

"John, this is Rocky."

Lennox swore again. Crudely. Cole smothered a laugh of his own. And decided that perhaps bringing that damn cat along hadn't been such a dumb idea after all.

Chapter 8

Tory stole a sideways glance at Cole. He was looking out into the distance, his battered hat pulled low to shade his eyes. He was riding easily, despite some obvious and wryly acknowledged stiffness that had lingered after the first couple of days of regular riding.

But more significantly—and somehow comforting and dangerous at the same time—he seemed to have become an accustomed part of life here, seemed, in such a short time, to have fit effortlessly into the pattern of her days.

He was so unlike John, she thought, who, with his designer suits and fancy car had never quite fit in. She had to keep back a chuckle as she remembered the night before last, when he'd driven in and been promptly attacked by Rocky.

John hadn't reacted well to that at all. Tory had never heard him use such language before. It had taken her nearly an hour to soothe his ruffled feathers, and they had never gone out for the dinner he'd come to offer. She didn't mind, since the distraction had kept him from probing too deeply about Cole, and what she had been doing wrapped in the arms of the "hired help" she'd known all of a few days.

If she'd thought John's casual invitations to dinner or a show had been serious, she might have been more concerned; he was their best client. But it was hard to be anything but amused when she remembered what Cole had done that night. He might deny to the death that Rocky was his, but when John had taken a swipe at the cat with his other foot, Cole had reacted instantly.

"Now," he'd said, the Texas drawl suddenly so thick Tory knew he was putting it on, "a fancy dude like you isn't gonna let a little ol' cat get to him, is he?"

"Get that damned thing off me before I—"

"I wouldn't be makin' any careless threats," Cole said as he leaned over and scooped Rocky up, not being particularly careful of John's suit pants, which had also fallen victim to the cat's claws. Rocky yowled in protest, but Tory noticed he didn't claw at Cole. "Cat here's just got a terrible dislike for boots like that, you know?"

That startled John into momentary silence. "What?"

"Those boots of yours. Snakeskin, right?"

"Thousand dollar imported anaconda," John retorted, some of the anger returning to his voice.

"Hmm." Cole tugged at the leg of his own jeans, revealing his own boot, and Tory suddenly realized the origin of those odd-looking scars. "Now, these are only domestic rattlesnake, but he don't like them any better."

"Oh."

Tory had had to cover her laughter with a cough. Domestic rattlesnake? Didn't John even realize that Cole was taking a swipe of his own at John's pretentious declaration of the price of his boots? But she shouldn't have laughed. God knew they couldn't afford to lose another horse, and John wasn't the type to take being made to look foolish lightly.

"What's so funny?"

Cole's question yanked her back to the present. She focused on his face, at least, what she could see of it. The sun was almost directly overhead and the brim of his hat cast his eyes and nose into shadow. Only the sensual line of his mouth was lit by the sun, and she'd found herself staring at it far too often today. She'd been pleased when he'd suggested riding out to see if there was any more sign of her trespasser. Now she was wondering if she would have been better off saying no.

"I was thinking about domestic rattlesnake boots," she said hastily.

Cole grinned. Tory felt that crazy flutter in her chest, followed by the tightness that seemed to seize her whenever she looked at him. He'd forgone shaving this morning, and the tough texture of beard that stubbled his face only made his lips seem smoother, softer, and the sunlight made her think of how warm they would be.

"Sorry," he said, not sounding at all apologetic.

"Don't be. Sometimes John gets a little..."

"Pompous? Haughty? Pretentious?"

This time the giggle broke free. "Yes. But Rocky brought him down to earth in a hurry."

Cole nodded sagely. "Attack first, ask questions later. Good strategy."

"The best defense is a good offense?"

"Yep." Cole's grin widened. And Tory thought that if she didn't stop watching his mouth like this, she was going to be in real trouble. She wondered what he'd say if she asked him to push his hat back. Not that being able to see his eyes would help much, she admitted ruefully.

"John's not really that bad." Tory felt compelled to explain. "And he's been very nice. Concerned. About all three horses who died, not just his own." She shrugged. "I don't think he believes they were killed, but he's always calling to see how I'm doing."

Cole made a sound that could have been grudging acknowledgment, or just as easily disgusted dislike.

"He's just very rich," she said. "He runs in my father's kind of crowd. They even met here at the ranch once. They talk the same kind of talk. And John's used to being deferred to, just like my father."

"He's like your father, and he's a good-looking guy. So why doesn't he get tarred with your father's brush?"

The unexpected question caught her completely off guard. "He's not *that* good-looking. Besides, I don't—"

She cut herself off with a gasp as she realized she'd been about to say she didn't go all weak in the knees when John was around.

"You don't what, Tory?" His voice was soft, oddly husky.

"I don't think of him that way," she amended lamely. She waited for him to take advantage of the admission, only slightly less damaging than what she'd been about to say in the first place.

"I'm glad," was all he said.

"Why?" she asked, feeling suddenly reckless without understanding why. "Because Rocky didn't like him?"

"I'm beginning to appreciate his taste."

"Since he chose you?"

"In spite of that."

He was still smiling, but Tory got the feeling there was more seriousness in the words than he would admit to.

Too many people died.

His words that day on the hill echoed in her mind. She supposed death wasn't a rarity in his kind of work. And Hobie had said he'd been in the army, special forces of some kind. Yet when he'd said those words, Tory had felt a chill unlike anything she'd ever felt before. And she still didn't know if it was from the stark, grim simplicity of the words, or the sound of throttled pain in his voice when he'd said them.

"Hobie seems better," Cole said, so casually it was hard to believe this was the same man she'd just been thinking of.

"Yes, he does." She hesitated, then added, "Thank you."

He looked surprised. "Me? For what?"

"For coming here. Even if we never find out who...did this, it was worth it for the change in him."

"Worth what?"

She gave him another sideways look. "Bearding the lion in his den. So to speak."

His smile was wry. "Was it that bad?"

"It felt that way at the time." She hesitated, then decided she had little to lose and plunged ahead. "At first I thought Kyra was your girlfriend."

If her words disturbed him, it didn't show. "And you thought I was making time in the office?"

"Something like that. Then, when she said she was pregnant, I thought maybe she was your wife."

This time a flicker of something darkened his eyes for a moment. "I'm not her style. For different reasons, she has the same feeling about guys like me as you do."

She barely stopped herself from saying she wasn't at all sure she felt that way any longer. "But you...care for her."

He reined Buck in sharply. The buckskin tossed his head in protest. He patted the horse as if in apology, then turned to look at Tory, his eyes fastened on her steadily.

"Yes, I do. A great deal. She's a very special lady, and a damn good friend. There was a time when I wished it could have been more, but she was too afraid of me to trust me until it was too late."

She wasn't sure if the edge that came into his voice then was aimed at her or not, but there was no doubt about the direction of his fierce gaze.

"Besides," he persisted, "she'd found Cash by then, and that was that. They're crazy about each other, and I wish them both well. Now, is there a point to this?"

"I was just...curious. She seemed very nice. I'm glad she's happy."

He seemed to relax a little then, and she breathed a silent sigh of relief that she hadn't blurted out something irretrievably foolish.

By the time the sun hit its peak, they had found no more signs of Tory's trespasser. It was turning into a scorcher of a day, and she suggested they stop for a while in the cool shade near the spring before heading back. Cole agreed, saying he'd like to check there, anyway. They hadn't really stopped there the day they'd moved stock, and it was a likely place for the trespasser to go to if he'd been in the area long enough to stumble across the water source.

"I hope not." Tory's brow creased. "That's one of my favorite places. I don't like to think of him being there."

"I wouldn't worry about it. It's pretty hidden. If you didn't know it was there, you'd probably never go back up in that draw that far."

She supposed he was right, she thought as they began to ride. The gap between the hills narrowed down twice to where a horse and rider, especially somebody Cole's size, could barely squeeze by. To a stranger it would no doubt seem hardly worth the effort of exploring. So they would never find the treasure she had found following a recalcitrant young steer one day—a tiny sheltered glade where trees and grass grew green right up to the edge of the little pool, and the air seemed cool even on the hottest of California days. She supposed there were more places like this. The little town wasn't called Summer Springs for nothing.

They rode up to the edge of the unexpected oasis, stepped down and loosened the cinches for the horses. They also slipped the bits, so the animals could indulge slightly in the lush greenery. Tory knew too much wasn't good for them, but the cattle kept the growth down to where there wasn't enough left for them to get sick in the short time they'd be here. And it would be a treat after their usual diet of hay and pellets.

After letting the horses drink, they knelt beside the precious water. Cole used his hat to pour the cooling liquid over his head while Tory wet her bandanna and wiped her face, neck and arms before rewetting it and tying it back around her throat. Then they sat in the shade of a scrub oak that had miraculously taken root in the split of a large boulder. Or perhaps it had caused the split with its inexorable growth. Tory closed her eyes and leaned back against the warm stone, listening to the munching of the horses, and the occasional buzz of a June bug as it went about its beetle business.

And, although she couldn't see or hear him, she could feel Cole's presence as surely as if he were touching her.

Maybe she was wrong about him. He was Hobie's friend, even all these years after their lives had taken different paths. But then again, she'd be a fool to believe that a man's dealings with other men were any indication of how they dealt with women. One of her father's friends, a man he swore he would trust with his life, had made a heavy pass at Tory when she'd been home from college one spring. At the time, it had been yet another nail for the coffin she was building for her childhood image of her father.

"Are you ever going to talk to your father?"

She nearly jumped at the uncanny connection between his out-of-the-blue question and her thoughts. She sat up and stared at him.

"What?"

"I just thought you might be curious about why he all of a sudden wants you home."

"I don't care," she said shortly. "I've only talked to him twice in five years, when I had the misfortune to be expecting another call and it was him." She leaned against the rock again. "Not exactly your typical, loving family."

"Who said a loving family is typical these days?"

"You're right. You have to work at that. My father never worked at anything. He didn't have to. He used his charm."

"So where did you learn to work?"

She smiled. "Hobie. He taught me about the real satisfaction of doing a good job. In fact, he taught me just about everything worthwhile that I know. In school, I was smart enough to slide through with the minimum of effort. Or bluff my way through. But you can't bluff horses." Her smile became a grin. "Or cats."

"Don't start with me about that damn cat."

"I think it's sweet."

"Fine. Let him sleep with you."

To her amazement, the minute the words came out, she saw a faint tinge of color stain his cheekbones. He turned his head quickly to stare at the clear little pool. She couldn't believe he was embarrassed. They had, after all, been talking about Rocky. Hadn't they?

After a long, silent moment, he asked, "Just how badly does your father want you home?"

Her forehead creased. "What do you mean?"

"You've been gone five years. Why now?"

"I don't know." She laughed a sour little sound. "I'm probably the only woman who ever really walked away from him. Even my mother stayed with him until it killed her."

"Why? Why didn't she just leave?"

"She didn't want to leave me."

"So why didn't she take you and leave?"

For once, it was she who felt old and wearily experienced. "My father owns a firm of high-powered attorneys. He has lunch with judges. And family-law arbitrators. He told her if she ever tried, he'd make sure she never saw me again." She grimaced at the painful memory, but felt she somehow owed it to her mother to finish it. "Then, to drive it home, he played his ace in the hole."

"Which was?"

"Me. He brought me in, made up some story about a little girl who had to choose between her parents, and if I had to, which would I chose. In all innocence, of course. But my mother knew what he was doing."

"And you chose your father."

She couldn't look at him. "Of course I did. I've already told you about the kind of kid I was. So she stayed. She started drinking. Then pills. But when she died, it wasn't from that. She just...gave up. I didn't realize until years after she was gone that what she'd given up on was me. She'd hung on for so long, hoping I would someday see the truth, and that she could be there for me when I did."

"Why didn't she just tell you about your father, about the affairs?"

Tory let out a long sigh as she stared at the glistening surface of the water. "I've often wondered that. I think, in a crazy sort of way, she couldn't bear to be the one to destroy my image of him. Maybe she thought I'd blame her."

She shivered, her skin rippling as if that chill wind were still encircling her. She wrapped her arms around herself.

"And you know what scares me the most?" Her voice had dropped to barely a whisper. "The fact that she was probably right. Then. I would have blamed her. I would have hated her for saying such awful things about Daddy." Her throat tightened up at the painful knowledge. "God, I was such a blind, foolish—"

"Child," Cole said from beside her. She'd been so wrapped up in her misery she hadn't realized he'd moved. "You were a child, Tory. I'm sure she understood."

Tory shook her head, tears welling in spite of her efforts to stop them. "She died all alone. My father and I were in St. Moritz for my birthday. Skiing. He didn't even tell me until it was time to go home. A week after she d-died."

In the moment that her voice broke, Cole's arms came around her. And in that moment, she needed that closeness, needed to feel the strength of him, more than she'd ever needed anything in her life. So she let herself go slack against him, as if he held the answers to the problems of her life instead of the likelihood of more. But he was the only thing powerful enough to drive away the old pain. And she welcomed the quelling of the ugly memories, even as what was left of her functioning mind warned her that she was only inviting more torment.

His heat made the sun seem a distant thing, and the solidness of his body made the hills around them seem insubstantial. She heard an odd, muffled sound, and realized it was her own breath escaping on a sigh as, just for a moment, she let one thing fill her world completely—the feel of the man holding her.

And as the troubles of her mother's death, her father's betrayal, Hobie's humiliation and the death of the horses faded, something began to take their place. It was something that changed her need from a simple desire to be held by someone much stronger than she to a need for something else, something far more intense—and far more dangerous.

A little frightened by what was happening to her, she drew back, and caught a glimpse of Cole's face. In the instant before he schooled his features to that unreadable mask, she saw it again—that stark, ravenous heat she'd seen in that electric moment when she'd suggested a rubdown. But this time it had been banked, controlled. And she wondered with a little shock if he had reined it in because he'd known that at that moment she'd just needed to be held.

But now, in this quiet place where she had so often retreated for stolen moments of solitude, she was no longer sure that that was all she needed. Or wanted. Her gaze focused once more on his mouth, on those sexy lips that had teased her all day as they rode. And she found herself wondering what it would be like to be kissed by a mouth like that—to be kissed by a man like Cole Bannister. Did he really know something lesser men didn't? Did knowing that you were kissing a man who must have been God's prototype for male beauty make it different?

"Tory."

It was short, husky and undeniably a warning. Her gaze flicked up to meet his. She felt color tinge her cheeks.

"I . . . was just wondering—"

"I know what you were wondering. It was written all over your face, little girl."

She went very still in his arms. "I'm twenty-seven years old, Cole. I'd been to nearly every industrialized nation in the world by the time I was eighteen. I've been on my own since I was twenty-two. I'm *not* a little girl."

She heard and felt a low groan rumble up from his chest. "A world tour isn't going to help you here, Tory Flynn. You're playing with a different kind of fire."

Her chin came up. She'd had quite enough of feeling naive next to his weary worldliness. "I'm not a virgin, either, if that's what you're thinking." She smiled rather shakily. It was true, but nothing had come even remotely close to making her feel the way just thinking about this man did. "Not physically, anyway," she amended.

"Damn." It came out on an explosive breath. He jerked away from her. "Don't you get it? We're talking sex here. Not love, not romance, just raw, hot, out-of-control sex. That's all I deal in, little girl. And if you throw me another look like that, you're going to find out firsthand."

Tory's breath caught in her throat, not so much at the sensual threat inherent in his voice as he spoke the rough words, but at the little thrill that raced through her at the idea of this man feeling this way—over her.

The best defense is a good offense.

The words popped into her head with startling clarity. True, they'd been talking about Rocky then, but she knew with a certainty she couldn't explain that they applied now, as well.

"Tell me," she said quietly. "Is calling me 'little girl' your way of making sure that doesn't happen?"

He went very still. He turned his head away. He stared at the little pool of springwater as if the future was held there. When at last he spoke, his voice was thick, almost raspy.

"Remind me to run the next time you start a sentence with 'tell me.'"

"I learned it from you."

He let out a long, harsh breath. Then he looked at her, his face once more settled into that unreadable mask.

"Is that what you want, Tory? You want to play with that fire and get yourself burned?"

"No. But you can warm yourself at a fire, too, can't you?"

"If the fire's under control."

She studied him for a moment, daring to wonder if there was something personal in that assessment, but his expression didn't change, gave her no hint. At last she shrugged.

"I doubt I'm in any danger. I'm hardly the type to send a man's hormones on a rampage."

"Damn."

This time it was low, throttled and came out through clenched teeth. Before she could move he pulled her a little roughly into his arms again. And before she could catch her breath, his mouth was on hers—hot, hard and fierce.

She'd been wrong about her state of naiveté. Nothing in her limited experience, in fact nothing in her entire life, had prepared her for this. Perhaps nothing could have. Heat built up in her until it seemed to burst loose under its own pressure, tumbling through her in waves. And when his mouth suddenly gentled, and she thought the sensation would ease, it instead gained another dimension, adding a series of tiny frissons of excitement that raced along every nerve.

When his tongue gently probed, she opened to him without resistance. Her sense of self-preservation seemed to have been the first casualty of the inferno Cole Bannister was igniting in her. She shivered as he tasted her, running the tip of his tongue along the even ridge of her teeth. It became a shudder when he went deeper—when the rough, wet velvet of him brushed her own tongue.

She heard her own sigh once more, but this time she recognized the sound for what it was—the sound of surrender. And this time it was muffled against his mouth, and he seemed to breathe it in, even as his mouth continued to plunder hers.

She should be worried, she thought vaguely. Worried about stopping this conflagration before it was too late. But for the first time in her life her body seemed beyond her control, and she couldn't do anything but cling to him. So she did just that, lifting her arms to thread her fingers through the thick strands of his still-damp hair.

She felt his hands, sliding down her back to her hips. She barely had time to marvel at the trail of heat they left behind before her wayward imagination supplied her with a vivid image of what it would feel like if it had been her bare skin he was stroking.

And then that image was shattered as one of his hands moved up her body to cup a breast. He massaged the soft curve as he teased her tongue with his, and took in the tiny cry she made when his thumb brushed over her nipple. The

little dart of fire that shot through her at that intimate touch
seemed to rocket around inside her until it settled someplace low and deep—the place that made her welcome the
moment when his other hand pulled her hips hard against
his.

She arched to him, wanting without knowing what she
wanted. When she felt the pressure of his aroused flesh
against her, heat swept through her in a billowing wave, and
that glowing place within her became an inferno.

She felt another odd sensation, a sort of distant ripple or
movement, and it took her a moment to realize that it
seemed distant because it wasn't her, it was Cole who was
shaking. For her.

Stunned, she broke the kiss. She stared up at his face.
There was nothing of that practiced mask there now. Nothing but need and heat and an arousal that almost frightened her. And something that did frighten her: a trace of
that stark self-loathing she'd seen that first day.

"Damn."

This third time the oath was delivered without heat. In
fact, it was the coldest, bleakest thing she'd ever heard.
Without another word he rose to his feet, grabbed his hat
and slammed it on his head in a choppy motion, so unlike
his usual streamlined grace that it gave away a great deal
about his state of mind.

He turned his back to her and walked stiffly over to the
horses without looking back. He pulled up Buck's head and
slipped the bit back into the buckskin's mouth. Mac's head
came up, as well, watching the proceedings, then turning to
look at Tory as if to ask if they, too, were going to leave.

I guess we are, she silently answered the horse. And I
suppose I should be glad, she added to herself. I probably
just got saved from handing my heart over to be broken by
an expert.

Chapter 9

Cole shut off the notebook computer and leaned back in the chair. He'd hooked up to the office network to do a little probing of his own, had turned up some interesting but not particularly useful facts and had left some instructions that would be found when the crew came in in the morning.

He looked up at a sound, and saw Rocky stroll into the office, a piece of red cloth caught in his mouth and trailing behind him.

"Now, what?" he muttered, then smothered a groan when he recognized it as a bandanna like the one Tory had worn today.

Well, if she wanted it back, she could get it herself, he thought. She's the one who always just laughed at Rocky's troublemaking. The cat leapt up to the desk top, dragging the bandanna along. Cole ignored him.

He sat there for a while, thinking. He hadn't been convinced by Eric and Kurt when he'd talked to them this afternoon. The two teenagers' vehement denial of any knowledge at all of any of the deaths was very interesting, since their denial had come before he'd even asked them. He'd merely mentioned what had been happening, in a conversational way, and out had come the disavowal, followed shortly by their rather abrupt departure.

Nudging Rocky out of the way, he reached over and picked up the envelope that held the autopsy reports on the first two horses. He'd read them once, but quickly. It wouldn't hurt to go over them again. A half an hour later, he let his head loll back as he mulled it over.

Traces of moldy feed were discovered in the stomach of the first horse. Not a lot, but enough to point toward the eventual diagnosis of cause of death. No trace of mold in the contents of the second horse's stomach, but the same kind of feed, and no other indications of illness or injury to explain the sudden death. Colic was presumed to be the culprit in this case, also.

"Nothin' new?"

Cole raised his head to look at Hobie. "No. But I didn't expect to find anything."

Hobie looked at him for a long moment. "Tory'd die before she'd give a horse bad feed."

Cole sighed. He didn't doubt Hobie. It was just that he'd been here long enough already to see how hard she was working. And under enough pressure, *anyone* could make a slip. But he didn't say it to Hobie.

"At this point," he said, tossing the reports on the desk, "I'm not sure the cause of death really matters. What does, is that whoever this is has been able to come and go without attracting any attention."

"Or is already here," Hobie said.

"It's a possibility we can't afford to ignore," he agreed.

And he couldn't afford to stall anymore. He'd waited far too long to get his sorry butt in gear. He'd come here hoping for a miracle, that something would turn up to point him in the right direction without him having to do anything. But after this morning with Tory, he knew he couldn't wait any longer. Things were getting too tangled up. *He* was getting too tangled up, too enmeshed in life here. He had to get moving. He had to stir things up and see what floated to the top. He had to poke and prod until somebody reacted.

But most of all, he had to get Tory out of his mind. He had to forget the shock that had jolted him to his toes when he'd kissed her, when he'd let himself touch her. If she hadn't pulled back when she had, if she hadn't looked at him like that, in such wonder, as if stunned by her own response, God knows if he could have stopped himself.

He could have taken her, then and there. It had been in every motion of her slender body, in every tiny sound she'd made and in her wide-eyed astonishment when she'd looked at him. Looked at him in a way that had made him want to do just that, to skim that T-shirt off of her and bury his face between her breasts, to tug her worn, tight jeans down those legs that went on and on, and bury his aching arousal between her taut thighs. He'd wanted to ride her with all the ferocity he'd once brought to the rodeo, and then he wanted her to ride him the same way.

And wouldn't that just shock Ms. Flynn? She might not be the little girl he'd called her—in his futile effort to do just as she'd cleverly discerned, relegate her to a safe, untouchable niche—but he knew damned well that she was far removed from the kind of women he usually relieved his urges with.

But then, this urge was also far removed from the usual. It was stronger than anything he'd known in years, perhaps ever. And he didn't know if the impossibility of anything between them made things better or worse. Either way, he had to put a halt to it.

All he had to do was figure out how.

Tory sighed, and leaned against Mac's muscled shoulder, taking comfort from the silky warmth of his coat. She felt weighed down, not just by the horses' deaths, but by the feeling that her world was once more caving in on her.

Was there some lesson she hadn't learned the first time this had happened to her? Some reason why—after pulling herself back together after the shattering of her perception of her father, indeed, her entire life—she had to go through it again? She wouldn't care so much, if it wasn't for the fact that this time, Hobie was going to lose, too…lose the thing he'd worked so hard for, risked his very life for.

She desperately wished there was someone she could turn to, someone who would just listen. She'd always gone to Hobie before, but he was hurting enough about all this without having to carry her load, too.

Maybe that was the lesson she needed to learn, she thought sadly as she walked across the pasture to the barn. Not to cut herself off so completely. When she'd first come here, some of the local women had made overtures of friendship to her. But she'd been so wrapped up in her misery, so consumed by her fury at her father, that she had ignored them. Eventually they'd given up. And once she'd got herself back in balance, she had found herself content enough with just Hobie and the horses, and hadn't tried to change things.

Now five, almost six years had gone by in relative peace. It startled her sometimes, the time that had passed. She hadn't really thought about being twenty-seven, until it had come up with Cole the other day. It hadn't seemed that old until she had wondered if he, like her father, usually limited his sexual forays to younger prey. Jack Flynn preferred them closer to twenty-one, just old enough to keep him out of legal trouble when he took them out and charmed them into his bed with champagne and roses and diamonds.

Not that she doubted that, at that moment at least, Cole had wanted her. She might truly be as naive as he seemed to think she was, but even she couldn't have misunderstood the ferocity of that kiss, his aroused state or the shudder that had racked him in the moment before it had ended.

No, she knew it had been real. It was the reason behind it she questioned. And no matter how she looked at it, being the only female handy kept coming up on top of the list. More than once she'd heard her father joke about all cats looking alike in the dark.

She rounded the corner of the barn in time to see the blue-and-white truck of an express-delivery service pulling away. Hobie stood on the front porch of the house with a large, thick envelope adorned with priority stickers in one hand as he ran the other hand through his silver hair. Rocky lay nearby, exquisitely balanced on the porch rail, and completely unconcerned by the interruption. He was lying on something red, and when she got closer, she laughingly realized it was the bandanna she hadn't been able to find.

"It's for Cole," Hobie said when she reached him. "Looks important, too. Hope he gets back soon."

"He's gone?" she asked, bandanna forgotten.

They'd communicated so little in the two days since he'd kissed her, she had no idea what he was doing. She didn't really wonder why, she had a feeling she already knew. That kiss had sent him running like a jackrabbit, no doubt appalled that he'd become that hard up for female companionship.

"Left about an hour ago." Hobie tugged at his mustache. "Forgot about it, or I would have had him pick up those blamed pills of mine at the drugstore."

"You're out?" The doctor had prescribed the medication recently to ease Hobie's breathing at night, and it at last seemed to be kicking in.

Hobie nodded. "Took the last one last night, but I was half asleep and forgot it until just now when I saw Joey."

"Oh." The express-delivery driver was the son of Marcy Redman, the Summer Springs pharmacist. Tory stifled a sigh. Hobie needed those pills. For that matter, so did she. She didn't want to go back to spending the night with her heart in her throat, listening to him breathe.

"I'll go get them. Just let me get cleaned up."

"Now, don't you worry about it. It's been a rough day for you. I can get through one night. I only mentioned it so's at least one of us would remember to get 'em soon."

"No, I'll go. I need to pick up a couple of things, anyway."

What she needed could have waited, she thought later as she wheeled the Jeep down the street that bisected the more modern shopping district of the small town. But she didn't want Hobie without those pills. And besides, she found herself glad to be out and away, even if it was only for a short trip to the drugstore. It was even nice to be out of her jeans. Her light-cotton, sleeveless dress was pleasantly cool in the still-warm evening air.

There were a couple of people ahead of her, but when she stepped up to the counter, the petite, blond-haired woman—who didn't look at all old enough to have a son Joey's age—handed her a small white bag that had obviously already been prepared.

"Hobie called ahead," she explained.

"Oh. Thanks, Marcy."

"Hear you've been having some trouble," Marcy said sympathetically as Tory wrote out a check. Tory's pen halted, then went on. Marcy had been one of the women who had tried to make friends, but unlike some of the others, she had never seemed to hold it against Tory when she'd been ignored, so Tory tried not to read any malicious intent into the simple comment.

"A little. It'll pass," she said, tearing off the check.

"Well, I'm glad you finally got some real help." Marcy's eyes twinkled. "And I must say, you have superb taste."

Tory blinked. "I do?"

"That is one prime hunk of male," the woman teased.

Tory knew she was gaping, but couldn't help it. "Cole? Cole was here?"

"If that's his name. Tall, built, gorgeous blue eyes with eyelashes a woman would kill for and a backside that—"

"Yes," Tory interrupted, knowing exactly what that backside could do to an otherwise sane woman. "That's him."

"Like I said, you've got superb taste."

And he tasted superb. The silly phrase flashed through her mind before she could stop it, just as a blush rose in her cheeks before she could fight it down.

"Mmm-hmm. That's what I thought. He got this look in his eyes when I mentioned you. Oh, I do hope you're... enjoying yourself, Tory. You've been alone far too long. And what a way to break the dry spell!"

Tory nearly gasped. She stared at the woman, but there was no sign of anything other than a teasing goodwill in her face or voice. Still, the memory of that kiss by the spring made her voice a little sharp.

"I'm not 'enjoying' anything. He just... works for me, okay? There's nothing... like that going on between us."

"Hmm" was all Marcy said.

Tory's brows furrowed. "What was he in here for? He's not sick, is he?"

Marcy's eyes twinkled. "Er... no. I just helped him find something."

"Oh." Something about Marcy's smile made her feel awkward. "Thanks for having these ready," she said, picking up the package of pills.

"No problem."

She started to turn away, then remembered that awful feeling of isolation she'd felt this afternoon. She turned back.

"And thanks for... everything else, too, Marcy. I didn't mean to be rude. Things just are... a little complicated right now."

Marcy smiled brightly. "That's okay. I understand. You take care of that sexy uncle of yours, now."

Tory laughed, feeling much better. "I'll tell him you said that."

"You do that," Marcy said. "I declare, if I was single, I'd set my cap for him in a minute."

"I'll tell him that, too," Tory said, grinning as she waved a farewell to the woman. And she would, just to see Hobie turn red. Feeling much more cheerful, she left the store.

"Cindy, darlin', I just knew you were the one I've been lookin' for," Cole said, slipping easily back into the heavy drawl of his rodeo days. It seemed to be working as well now as it had then. The platinum blonde who was draped across his lap was eating it up. That he wasn't enjoying it at all was another matter.

"Honey, all your lookin' just ended," she drawled back, running a finger—tipped with a long, bloodred nail—along his cheekbone.

There was no reason for him not to enjoy it. True, this hadn't been his intent when he'd strolled into this bar. He'd come because Hobie had told him about the place. Whitey Whitson's tavern was notorious for two things in Summer Springs—the purity of the booze, in particular the home-made variety, and the general impurity of its patrons, male and female. This was where the working people came, con-trasting with the upper-crust tendencies of many of the ranch owners themselves. Despite the clientele, Whitson's formidable presence—the ex-marine was actually bigger than Cole—kept the place orderly; no one dared argue with his rules.

Hobie had explained that, kept from fighting, the pa-trons were generally reduced to talking—about anything and everything. Cole had meant merely to probe the clientele for what information they had about what was going on on the Flying Clown. But when the blonde had made her invita-tion so blatantly clear, he'd decided she could provide what he needed as well as anyone.

She looked like a regular, judging from her seeming familiarity with the bartender, and the knowing glances he was getting from the men over at the pool table. She should know as much as anyone here. Probably more. Besides, maybe this was what he needed—a reminder of the kind of woman he should stick to. He had no business sniffing around Tory Flynn, no matter what effect she had on him.

And the blonde was certainly an adequate substitute, he told himself. She had a nice figure, perfect features and a mouth that made a man think of things that were still ille-gal in some states. By rights he should be in cowboy heaven, anticipating all kinds of heated activity later.

He wasn't. And it was all he could do to keep it from showing. Even his usually cooperative body wasn't participating. No doubt, he thought dryly, because his mind was running at a full gallop. And in a direction the lounging Cindy would hardly appreciate.

She'd probably wail if she broke one of those nails, he thought. And even though he knew it wasn't any worse than what he saw every day in L.A., her makeup seemed a bit heavy-handed to him. He doubted she ever pulled that full, fluffed and, he had to admit, striking fall of pale curls into a bouncy ponytail. And he'd be willing to bet she never bit those soft, red lips. But then, he'd bet those lips would never curve into a full, joyous smile at the sight of a frolicking horse, either. He doubted that they ever responded so innocently, so delightedly to something so simple. And he couldn't quite picture her letting that horse drench her with water. Unless it was for a reason.

Purposely, he let his gaze lower to her breasts, trying to picture her in a wet shirt, nipples taut. It wasn't difficult; her cropped blouse made the most of her generous attributes. And the minute she saw where his gaze had moved, she seemed to try and make certain he noticed she was braless.

Nothing. Not even a twinge of interest. With her breasts in his face and her bottom rubbing all over him, he didn't feel a damned thing. And that was enough to scare him out of thinking about it any longer. It was time to get to work, anyway.

"So, tell me, darlin'" he said. "You live around here?"

"All my life." There was a sour note in her voice that told him she wasn't happy about the fact. But she brightened a little when she bragged, "My daddy owns one of the biggest thoroughbred ranches in the valley."

And I'll bet you're a trial to him, Cole thought. "Congratulations," he said, then winced inwardly. That had sounded a bit sarcastic. He thickened the drawl. "You must know pretty near everybody around here, then."

"Oh, I do," Cindy said, snuggling closer. "And I know you're new. I'd *never* forget seeing a man like you."

"Why, thank you, darlin'. You're pretty unforgettable yourself." He cleared his throat; this wasn't quite as easy as it used to be, after all. He gave her what he hoped was a suggestive look. "I might even want to look into staying around here for a while. Know where a man might find work around here?"

She seemed to light up at that. "Oh, I'm sure my daddy could find something for you." She leaned forward and batted her eyelashes at him. He'd never really seen that done before, and he had to smother a laugh. "I usually don't get involved with that boring old ranch, but for you, I'd ask him."

I'll just bet you would, he thought. But he gave her the slightly crooked smile that had always worked before, in the days when he'd been young and had had no compunction about using his looks as a tool.

"Now, that might not be such a great idea, honey. I mean, I'm not much for messin' with the boss's daughter, if you get my drift."

Amazingly, she blushed prettily. Or maybe she didn't, maybe it was just that she was acting like she was blushing prettily. He couldn't tell here in the bar's low light.

"I drove in past a neat lookin' little place. Kinda liked the name. 'The Flying Clown,' it said."

Her brows—considerably darker than the silver-blond of her hair—furrowed. "The Flynn place? Oh, no, baby, you don't want that. They used to be hot stuff, but there's been some bad things going on there lately, and they may be in big trouble soon."

Cole's stomach knotted. It was clearly general knowledge now. "Bad things?"

She nodded. "Couple of horses died, or maybe three, I don't recall."

"Died of what?"

She shrugged. "Colic, I think. Bad feed, people say. Folks are saying it's their fault, and are pulling their horses out of training there. They're probably gonna get sued and everything. Believe me, you don't want to get tangled up with them.''

Cole tried to look suitably appalled. It wasn't hard. He was feeling a little sick to know the rumors had gone so far. Hobie and Tory's troubles were getting deeper fast.

"Didn't look like the kind of place where they'd get that sloppy," he said.

Cindy's nose wrinkled. "It seems strange to me, too," she admitted. "That Flynn girl, she's an odd one. A loner, you know? Kind of prissy, but she lives for those horses. That's all she does. Doesn't seem like she'd let something like that happen."

At her words, Cole felt a twinge of guilt for feeling so rancorous toward the woman. And the smile he gave her then seemed to show it, because she smiled back widely. She leaned in closer. Cole heard the bar's door swing open, and had the fleeting wish that whoever it was would stand there for a minute and let in some air. In close quarters, Cindy's perfume was a bit overpowering.

"But let's not talk about that," she said, practically purring. "Let's talk about us."

She punctuated her words with a tiny nip of his earlobe. Cole knew it was meant to be arousing. He knew it had been, for him, in the past. But he felt nothing more than a mild annoyance. And a stronger annoyance at himself as he wondered what the hell was wrong with him.

Cindy seemed to be wondering, too. She drew back from him a little, frowning. Then something over his shoulder seemed to catch her attention. Her eyes widened.

"Well, speak of the devil," she murmured. "*She*'s never been in here before."

Cole froze. He knew, without looking. But still he made himself turn.

Tory stood there, looking at him with an expression that ripped at his gut. What she was thinking was obvious, written all over her honest, ingenuous face. And before he could even remember to breathe, she turned and ran out.

Chapter 10

Tory's fist ached where she had slammed it against the Jeep's steering wheel.

God, she was such a fool.

She could forgive that in anyone else, she thought as she fumbled with her keys, but not herself. Not a woman who'd grown up with a prime example of the worst kind of using male. Not a woman who knew all too well about too-charming Texans with only one thing on their mind: all the women they can notch on a tooled, silver buckled belt.

And she'd reacted to the sight of him with another woman like a jilted lover. She didn't want to think about what that meant, about how far down that primrose path she'd strayed.

And she had no one to blame but herself. She'd known in the first moment she'd seen him that he was cut from the same cloth as her father. Her instant, gut reaction had been right, and she'd been a simpleton to ignore it just because he made her feel things she'd never felt before. She'd convinced herself there was more to this man—that those flashes she'd seen were real feeling, not the result of a practiced, polished act. And now she was paying the price.

She swiped at her eyes, furious at the moisture that was pooling there. Then she tried the keys again, managing to slip them into the ignition this time, and swore as a hot, salty tear fell on her bare leg below the hem of her dress.

She would *not* cry over this, she ordered herself. She would not cry over him. She wasn't hurt. She was just... disappointed. That's all. Disappointed. In him. And much more than disappointed in her own judgment.

And she was more than a little humiliated at how easily she'd forgotten the hard-learned lessons of her life, as if all it had taken to burn them away was the heat of his kiss.

She turned the key. The engine fired.

The Jeep's door swung open.

"Tory."

She started, her head snapping around to gape at him. She'd been so wrapped in her misery she hadn't seen him approach. Swiftly she looked away. She would just die if he saw how close she'd been to crying. And she didn't dare speak, for fear her voice would give her away.

"Tory, listen, that wasn't... what it looked like."

Fury rose up out of seemingly nowhere, flooding her with nerve-steadying strength. How many times had she heard Jack Flynn say that to her mother? And how many times had she wondered how her mother could ever doubt the wonderful man who was her father?

She met his eyes then, her own suddenly clear and dry. "It looked like Cindy Crain to me. Which generally means it was *exactly* what it looked like."

His dark brows lowered. "Crain? The Crain you mentioned that might want the ranch? And owned the second horse?"

So he hadn't even known that. And she rebuked herself scathingly for even having considered that he might have been romancing the always available Cindy for a reason other than the obvious. *Fool,* she repeated to herself.

"Well," she said with a cool nonchalance that she found, to her surprise, she didn't have to work too hard for, "that blows that excuse, Mr. Bannister."

"What excuse?"

"That you were working."

His brows came up. "I was. I just didn't know how close she was to the situation."

"Close," she said bitingly, "is Cindy's specialty. Speaking of which, I'm sure she's getting impatient."

"Look," he said, sounding exasperated, the same tone her father had perfected, "I *was* working. I wanted to hear what people were saying about what's been happening."

That made sense, she supposed. And Cindy would be a good source—she never had known how to keep her mouth shut. *Lord,* she thought, *she was* still *making excuses for him!*

"Hobie told me about this place—" He broke off, looking puzzled for the first time. "Did he send you?"

She answered the unexpected question without thinking. "No. You got an express package, and I was in town, and I saw your truck, so I was going to tell you. It looks important."

"From the office?"

"Yes, it's—" She broke off, realizing in disgust that he'd diverted her. Just as her father used to divert her mother when she had asked him where he'd been. "It's not going anywhere. You'll see it when you get back." Her gaze flicked to the door of the tavern. "Or if."

"Right," he muttered. He let out a harassed-sounding sigh, looking as if he regretted having come after her. And then, slowly, something that looked like resigned determination turned his eyes that steel blue color once more.

"I'll get there when I get there," he said, his voice now cool and indifferent.

"I'm sure you will," Tory retorted, hating herself for being stung by his tone. "And not a minute sooner."

"What's wrong, little girl? Don't like finding out you were right?"

She straightened up; she'd betrayed enough to this man already. "I don't like finding out Hobie can be as poor a judge of people as I can."

Something flickered in his gaze then, but it was gone so swiftly she couldn't put a name to it. "People change," he said flatly.

"Yes, I suppose they do. Too bad you changed from whoever it was Hobie trusted to...to..."

"A shell, darlin'." His voice was an exaggerated drawl now. "Just a big, strong facade, without a damned thing behind it. It'd pay for you—and Hobie—to remember that."

He turned on his heel then, and strode back into Whitey's without a backward glance.

Tory sat staring after him, shaken, both by his words and the devastating conviction of truth that had rung in his voice. No matter how damning the words he'd just spoken of himself, Cole Bannister believed every one of them.

And, perversely, that very conviction shook Tory's own belief in his innate emptiness. She couldn't deny what she had just seen. And now she wasn't sure she'd been wrong about the feeling of self-loathing she had sensed that first day in his office. Any man capable of being that down on himself, of speaking of himself so acidly, had to have emotions that ran deep. Real emotions, the likes of which she would have thought impossible to find in the kind of man she thought he was.

And suddenly she thought of Rocky. The last thing she would have expected was that that kind of man would show up with a pet cat, too. Rocky was his, whether he admitted it or not. She hadn't missed the dish he'd been using to feed the animal, despite his efforts to keep it hidden.

She sat there, her thoughts whirling. When she realized that some of the men heading for Whitey's were noticing her presence in the parking lot, she hastily put the Jeep in gear and pulled out, steadfastly not glancing at Cole's truck.

Maybe she'd been looking at this all wrong, she thought as she drove. Maybe she should look at the evidence that proved he wasn't what she thought he was, not the evidence that proved he was who she thought he was. Maybe instead of only seeing what she'd expected to see, she should be looking at what she hadn't expected. What had just happened, for instance. And his surprising perceptiveness when he had prodded her into talking about her father; his anger about the way Hobie had been treated; and the way he'd held her, nothing but gentle reassurance in his touch when she'd needed it so badly. And his refusal to claim Rocky. All his gruff talk about the "damn cat," while at the same time he was secretly feeding him.

And finally, there was what had happened at the spring, she added, not at all certain now how she felt about that fierce, shockingly arousing encounter.

So maybe she should have her head examined. If they could find anything inside to look at, she amended wryly.

She drove around for a while longer, aimlessly, needing to think. On the surface, it seemed simple. She was contrarily attracted—fiercely, she admitted reluctantly—to a man who was the image of everything she'd always avoided.

But was it just that, an image? An image concocted not, as she'd assumed, to charm and finagle, as her father had done, but a facade designed to hide the fact that he really, truly felt there was nothing behind it? And for the first time she really thought about his words the time he'd spoken so viciously about his looks.

My looks didn't matter a hoot to any of the horses or bulls I rode. Or to my DI's . . . except to make them want to push me even harder. . . . And my looks sure as hell didn't stop that bomb. . . .

She'd wondered then, with a kind of morbid curiosity, what he'd been about to say when he'd let slip those last words about a bomb. But now she found herself thinking unexpectedly that looks like his could be a curse. She'd heard enough about women who weren't taken seriously because they were too attractive, but she'd never thought of that kind of thing in a male context.

And Kyra, at least, had chosen another man despite Cole's obvious attractiveness. Or maybe, Tory thought suddenly, because of it.

For different reasons, she has the same feeling about guys like me as you do.... She was too afraid of me to trust me until it was too late.

Guys like me.

She'd spent too much time acknowledging that she was different from many women not to hear the isolation in those simple words. She'd just never thought of Cole like this before.

She'd never thought about any man at all as much as she'd thought about him. And she'd never been so confused, either.

And on that thought, she knew what to do—what she always did when she couldn't seem to thrash her way through a problem. She would go to the one man in the world she trusted completely.

She couldn't get the words out. She sat there looking at Hobie as they swayed slightly on the porch swing, and didn't know what to say. Never before had she felt constrained like this. Since she'd come to him at twenty-two, humbly apologizing for having taken her father's word about him—since he'd opened his door and his heart to her without judging, without a trace of vindictiveness for the humiliation her father had heaped on him—she had been able to talk to Hobie about anything.

But then, she'd never been in the position of trying to find the words to tell him she was a confused mess because of a man, a man who happened to be an old friend of his.

"You're looking a mite distracted tonight, honey."

She managed a faint smile. "Perceptive of you," she said ruefully as she tugged off the strappy sandals she'd worn to town.

"Nope," Hobie denied. "I just know my girl."

Tory sighed. "I wish I was your girl. Really, I mean."

She'd said it more than once, that she wished he'd been her father, but before it had always made Hobie smile. Never had he responded with the thoughtful, almost wistful expression he wore now.

"You could have been, you know." His mouth quirked beneath the mustache. "Always thought it'd happen that way."

Tory stared at him. "What . . . What do you mean?"

He didn't answer right away. He tugged at his mustache as he stared out over the ranch. Then, at last, he met her puzzled gaze.

"I loved your mother, Tory. I'd loved her since we were in high school together."

Tory smothered a gasp. She'd never known. True, her mother had done her best to counteract Jack Flynn's diatribes about his useless brother, but never, even after she'd realized the truth about Jack Flynn, had Tory ever suspected there was more to it than simply her mother's desire for fairness where there was none.

"We went steady for years." Tory's eyes widened as he continued to astonish her with his quiet words. "Used to talk about when we'd get married. How we'd settle down on our own place someday, raise cattle and horses and a passel of kids."

"I never knew," she whispered, shaking her head in stunned slow motion.

"I know you didn't. It wasn't something your father would advertise."

Hardly, she thought, somewhat numbly. Jack Flynn would never want anyone to know that his wife had once dated his despised little brother.

"My God," she said in sudden realization, "that's why, isn't it? He hated you because mother was yours first."

Hobie shrugged. "I don't know. I never thought I mattered to him that much. But maybe."

"No wonder it galled him when Mother defended you."

Hobie's eyes, so like her own, widened. "Jeanie defended me?"

"All the time. He would get off on these tirades, you know the kind, and she would just sit and listen. Until he started on you. Then she would tell him to be quiet. That it was all lies, and he knew it." Tory tried to smile, but she knew she didn't quite succeed. "It was the only time, other than for me, that she ever stood up to him."

Hobie lowered his head, and Tory pretended not to notice when he made a quick swipe at his eyes. It took her a long, silent few moments before she worked herself up to go on.

"What happened?" she finally asked, already certain she didn't want to hear this. But if Hobie was telling her this now, after all this time, he must have a reason.

"We were in love, but we knew we had to wait until we graduated school. So the day afterward, I brought her home with me. Like they say, to meet the family." He tugged at his mustache again. "Well, she did. She met your grandma and grandpa. And your great-grandma, Martha." He let out a breath. "And then she met Jack."

Your uncle Hobie has been hurt badly in his life, Victoria, but he had the gumption to go on. He deserves respect, not the misery your father heaps on him.

Her mother's voice came back to her as if from a tape played so often the words were becoming faint.

"You were engaged . . . and she left you for him?"

"Now, don't be looking like that, honey. We were young, and naive. And Jack was home from that fancy east coast college. He'd always been high, wide and handsome, but now he was sophisticated too, and flashier than anything either one of us had ever seen. And when Jack put his mind to getting a woman, he usually got her."

"But if she loved you—"

"I know, it sounds like it was pretty simple. But it wasn't, Tory. It never is as simple as it seems. People's hearts tangle it all up with old ideas, old hurts, until you're not sure what you're really seeing now."

Tory went very still. She stared at her uncle, wondering if he'd somehow read her mind and understood her confusion without her having said a word.

"Jack swept your mother off her feet. She had stars in her eyes so fast, I don't think she ever had a chance." Hobie shrugged. "Neither did I, once Jack set his sights on her."

Impulsively she slid over to hug him. "I'm sorry, Uncle Hobie. My mother was a fool."

"People make foolish choices, honey. That doesn't always make them a fool."

"She was," Tory said sadly. "Because she was unhappy for most of the rest of her life."

"And that's the saddest part of all."

She pulled back, and sat up to look at him intently. "You can say that? After what she did to you, after the way my father treated you?"

Hobie reached out and took her hands in his. "I've had five years of loving the woman who could have been our daughter. That's more important than any old hurts, Tory. Much more important."

Moisture sprang to her eyes, and in seconds she was blinking away tears at her uncle's simple declaration. This time she hugged him fiercely.

"She *was* a fool. She went for the flash, when she could have had the best man in the world."

"Thank you for thinking that, honey."

Hobie hugged her back, tightly, and Tory felt a moment of thankfulness as she realized his strength was returning. For that alone, for the hope he'd given her uncle, she owed Cole Bannister a great deal. But not, she thought, her heart.

"I won't be that kind of fool," she murmured, half to herself, as if saying the words made it true.

Hobie seemed to go very still then, and she knew he'd heard her. She almost wished she hadn't said it at all, but when he spoke, it seemed he was going to let her words pass.

"I've been thinking about Jeanie a lot lately," he said quietly. "Hell, I haven't been able to do much else but think.

And I know some would say I should hate her. But I can't, Tory. I loved her then, and I love her now."

"Oh, Hobie," Tory began, aching for him.

"And I'll tell you something else. I'd trade everything I've got, except you, just to have one night with Jeanie to look back on."

This time it was Tory who went very still. "One...night? You mean you never...?"

"No. Oh, it was a close thing, and God knows we were young and hot, but I wanted to wait until we were married." He made a small, pained sound. "In case she got pregnant. Birth control wasn't so easy, back then." He let out a deep breath. "If I hadn't been so damned careful, you might really have been mine."

She snuggled closer to him. "I wish you hadn't been."

"Think about that, too, honey. I know you've been looking at the world through glasses colored by your father. But don't paint every man you're attracted to with that brush."

Why doesn't he get tarred with your father's brush?

Cole's question echoed in her mind. God, was that it? She'd known her father had skewed her outlook, but since she didn't react that way to all men, since she'd been able to see some as decent and honest, she had thought herself fairly balanced. But was Hobie right? And Cole? Was it only the ones she was attracted to that caused that reaction? Was it some sort of instinctive, automatic self-protective urge that had made her so certain Cole was just like her father? Because she was more attracted to him than she'd ever been to a man in her life? She didn't want to believe it, but it made a sort of painful sense.

But not nearly as painful as the sight of Cole in that bar, with Cindy wrapped around him. She was probably a fool for even looking for an innocent explanation. After all, Cole had told her straight out she'd been right, hadn't he? It was only her obviously too-fertile imagination that had her half-believing there was more to his words than that.

"I wonder when our crack investigator will wander in to take a look at what his office sent," she said sourly. Only after the words were out did she realize what she had given away by bringing Cole up after the conversation she and Hobie had just had. Hobie, bless him, merely looked at her curiously.

"He's been back for a long time."

Tory straightened up to look at her uncle. "What?"

"He came back long before you did. Nearly two hours ago."

Two hours. That meant he'd left almost right after she had, and had come straight here. No time for dallying with the available Cindy. But had he meant to, before her interruption? Or had he been telling the truth, and merely been probing for information?

He'd told her that, but she hadn't believed him. And only after she'd continued to needle him had he finally gotten that resigned look in his eyes and told her she was right. On all counts.

"I...didn't see his truck," Tory said lamely, knowing that Hobie knew as well as she did that Cole had taken to parking the slightly battered vehicle out of sight behind the house.

"Hmm." Hobie lifted a brow, but said no more about her obvious dissembling. "He's in the office, going over the files that were in that package. I've been feeding him coffee. He didn't want to eat. Seemed in a pretty poor mood."

Because she'd interrupted his liaison? Or because she'd misjudged him? God, she didn't know. She felt like she didn't know anything anymore. Maybe he'd meant to take Cindy up on her offer. But the point was, she supposed, that he hadn't. For whatever reason, he'd walked away.

"He's a good man, Tory," Hobie said gently. "He may be a little confused right now, and he's like that cat of his, been through some hard times he ain't talking about, but that doesn't change what he is at the core."

With that, Hobie said good-night, and went inside to bed. Tory stayed on the swing, staring out into the darkness, trying to sort through her tangled emotions.

What had Hobie been trying to tell her? Obviously he'd realized she was attracted to Cole. But then, that would only be reasonable. Take any woman, let alone one who'd been tucked away on this ranch, isolated for most of the year except when she went to shows and competitions, put her in the same room with Cole Bannister, and there was a darned good chance she was going to react. If she was still breathing, anyway.

But it had almost seemed as if Hobie had been reassuring her about Cole, almost as if he'd been encouraging her. She grimaced at that thought. Hobie looked at Cole as an old friend. He was that, but she doubted he was still the man her uncle remembered. And Hobie would hardly look at him the way a wary woman would.

She sighed, knowing there were no easy answers. But she stayed, liking the comforting rock of the swing. She stayed even when the air at last began to cool, and she felt the chill on her bare arms. She was still there when Rocky, finished for now with the excursions that were playing havoc with the local mouse population, glided up onto the porch to sit in front of her.

The cat waited, head tilted to one side, until Tory, smiling despite her distraction, reached down to pet him. One long stroke over the soft fur, and a passing tickle of the ragged ear was all that she was permitted before the cat disappeared behind the swing, came out dragging the now dusty red bandanna, leapt to the porch rail and settled down to survey his new domain. She'd found Rocky disliked sitting on the swaying swing, finding such movement excessive and unnecessary and not conducive to peaceful napping.

"You have been through some hard times, haven't you, Rocky?" she whispered.

The cat turned his head to look at her, his distinctive, pale blue eyes seeming to gather what light there was and reflect it eerily, giving him a wise, almost mystical look. It made his ragged ear, and the other scars that marked his body insignificant.

"But you've made your peace with the world, haven't you?" she said. "That's the difference between you and Cole. You've come out of the dark. He hasn't."

Rocky blinked. And slowly, uncannily, inclined his head as if nodding at a particularly bright human who had reached an enlightened thought.

Tory nearly laughed at her own fancifulness. But Rocky truly was a most expressive cat. And right now, lying atop her old bandanna, he seemed utterly at peace with his world. She wished she could claim the same state.

Hobie's words spun in her mind. There had been little less than pain in his voice when he'd spoken of trading everything except her for even just one night with the woman he'd so loved. It was hard for her to think of her mother as that woman. She'd been such a quiet, shadowy figure in Tory's life for so long. But to Hobie, she'd been...young and hot, he'd said.

She herself had been young, Tory thought, but never... hot. Until now. Even sitting in the dark with only a cat for company, color flooded her cheeks. But it was true, she admitted honestly. For the first time in her life, it was true. Cole made her feel things—hot, swirling, frightening things that—were at the same time so tempting she woke in the night reaching for him, a moan of pleasure already on her lips.

Would there come a day, years from now, when she would regret this missed chance? When she would look back and sadly mourn not having at least one purely passionate fling to remember? That with Cole, that was all it would be, she knew. He would be gone soon, as soon as this mess was over. There would be no future in a relationship with him. But was that bad? Wouldn't knowing that help her keep her heart intact?

We're talking sex here. Not love, not romance, just raw, hot, out-of-control sex.

A shiver rippled through her as she remembered his words. It would be that way with him. Raw. Hot. The words repelled and drew her at the same time, just as the man did. Made her weak in the knees while making her nerves quail. Made heat build in her, low and deep, while her mind screamed a warning her body didn't want to hear.

No, she had few illusions about Cole. But then, it was the shattering of the illusion that hurt, wasn't it? Like the shattering of her image of her father had hurt. If you don't have the illusion in the first place, she told herself, you won't be hurt when it vanishes, as it always does.

What she did have was the grim knowledge that she was twenty-seven years old, and had never really, truly wanted a man. Had never been possessed by the urge to touch, to hold, to caress...and to give whatever he asked. Until now. She'd never thought it would happen to her. Perhaps it never would again. And that thought filled her with a sadness that verged on desperation. That, and the memory of the quiet sorrow in her uncle's eyes, decided it for her. She got to her feet.

Rocky looked at her.

"Am I a fool, Rocky?" she asked. "Is he really just an empty shell, like he said, or is he just lost, like you once were?"

The cat merely began to groom his coat with a rough, pink tongue, providing no answer this time. Or perhaps he was answering, Tory thought. Showing her that even a battered street fighter like himself could find enough peace to care about something other than simply staying alive.

She was going to find out, she thought, surrendering to a sense of inevitability. And if Cole truly was that empty shell, she could only hope she didn't get cut to ribbons by the fragments if it shattered.

Chapter 11

Maybe his instincts weren't as rusty as he thought. He'd known the instant the office door opened that it was Tory, long before he'd caught the faint trace of that sweet, jasmine scent she wore. And the moment she started across the room, he recognized the faint sound of bare feet on the polished wooden floor. It didn't take her long. The ranch office was small, barely large enough for the big rolltop desk, the desk chair and the file cabinets against the wall.

Cole stifled the urge to shut the file he'd been reading—the one he'd asked the office to put together on her father, more out of curiosity than anything—and hide it from her. He didn't move, just kept staring at the file in his lap, his booted feet up on the corner of the desk as he leaned the chair back on two legs, balancing somewhat precariously.

He was surprised at the effort it took not to raise his eyes. But the memory of the look on her face when she'd walked into Whitey's and seen Cindy clinging to him like a wet shirt tipped the scales, and he kept his eyes fastened on the financial report he'd been reading. Even when she halted near his crossed ankles, he kept reading. Or trying to.

"Is that what came today?"

"Mmm-hmm."

With his peripheral vision he could see the pale blue color of her dress, that dress that hugged her shape, left her long, trim legs and arms so lusciously bare and turned her eyes the purest big-sky blue. He saw her run a long, slender finger along the edge of the desk. He kept his eyes down. His peripheral vision had always been too damned good, he muttered silently.

"Are they the files you were expecting?"

"Mmm-hmm."

Her finger slowly traced the S-curve of the desk's top portion. He found himself thinking of how strong her hands were, tanned, steady, nails trimmed neatly for work, not exaggerated for show. Yet they were gentle hands, utterly feminine in movement and grace. He'd seen them caress a horse's velvety nose, and an aloof cat's chin until both were reaching for more. He knew the feeling.

"Are you finding anything?"

It was all he could do not to let his gaze follow the unconsciously sensual movement of her hand as she touched the smooth hardness of the wood. His jaw tightened. He consciously relaxed it.

"Yes."

He thought he heard her sigh, but he couldn't be sure. She leaned her head against the side of the rolltop, her cheek pressing against the wood. It was, as all her movements had seemed to him since she'd come into the room, a slow, seductive kind of pose. But he knew it was in his mind. After this afternoon, seducing him would be the very last thing she would have on her mind.

He could almost feel her steeling her nerve to speak again. "Anything that could be...a motive?"

He slammed the file shut. She jumped. He lifted his head at last, to glare at her. "Exactly what is it you want from me?"

"I..."

Her voice trailed off, the oddest look coming across her face. Then a slow flush rose in her cheeks, and when he thought about how he'd worded that question, he sucked in a breath at the possibilities that could have caused that blush. Coupled with the almost caressing way she was holding on to the old desk, the images that popped into his head stopped his breath in his throat.

She seemed to recover, drawing herself up straight and then meeting his gaze and holding it steadily. "I want to know what progress you've made, if any. I have a big stake in this, after all."

Nerve, he thought again. She was facing him down again. And he'd been way out in left field. Again.

"Some," he said, admitting that she had the right to know. "Ralph Hudson, for example. Did you know that his wife's brother just opened a trendy new cutting horse training facility in Arizona?"

Tory's expression gave him his answer before she shook her head. "No. I didn't know."

Cole nodded. "And your contract has an escape clause that enables him to pull out without paying the rest of the contract if conditions here become unsafe for the horses."

Her brow furrowed. "But that's only for natural disasters, like a fire, or—"

"The way this is worded—" he held up a copy of their standard contract "—you'd have trouble making him pay."

"But who would ever expect anything like this to happen? And we've had Starwalker for nearly a year. Or we did," she amended glumly.

"But his brother-in-law didn't open a training stable until now."

She gave him a puzzled look that gradually changed to one of shock. "You're not saying you think Ralph killed those horses just so he could pull out? To go to his brother-in-law's?"

Cole shrugged. "I've seen worse done for less."

"Cole, no. I know I've been . . . naive about some things, but that's really too much."

"Okay, then, how about Crain, for instance? Did you know he has a second and third mortgage on his place? Maybe he could have used that insurance."

That look he'd come to recognize, a sadness at the mention of any of the dead horses, crossed her face. "Firefly wasn't insured for nearly as much as John's Prize. She wasn't nearly as much horse. Harry's a thoroughbred man, and he only bought her because he wanted the cachet of saying he owned a cutting horse."

She smiled wryly. "And besides, it's been a standing joke around here for a long time that Harry had to mortgage the place to the hilt just to keep Cindy out of trouble."

He couldn't believe she'd so casually mentioned the woman, not after the way she'd reacted this afternoon. She'd looked like a wife who just walked in on her cheating husband, and that realization had made him as edgy as Rocky when the Santa Anas were blowing.

"What about your buddy Mr. Lennox, then?" he asked hastily.

"John?" she said, looking wary now. "What about him?"

"He's strapped right now. Overextended, because he bought that new software-development company last year." He gave her a sideways look. "But maybe you already know that."

Her mouth twisted. "Hardly the kind of information I'd be privy to."

"You mean he didn't mention it over any of those cozy dinners you shared at his country club?"

Her eyes widened. "How did you... Never mind. Hobie, I suppose."

"He did mention it. And that Lennox wants more than you're willing to give him. Personally."

"John just sees me as a challenge," she said dismissively. "He's used to getting what he wants."

Cole couldn't help the sudden tension in his voice. "And he wants you?"

"So he thinks. For now. He'll get over it soon enough. It's not real. He's just not used to anyone telling him no." She shrugged. "I'm hardly his type, either."

Either? Cole's stomach seemed to take a tumble. He tried to ignore the feeling.

"Tell me something," he began, and saw her tense slightly. It was an odd habit they both had, of giving off this warning when a loaded question was coming. "Is there any male in the world you trust, besides Hobie?"

She grinned unexpectedly, and widely. He nearly bit his tongue in his surprise. "Sure. Mac. I'd trust him with my life."

Fighting down the surge of heat that grin had roused in him, he said warningly, "I wouldn't get any more attached to that horse if I were you. If Lennox needs cash..." He ended on a shrug.

Her forehead creased. "What? You think Mac is..."

"A convertible asset. One way or another. He's insured, too, although not for as much as the other horse."

The moment the words left his lips he wished he hadn't said it. She went pale. "No. Not Mac. He wouldn't."

"How much could he have gotten for the other horse, if he'd tried to sell him?"

"I...don't know. A lot, I suppose."

"As much as the insurance paid off?"

With obvious reluctance, she shook her head. "But he wouldn't. Not John."

"Why? Because he's rich? Charming?"

He didn't know where that had come from. What did he care what she thought of Lennox? What sour well had those biting words risen from? He knew she'd heard the tone, because her chin came up as she looked at him stubbornly.

"He was too proud of John's Prize. And he wouldn't hurt Mac. I know he wouldn't."

She bit her lip fiercely. Cole wanted to tell her to stop it, to keep that soft flesh unbruised for him. He wanted to tell her she looked wonderful in that dress, but that it made him want to take it off her and learn every slender line of her body. He clenched his jaw against the words of want and need that were getting harder and harder to hold back.

With an effort, he tore his mind out of that dangerous track. And tried, in a roundabout way, to make up for what he'd said.

"You're right, if he is behind this he probably won't. Losing two horses would make him a prime suspect, and he's smart enough to know that. Besides, 'John's Prize'—" he couldn't keep the sarcasm out of his voice as he spoke the name "—was insured for a full million, right?"

Still biting her lip, she nodded.

"That's a lot of cash flow, even at that level."

He saw a shiver ripple through her. Then he saw her tense again, fighting it down. "I just can't believe he would do something like that. And he's always...spent like he had plenty of money. Are you sure he's...in trouble?"

"My people are good. If they say he's in a bind, he is. They're working on finding out how bad it is."

"Maybe if I ask John—"

Cole came up out of the chair so quickly she stepped back with a startled little movement. "No. Don't mention anything to him."

"But—"

"No buts, Tory. If he isn't behind this, you'll just lose a paying customer. If he is behind it, you could put yourself in more trouble than you ever dreamed of. Don't say a word."

"All right," she said, with a meekness that made him instantly suspicious. Lennox was a friend who wanted to be more, and Tory was still having trouble believing anyone that she knew could be behind this. If she came to believe it, it would be just like her, in outrage, to ask Lennox flat out if he'd killed his own horse for money. She was like Hobie that way—more guts than common sense, sometimes. Of course, if Hobie hadn't been that way, Cole wouldn't be here now to worry about it.

"I'm not joking about this, Tory. Not a word."

"I said all right."

"I mean it. You don't want to have to explain to him why you suddenly know about his troubles. Or how you found out. Do you?"

She let out a long breath. "Cole, I said all right. I won't say a thing to him. Why don't you believe me?"

His mouth quirked. "Maybe because you're as stubborn as Hobie and it's not like you to give up so quickly."

She lowered her gaze, as if comparing the toes of their boots. "Maybe I'm trying to apologize."

"Apologize?"

Her head came up then. She looked at him, openly and so honestly it hurt somewhere deep in his chest.

"If you say it was business this afternoon, I believe you. Cindy would be...all over you the minute you walked in, whether you wanted it or not."

The sheer simplicity of it staggered him. Just like that, he was forgiven. Despite what she'd seen, despite what he knew had been a life that had made every man suspect to her, despite what he'd told her, she'd decided to trust him. It made no sense.

And it scared him. Because it had been the truth when he'd told her there was nothing behind the facade. But not the truth he knew she had believed, the truth he'd meant her to believe. He hadn't been talking about women like Cindy, women he was sure she thought paraded through his life. He'd been talking about himself. Somewhere along this road he'd been on, he'd lost himself. These days when he looked in the mirror, he had a habit of thinking about the reflection in the third person, like it was somebody else. And somebody he didn't like much.

But Tory Flynn trusted him. He'd told her something that contradicted the evidence of her own eyes, and she believed him. He had a sudden sense of rolling headlong and out of control toward some kind of inevitable outcome. He didn't like the feeling.

"Maybe you shouldn't be so quick about that." His voice was flat. "How do you know I didn't want it? In fact, how do you know I wasn't the one all over her?"

"Because you left right after I did. Hobie said you got here hours ago."

He expelled a compressed breath. "Yeah. And I'm beginning to be sorry I did." That sense of helpless compulsion swept over him again, and in a desperate effort to scare her off, he added crudely, "I've been horny as hell lately."

She colored again, but she didn't look away. "I know."

He nearly choked. "What?"

"Well, the way you kissed me, I... You'd hardly do that if you weren't... I mean, I felt..."

He knew exactly what she'd felt. He'd been as hard as a fence post. His body began to tighten again simply at the memory of that day by the spring.

She stumbled on. "I knew you were—"

"Horny?" he suggested again, his voice tight.

She nodded. "And I know it's not any of my business, what you do, personally. I mean, just a kiss doesn't give me any... claim on you, but—"

Perversely, her characterization of what had happened between them stung. "*Just* a kiss?"

Her color deepened. "I...don't know what else to call it," she said with that disarming honesty. "Nothing like that has ever happened to me before."

Me, either, he thought grimly. He watched as she took in a deep breath, thinking that he wouldn't dare speak or he'd say something that would somehow make him pick up more speed on this headlong run. He knew it was headed toward something irrevocable.

"That's what I mean, I guess. I've never felt like that. Ever. I didn't know I...could. All this time, and I didn't know..." Her next breath was shaky, as was her voice when she went on. "I know I'm not...what you're used to, that somebody who looks like Cindy is probably more your style, but..."

Her voice faded away, he saw her hands knotted together, her knuckles white. He steadied his voice before he asked, "But what?"

"I know it was just because I was the only woman handy, but it…didn't seem to matter to you that day, at the spring, and I thought… It seemed like you…wanted me then, and if you still—"

"What the hell are you saying?"

It broke from him on a rising note of disbelief. He was reading her wrong. He had to be. Tory Flynn wouldn't do what she seemed to be doing. He couldn't handle it if she was. He was already having trouble reining in a body that wanted what she seemed to be offering more than it wanted to keep breathing. He stared down at her.

He saw her shiver again, then make herself hold his fierce gaze. "I mean that if you still…if you … can forget that I don't have Cindy's looks…" She made an eloquent little motion with her shoulders and hands. "I'm still handy."

He wanted to shake her. Not for himself, but for her, for the insult she'd just so quietly, devastatingly delivered to herself. What the hell had gotten into her? Even the suggestion of what she was doing was so obviously against her nature that it almost made him ill to think about it, even as his body raged to full attention at the suggestion.

And that she truly thought so little of him, to think that he would take her up on her offer because, God help him, she was *handy*? To think that a practiced, calculated beauty like Cindy's would mean more to him than her own sweet, honest loveliness, was—

Only to be expected, he realized suddenly. What Tory thought of him was exactly what he'd tried so hard to make her think. He'd needed a buffer between them, a way to bolster the self-control he was no longer sure he could count on. And he'd built it the only way he could think of. He could hardly complain now because she'd believed him. He'd given her little choice but to believe he was the kind of man who would never turn down a no-strings-attached opportunity for sex.

"Don't worry," she was saying, in a voice that was much too small to be causing the tearing he was feeling inside. "I don't...expect anything. When this mess is over, you'll be gone, and I know that."

"Just like that, is that it?" he asked, his voice taut with suppressed emotions. "We hop in the sack, have a little fun, and then I take off?"

She looked startled. "I...isn't that what you wanted?"

"What I want," he said harshly, knowing that all the things he was thinking would shock her mind and her body, "isn't anything like what you want, little girl."

It took her a moment, but when she answered, her voice was steady and calm. "You don't know that. And calling me little girl doesn't change anything. And the fact that I'm Hobie's niece doesn't change the way you make me feel. I thought no strings was what you wanted."

Her use of the words he'd just thought put an even harsher edge in his voice. "And just what is it that *you* want?"

She looked away then, lowering her gaze for the first time since she'd begun this. "What you...talked about. That day. What I've never had. Something...hot. Out of control. You're the only man who's ever made me want that. Or feel that it could be like that, even for me."

"God, Tory!" It broke from him on a harsh, compressed breath. "Do you have any idea what the hell you're doing?"

Her gaze met his then and held. And in the turquoise depths was a heat he couldn't deny, just as he couldn't stop his own response to it.

"No," she said simply. "That's why I want you to teach me."

His heart was hammering in his chest as he stared down at her. His body was echoing the slamming beat, already aroused to the point of pain. She wanted it hot. Out of control. And just the thought made him want to show her just how out of control she made him.

Somebody who looks like Cindy is probably more your style. If you can forget that I don't have Cindy's looks.

She'd meant it. He was as certain of that as he'd ever been of anything. She was too innocently easy to read for a man like him. She hadn't been fishing for compliments, or feeling sorry for herself. She'd meant it. She knew she wasn't that kind of beauty. What she didn't know was how glad he was—how glad any man with a brain would be—that she wasn't. Glad that she was real and honest and so sweet it could nearly burn a hole in you.

And he knew exactly what she'd think if he turned her down now. She'd think it was because of that. Because she wasn't that kind of beauty. He opened his mouth to tell her the truth, to tell her she outshone and would far outlast Cindy's kind of fleeting perfection. But he didn't say it. He was afraid once he started he wouldn't be able to stop, and that telling her in words would too quickly progress to showing her with his body exactly how beautiful he thought she was.

And some mocking part of his mind was jeering him, telling him that he was lying to himself, just looking for an excuse to take what he already wanted so badly he could hardly stand it.

And then, with a steeling of her nerve that was so obvious it tightened his chest unbearably, she took a step toward him.

"Will you teach me, Cole?"

Instinctively his hands came up. He'd meant to fend her off. He knew he had. So why had his hands gone instead to her shoulders, his fingers practically shaking as they curled around her?

"Tory," he said, shocked at the break in his voice, at the painful lump in his throat. "I don't...I can't..." He took a deep, shuddering breath and tried again. "You deserve more than this."

"I'm twenty-seven years old, Cole, and I never knew there was this much. I don't want to take the chance there never will be again."

His fingers tightened on her shoulders, and it was all he could do not to pull her into his arms right then. He heard a harsh sound and realized it was his own breathing, coming fast and deep. He felt an odd coolness on his forehead, and realized he was breaking into a sweat. Small wonder, with the thoughts, the possibilities, the visions that were racing through his mind.

Desperately, he tried to give her one last warning. "You don't want to do this, Tory. Not with me. Not now. I'm not going to deny I want you—" His gaze flicked downward to where flesh taut and ready, strained against his zipper. Tory followed his glance as if instinctively, and when she looked hurriedly back up at his face, the wonder that filled her eyes did nothing to ease the ache that was building in him. "I couldn't, anyway. Obviously. But it won't be soft and sweet, Tory. In fact," he added, hating the fact that his voice had become nearly a growl, "it would damn likely be right here, because the more I think about it, the hotter I get. We'd never make it to your bed."

Her lips parted as she stared at him. He'd done it, he thought. He'd finally scared her off. And his body was going to torture him for it for longer than he cared to think about it.

And then she was answering him, simple words that stole what was left of his breath. "That's what I mean," she said quietly. "It's not just...how I feel. How you make me feel. It's that...no one's ever felt that way...for me."

Cole knew it couldn't be true, knew that all the men in the world couldn't be blind to Tory's sweet appeal. More likely it was she who hadn't realized it, she who had kept such a distance between herself and any man who wanted her that it couldn't be bridged.

Until now. And for some perverse reason, she'd chosen to let him in. The one she should have kept the farthest from. And God help him, he didn't think he had the strength to keep that distance from her. Not when she was looking at him like this, not when she slowly reached up and touched his cheek, so tentatively it felt like the tiny breaths of the breeze that had brushed over his face that day by the spring.

Involuntarily he turned his head, touching his lips to her fingers. She hesitated, looking suddenly very shy, then even more slowly began to trace the line of his mouth. He shivered, unable to stop it, and that look of wonder came back into her eyes. It was his undoing.

With a throttled groan, he pulled her into his arms.

Chapter 12

Tory knew she'd begun this, had told herself she'd thought it through, that she knew what she was letting herself in for. But Cole quickly showed her she hadn't really known a thing.

At first it had been like that kiss by the spring—startlingly swift and fierce. She'd been expecting this, even telling herself it couldn't possibly have been as wild as the kiss she remembered. She'd been right. It was even wilder.

He pressed her back against the edge of the desk, his hands cupping her head and tilting it as his mouth devoured hers, as his tongue plunged deep. He tasted her as if she were the sweetest of springwater after a long day in the California sun. He seemed ravenous for her, and just the idea sent ripples of heat through her that made her feel as if he were that sun. He seared her, made her quiver, then shake as he took possession of her mouth.

It struck her then that he would take possession of her body the same way—hotly, fiercely and a little savagely. It should have frightened her, she supposed with what little part of her mind was still functioning, but instead she

longed for it. She was eager to know more, yet she wanted
to savor the feelings he was causing in her now. She wanted
to leap ahead, yet stay here in this delightful place. Her di-
lemma was the sweetest she'd ever faced.

She made a tiny sound of protest when he drew back a
little, depriving her of the rough heat of his tongue. He
traced her mouth with his tongue and drew back again.
Then he flicked the tip over her lips and withdrew it once
more.

At last she understood, yet she hesitated, nervously uncertain. This time his tongue slipped softly over her lower lip
and lingered for a moment. And this time she responded,
moving to taste him with her own tongue.

She heard an odd sound, a slight whisper of a moan that
she couldn't quite believe had come from him. She'd expected him to become the aggressor once more, but he
didn't, he simply let her tongue tease his, only occasionally
returning the caress, letting her take the lead.

When he pulled back again, it was to catch her lower lip
between his teeth, tug, then release it in a gentle bite that
unexpectedly sent little darts of fire racing through her.

With barely an inch between them, Tory was suddenly
aware that she was clinging to him. And that even that
wasn't close enough. Her breasts felt swollen, nipples tautly
rigid, as if begging for his touch. She felt an aching emptiness low and deep inside her, and instinctively she parted her
legs to let him closer. It took him only a split second to accept the tacit invitation.

She gasped as his body came up hard against her. She'd
seen that he was aroused, but somehow it was very, very
different, feeling that hardened ridge of flesh pressed so intimately against her that the layers of cloth that separated
them seemed to barely exist. Hesitantly she shifted her hips,
rubbing against him. He groaned, low and husky, from deep
in his chest.

"I'd say you've got about another minute to change your
mind," he said thickly. "Then there's no turning back."

Turn back? Her inflamed body recoiled at the suggestion. But she couldn't find the breath to answer him. Couldn't remember how to speak at all. So instead she reached up, and slid her hands around his neck and her fingers through the thick darkness of his hair.

He responded to that barest of pressures, slipped his hands around her waist and brought his mouth down to hers again. That alone—how easily he did as she'd asked with that faintest of urging—made her feel that little thrill again. And when he moved his hips harder against her, pressing convulsively, as if he couldn't help himself, that thrill was joined by a sense of feminine power she'd never experienced before.

When he at last wrenched his mouth away, he was breathing hard and fast. She could feel his chest heaving as if he'd just been on the longest eight-second ride of his life. For a moment she was afraid he was going to back away. But then his hands tightened at her waist and lifted, and suddenly she was sitting on the desk top. For a long moment he just looked at her.

"Is this another last chance to change my mind?" she whispered shakily.

She saw him swallow, as if he were having to force the words out. "Do you want one?"

A different kind of warmth flooded her then, born of tenderness. Different, but just as consuming as the heat he'd kindled.

"If I said stop, you'd walk away, wouldn't you?" she said, a new kind of wonder dawning in her eyes.

"Crawl, maybe," he muttered. "Are you...saying stop?"

She smiled shyly, shaking her head. "No. Hurry up, maybe."

He closed his eyes on a low groan. "It's liable to be fast enough, anyway," he growled. "I've spent damn near every night since I got here wanting this."

Her eyes widened. "You...have?" Then, ingenuously, "Why?"

He chuckled wryly, a painful little sound. He slipped a finger beneath her chin and tilted her head back. Then he kissed her, gently this time, stroking softly over her lips with his tongue. She parted her mouth for him immediately this time, and flicked at his tongue with her own. The heat was softer, rippling instead of racing this time, but no less intense for the difference.

"That, for starters," he said.

Then he reached once more for her shoulders, only this time it was to slip the straps of her sundress down. The fine fabric slipped away easily, only to catch on the taut points of her breasts. She felt color flood her face once more. If she'd been intent on seduction since the moment she'd dressed this afternoon, she couldn't have planned it better. The skimpy straps of the cotton dress had precluded her wearing a bra, and for coolness in the summer heat, she had worn no panty hose. She was suddenly very aware that she wore only panties beneath the dress that he could pull to her waist with only the slightest of tugs. She wondered if perhaps she had planned it, that somewhere in some part of her mind she had known this was inevitable. She waited for him to take the next step, to reach for the soft cotton material.

He didn't do it. His hands came down to rest on her knees, then slid slightly upward on her thighs, as if he'd only now realized her legs were as bare as her arms. He stopped, as if waiting. She held her breath.

"Tory?"

It came from him in a voice so hoarse it was barely recognizable as his. And suddenly she realized his hands were trembling.

She sensed then what he was waiting for. That even now he was giving her a chance to back out. Little did he know that the raw hunger in his face would have decided for her, if she had had any doubts left. In that moment she was as certain as she could be that no woman had ever been wanted more than this. It was a heady feeling for her, and powerful enough to wipe out any fears about what would happen afterward. Surely this hot, fiery soaring, was worth any price.

She reached up with a none-too-steady hand of her own and tugged the dress free. It pooled around her waist, baring her breasts to him.

"God, Tory."

It came out on a long, drawn out breath, his tone touched with a wonder and need that seemed almost palpable as his gaze swept over her body. She shivered as if he'd touched her, and felt the tingling flesh of her nipples draw up, tight and eager.

He groaned again, low and husky, and lifted his hands. They came up to cup and lift the soft, rounded flesh of her breasts. Tory moaned at the first touch of his strong, tough hands on her delicate skin. Her head lolled back and her eyes drifted closed, only to snap open again as he rubbed his thumbs over her taut nipples. She cried out, her back arching involuntarily as he did it again, and again.

She should be embarrassed, she thought vaguely through the web of pleasure he was spinning around her. She was half-naked atop the desk, wantonly offering herself to him, while he stood there fully clothed, caressing her body as if he owned it. But he was causing such intense sensations, making her feel things she'd never felt before, doing exactly as she'd asked, teaching her, that she couldn't feel anything but pleasure. More pleasure than she'd ever imagined. More pleasure than she'd thought possible.

And then he lowered his head to capture one hardened nipple in his mouth, and she cried out his name in shocked wonder as he gave her a whole new lesson in what was possible. He flicked at the puckered tip with his tongue until she was moving helplessly, thrusting herself upward, silently urging him on. Then he moved his lips to the other nipple, suckling deeply, making her cry out again, and then again when his fingers began to pluck at the other crest still wet from his mouth.

The exquisite tugging made her aware—in a way new and wondrous to her—of the connection between the ultrasensitive flesh beneath his fingers and mouth and that hot, swirling place deep inside her that seemed to have been born when he'd kissed her, and had been expanding ever since.

Heedlessly she moved, hands curved as she sought something to hang onto, some anchor in this maelstrom she was twisting in. Her fingers caught in the cloth of his shirt, the pearl snaps giving way beneath her frantic grasp. She let her fingers slip beneath the shirt, sliding over skin that felt like living satin stretched over muscle as taut as any fit, powerful animal she'd ever seen.

She heard him suck in his breath, then felt the muscles beneath her hands contract, felt the hammering beat of his heart. With some vague idea of returning the pleasure he'd given her, she moved until her fingers encountered the flat disks of his nipples, not expecting the sharp intake of his breath when she rubbed the tightened flesh there.

She did it again and, as if involuntarily, his hips moved, sliding that ridged hardness over the core of her once more. She felt an odd, spiraling, falling sensation that faded away to a throbbing ache, as if she'd nearly reached some unseen goal her body was clamoring for.

She clutched at him then, hanging on. Her hands slid around him, and she felt an odd series of faint ridges beneath her fingertips, just above his belt on the left side of his back. Scars, she realized. A web of them, crisscrossing the sleek skin. She barely had time to wonder what hell he'd been through before he sought out her breast with his mouth again and sucked just hard enough to make her arch upward with a cry.

When she could breathe again, she slid her hands up over his shoulders, pushing at his shirt. It slid away, and he moved his arms to let it fall to the floor. She moved her hands slowly down his sides, then over his belly. She felt a rippling contraction there as he let out a low groan.

He took her wrist then, and gently urged her hand lower. Her fingertips encountered the denim waistband, and she hesitated. He let go of her, but muttered something that sounded incredibly like a plea, and she was helpless to resist it. She moved then, tracing the rigid length of him uncertainly but lovingly through the worn jeans.

He made a choking sound, and his hips jerked as he pressed himself into her palm. She caught her breath at the way he seemed to expand beneath her fingers, obvious even through his jeans. She stroked him again, with more assurance. And again.

An explosive oath ripped from his throat. His hands slid up her legs, reaching, curling in the practical blue cotton of her panties much like her fingers had frantically caught in his shirt. He yanked at them, and she lifted herself to help him. She wasn't sure where they landed, didn't care, because he was touching her, stroking her, and teaching her yet another lesson.

She'd known he would touch her, had even guessed it might be even more shattering than when his eager lips had enveloped her nipples. But she hadn't yet connected the expansion of that heated pool of flame within her to the physical readying of her body for his plunge into it. Only when his fingers slid easily into her wet heat did she realize how very ready she was for this man.

And so did Cole. He groaned her name at his first touch of that slick, welcoming flesh, and in seconds he was yanking at the button at his waistband and clawing at his zipper. He tugged at the layers of interfering jeans and briefs.

Tory stared as engorged male flesh sprang free; she should have known, she supposed. Cole was a very big man. And she couldn't help a pang of trepidation. But she forgot it as she realized the significance of the small foil packet he'd yanked hurriedly from a front pocket. A memory knifed through her mind, and her gaze flew to his face.

As if he'd felt her stare, he met her eyes.

"That's why you were in the drugstore," she said in a tiny voice. "Before you went to Whitey's."

Understanding hit him visibly. "Tory, no," he said quickly. "I didn't...doesn't have anything to do with her."

She bit her lip, all her doubts flooding back.

''Tory, listen to me. I bought these—'' he gestured with the package, an almost grim look on his face ''—because I wasn't sure I'd be able to keep my damned hands off of you, after that day at the spring. And I was right.''

For a long, silent moment, she just looked at him. All the reasons she was here came back to her, all the decisions she'd made. None of them had changed. And even if he had bought them with the intention of using them elsewhere, he hadn't. He'd come home. And she didn't even think to cringe at that word she had instinctively used.

''A good thing you did, then'' was all she said.

''God, Tory,'' he said on a sigh of relief that seemed tinged with wonder.

And then he was touching her again, stroking, petting, until she was writhing there on the desk, aching for him to finish the lessons he'd begun. She had just enough sanity left to realize that he was perilously close to the edge himself. She'd never seen raging need so eloquently expressed as in the tight, rigid line of his jaw, the taut cords of his neck, the tensed quiver of his arms as he touched her.

Remembering what she'd learned moments ago, she tentatively reached for him. She wanted to feel the heat of him, wanted to trace the hardened length of him without the interference of cloth between them.

The moment he saw what she was doing, he froze. So did she, afraid she'd done something wrong. Without a word, but with a world of fevered need in his face, he again took her hand and guided it to him.

Tory shivered in amazed wonder at the feel of him, hot and hard and heavy against her hand. And sleek. And smooth. So very smooth. Maybe even smooth enough to make this impossibility, this joining of his body to hers, possible after all. But as she tested the size of him with unschooled fingers, she had her doubts.

But what she couldn't doubt was that he was taking pleasure from her touch. It showed in his face, in the tautness of his body, in the way he moved, urging her on. She touched him again, with more assurance, and then again, long, deep stroking caresses that, to her wonder, made him tremble. And then he began touching her yet again, gently, teasingly, sliding his fingers over her, finding and massaging a little knot of nerves that leapt to life with sizzling awareness.

It was incredibly arousing, this mutual touching, this learning about his response and her own. She could feel her heart pounding, could feel its pace increase whenever she could gather her nerve to steal a glance at his strong hands stroking her body—or at her own hands, capturing and stroking him.

At last he pulled away, shuddering at her last, lingering caress as he did so.

"Now, Tory," he ground out. "I shouldn't . . . not on the damn desk . . . but there's nowhere else here, and it's got to be now."

"Yes," she whispered, her body already crying out at the cessation of his touch.

She had a vague thought that it was lucky the desk was a heavy, solid piece, but it vanished as she watched him sheath himself, saw the unsteadiness of his hands as they moved over that part of him—familiar to him, so new and hotly fascinating to her—and found the process unexpectedly erotic.

"Next time," she said huskily, "let me do that."

"If I live that long," he muttered.

And then he was holding her, pulling her to the edge of the desk and steadying her as he guided himself forward. She felt the first probing touch of him, then the first moment of sliding entry, and her body clenched in anticipation, capturing the tip of him in a sweetly hot grasp.

"Ah, Tory . . . I can't . . . wait!"

On the last word he let out a guttural sound and drove home hard and deep. Tory cried out at the sudden fierce invasion that made her shudder to her toes. She clutched at his shoulders, and he froze.

"Did I . . . hurt you?" he rasped panting.

"No. Oh, no. Please," she whispered, "don't stop now."

With a low growl he began to move, thrusting, driving. He lifted her legs until she instinctively wrapped them around his waist, and then he drove even deeper, wringing a pleasure-filled cry of his name from her. The sound seemed to fire him further, and Tory saw his hand go up to grasp the top of the desk as if to add even more force to his thrusts. She didn't care, all that mattered was the exquisite pressure building, coiling inside her, stoked by the sweet friction of his body.

She moved with the powerful motion of his hips, discovering as she did so that rising to meet him only increased the raging heat. Her head lolled back as she lifted her hips. She saw his hand, gripping the top of the desk so tightly his knuckles were white, and realized he wasn't adding force, he was trying to hold back. And she remembered her first sight of that powerful hand on her breast, cradling the soft curve as if it were the most fragile of things.

It was that image of power reined in that sent her over the edge, unleashing the coiled pressure inside her in a sudden fierce burst of heat and wild sensation. She arched upward, crying out, catching him as he plunged into her and making him cry out in turn as her body clenched tightly around him. And suddenly he wasn't holding back any longer. He was the wildest of wild creatures, plunging, slamming himself into her, a harsh, driven sound breaking from him at the depth of each lunging invasion of her body, sending her spiraling upward until she convulsed, spasms undulating through her fiercely.

His name broke from her again and again as she nearly wept from the sweet force of it, wave after wave that kept on and on. Through the haze she heard him call her name in turn, first in pleasure, then in wonder, then in shocked surprise as he shuddered violently, his muscles contracting into rigidness as his body bowed into hers. She felt his hands slide down to her buttocks to hold her body tight to his, as he groaned again and she felt another shudder ripple through him as her own body sagged into sated exhaustion.

She was only vaguely aware of the movement as he turned them around, then realized they were in a tangle on the floor. She lay straddling him, cradled against his naked chest, his back half propped against the front of the desk. He must have held her as they'd slid down. If he felt anywhere near as limp as she did, it was a wonder he'd been able to cushion the fall at all.

Tory shivered, an echoing quiver of that astounding explosion of pleasure. She truly would never be the same again, she thought dazedly. She supposed it was trite to say it had been a life-changing experience. But no longer would she wonder how people got themselves in such a tangle over love. Or why it seemed to occupy so much of their time, why they sang songs about it, wrote poems about it, wrote entire books about it. Or why her uncle still regretted, after all these years, that he'd never had a moment like this with the woman he'd loved.

But this wasn't love. No matter what it felt like, Cole had made that very clear. But it had been exactly what he'd promised: hot, raw and out of control. And she'd loved it. Reveled in it. Right here on her uncle's desk, heedless of anything but the wondrous lessons this man was teaching her. And for that alone she knew she would never, could never, regret it.

But even as she told herself that, she knew it had been more than simply sex. She might be naive, but not naive enough to think that this happened to everyone. Or every time. And even if she hadn't known, Cole's shocked surprise would have told her.

But she wasn't naive enough to think this changed anything, either. She'd made this decision with her eyes wide open. And now she had more than most to look back on. More than Hobie had. She couldn't be sorry that she'd done it. Even if this was all she would ever have.

Cole felt the quivering of her body as she sagged against him. He barely suppressed a shiver of his own. Silence spun out between them. All he could hear was the pounding of his pulse and the still quickened sound of his own panting for breath.

A million things to say swirled in his head. All the usual things a footloose and fancy-free man said after great sex. Things that acknowledged the pleasure given while making clear it in no way impinged on his freedom. Things that made it clear that no matter how great the sex had been, he would still head down the road when the time came.

He couldn't say any of them.

There were no easy words for what had just happened between them. It had been beyond anything he'd ever known, beyond anything he'd expected, even when he'd awakened in the night haunted by a pair of turquoise eyes and erotic dreams such as he hadn't experienced since he'd been a teenager in heat at the mere sight of a pretty girl.

But he couldn't say so. He was afraid if he tried to put what he was feeling into words, he'd end up saying something he didn't mean to. Or, he'd say something that would lead her on, something that would make her think this meant more than it had, that it had been more than just the hottest, wildest sex he'd ever had in his life.

But he was even more afraid that it *had* meant more.

God, he was losing it. He wasn't even thinking straight anymore. He took in a couple of deep breaths, trying to steady himself.

She moved just slightly against him, and he felt a sudden leap of the pulse that had been beginning to slow. And an echoing shudder of sensation rippling through flesh he would have sworn too sated to feel anything, even the most intimate of caresses. And all she'd done was move. Barely.

He really *was* losing it, he thought. He tried to distract himself, tried thinking of the ludicrous picture they must make. He'd managed to keep them from crashing painfully to the floor when his knees had given out, but he wasn't sure how. And now here they were, sprawled in an awkward tangle of bodies and clothing, her dress twisted down around her waist, his shirt beneath them on the floor, his jeans halfway to his knees, boots still on, and her bare legs entangled with his.

And he could feel with searing clarity every place where naked skin touched naked skin. Her hand against his belly, the soft curve of her breasts against his chest, her hips against his, pressing intimately close. Only now was his flesh ebbing, slipping from her, reluctantly leaving the sweet, warm haven of her body.

Again he tried to speak, to say something, anything that would reduce this to something he could deal with. Anything that would convince her that this had been what he'd told her it would be, and no more. The problem was, he had the grimmest feeling it wasn't her he had to convince, it was himself.

"Thank you."

The words were low and husky, and he just managed not to shiver anew at the feathery brush of her breath across his chest. But the words themselves, so unexpected, and the sound of amazed joy in her voice were another matter. They sent a shock wave down his spine that he was helpless to resist, and his arms tightened around her.

"No regrets?" he asked, not knowing what he'd do if she said yes.

She made a little sound that was half sigh, half something he couldn't put a name to. "No. I asked you to teach me. You certainly did."

"Tory, I—" He cut himself off.

"What?"

"Nothing."

He left it there, knowing the words he would have said would have complicated things immeasurably. He wasn't at all sure who had done the teaching here. He'd mocked her, thrown what she could expect from him up in her face like a challenge. He'd told her how it would be, and then dared her to come after it. He'd told himself she'd never do it, but now, sitting with her clutched to him, he wondered if, deep down, he'd known all the time she would. He suspected so.

Tory Flynn was a strong woman. Maybe even strong enough to keep him from hurting her.

And in the end, it had been he who'd been out of control, he who'd been wild and raw and hot. He'd taken her on the desk, for God's sake, like a kid so eager he couldn't wait.

And she'd loved it. He had enough experience to know when a woman was just going through the motions. And he knew Tory well enough to know that that kind of pretense was beyond her. He knew the fierceness of what had just passed between them had shaken all his perceptions. What he didn't know was what the hell he was going to do now.

In a moment he was saved from that decision. A piercing yowl, a loud crash and a trumpeting neigh sounded from the direction of the barn. Tory went rigid in his arms.

"Mac!" she cried.

Before Cole could move, she was on her feet, tugging her dress around her and racing barefoot for the door.

Chapter 13

"Tory!"

She never stopped. He cursed, tangled in his twisted clothes on the floor.

"Damn it, don't go charging out there alone!" he yelled after her as he managed to get to his feet and yank his jeans up and zip them on the run.

By the time he got to the office door he heard the slam of the door in the kitchen, and knew she either hadn't heard, or hadn't listened. He heard Hobie's voice calling out to Tory, saying he was on his way, then the clatter of booted feet, moving fast.

Hobie.

God, it was happening all over again. Nausea roiled his stomach as he ran. Images, temporarily seared away by the savage heat of their lovemaking, rose to batter at him. Three times. Three god-awful times. People he'd tried to help. Women who had trusted him to help, and had wound up burying the ones they loved. Why hadn't he learned? Why had he come here, to set the twisted, evil dynamics in motion again—the deadly combination that had already buried two men and a child? A sudden vision of Tory weeping over Hobie's grave nearly stopped him dead in his tracks.

He stumbled, recovered, fought down the nausea and made himself go on. His faltering had given Hobie a lead, and Cole swore at himself as he heard the outer door slam closed again just as he rounded the corner into the kitchen.

He raced outside. Tory was nowhere in sight. He saw Hobie's wiry shape step from the shadow of the house out into the moonlight. He pushed himself and caught up with Hobie halfway to the barn. He grabbed the older man's arm and pulled him to a stop.

"Wait here," he said.

"But Tory's in—"

"I know." Cole clenched his jaw, trying to rein in the fear that threatened to swamp him. Still, his voice shook slightly when he went on. "Please, Hobie. Stay here. I'll go in and get her."

Hobie's brow furrowed, and he stared intently at Cole. Something he saw in Cole's face seemed to decide for him, and he nodded shortly.

"You got three minutes, boy."

"Just stay here," Cole begged, not even caring now how he sounded. Then he headed for the barn at a run.

He skidded to a halt at the big sliding barn door, still open from Tory's entrance. He spent a precious five seconds listening, and heard nothing but the natural movements of the horses, still restless after the disturbance. He stepped inside, hugging the wall to remain in shadow, using every bit of concentration he could muster to stay quiet.

Tory laughed.

It hit Cole like a blow to the gut. She was all right. It hadn't happened. Despite his panic, his hesitation, she was all right.

"You've really done it now, Rocky," she said, still laughing.

Rocky. That damned cat. Was he behind this chaos? Cole straightened up, only now realizing he had sagged against the barn wall in relief. He started toward her voice, which was coming, inevitably he supposed, from the direction of Mac's stall.

At last he saw her, inside Mac's stall, grinning widely at Rocky as she leaned against the bottom half of the stall door where the cat was precariously balanced. The cat's fur seemed to be standing on end, and his tail was twice its normal size.

The minute Cole got close enough Rocky let out a yowl and leapt to his shoulder.

"Damn, cat!" Cole yelped as claws dug into his bare skin. He grabbed the cat in the middle with one big hand and started to lift him away, wincing as the animal tried to dig in and stay put. The damn cat had drawn blood this time, he could feel it. Rocky yowled again, and Mac snorted.

"He just tried that with Mac," Tory explained, laughing. "That's what all the ruckus was. It's a good thing he thought better of using his claws that time."

Cole pried the cat's feet loose, then lifted him up and away. Rocky hissed, batting with his front paws like his namesake in the ring.

"Knock it off, cat," he said warningly as he bent to set the cat down, "or you'll be spending eternity on some violin somewhere."

"Trouble just seems to follow you, doesn't it?"

Cole went very still. He felt an echo of that earlier nausea churning low in his belly. Did she know? Had she somehow guessed about the trail of disaster he'd laid down over the last thirteen years?

Very slowly he straightened up.

"Yes," he said stiffly. "It does. I warned you about that."

She was very quiet for a moment before she said, "I meant the cat."

There was a tenderness, a soft note of compassionate gentleness in her voice that made him uneasy and angry at himself. All he could think was that had she really been in danger, that staggering moment of fear could have got her killed.

"I'd better go tell Hobie you're all right." He sounded even stiffer than before. He didn't care. He turned around and started to walk away, every second expecting her to say something, to call him back, to use what they'd just shared as a bond to hold him.

"You'd better take care of your shoulder. You're bleeding" was all she said.

"Yeah," he muttered, and kept going.

He had no right to feel stung, he told himself. He should be grateful she'd let him go so easily. He should be glad she hadn't insisted on indulging in a heavily emotional dissection of the sensual fever that had gripped them. So why did he feel like his shoulder wasn't the only place he was bleeding?

He ran into Hobie just outside the barn door. The wiry older man had a small rifle in his hands. A semiautomatic .22, Cole noted mechanically.

"You had about another ten seconds, boy," he said, "and I was comin' in."

And if there really had been a threat, you, too, could have joined the list of bodies I've left behind.

"You hang on to that," he said flatly, gesturing at the rifle. "She's all yours."

"I've been keeping it in the tack room since all this started— What do you mean, she's all mine?"

"Just look out for her. Until I . . . figure out what to do."

"I always look out for her." Hobie's bushy gray brows lowered. "You're not makin' much sense, boy."

"That," Cole said grimly, "is the truest thing you've ever said."

Hobie stared at Cole. "You're acting like a lizard strung up over a fire."

Yeah, Cole thought sourly. And the fact that he'd lit that fire himself made it even worse. "Well I'm going to go put it out," he muttered. "If there's enough booze in this town."

He strode back toward the house, never looking back. The chill he felt had little to do with the cool air on the bare skin of his chest and arms, and everything to do with the memory of that moment when he'd faltered, helpless against the fear that swamped him. Yes, he'd got moving again, but that moment could have made the difference between life and death for Tory. He'd seen it too many times to deny the possibility. That nothing had happened was merely luck. Hers, no doubt, not his.

He walked into the house, his jaw grimly set. If he'd ever had any doubts about his decision five years ago to pull himself out of the field, they were now erased. He'd lost it, that indefinable something that made a man quick enough, that honed his reflexes to that fine point where there wasn't even a split second of hesitation. It wasn't much, just the slightest blunting of a once razor-sharp edge. Just a few precious seconds of hesitation while he fought down the memories. But it was enough. Enough to get somebody killed.

And tonight that somebody could have been Tory. Or Hobie. He lived with the other ghosts of people he'd failed, only rarely resorting to alcohol to blur the memories. He knew he would never be able to live with the images that would haunt him if something happened to either of the Flynns. There wasn't enough alcohol in the world to blur that kind of haunting.

He walked into the office to pick up his shirt. His mouth was compressed with his determination to feel nothing as he crossed the room to where Tory had given herself to him so completely, for reasons of her own that he'd convinced himself were all that mattered. That determination wavered as, picking up his shirt from the floor, he saw the tiny scrap of pale blue cotton that were her panties, forgone in her fear for Mac.

A sudden image of himself tearing them from her body, of her letting him do it, helping him, flared vividly to life in his mind. A wave of renewed heat swept through him, cramping his body with a need he couldn't believe was so strong—so powerful—even after the wild coupling that had taken place between them.

He heard footsteps on the porch, and hastily stuffed the scrap of blue cloth into his jeans pocket. He would put them in her room, save her at least from that much embarrassment, should Hobie walk in here.

And it wasn't until he'd done so, until he was standing in the tidy blue-and-white room that managed to be cheerful and feminine in comparison to the rest of the businesslike house, that an explanation for how easily she'd let him walk away came to him. It made him feel nearly as nauseous as that swelling fear had. What if she'd gotten all she wanted? What if she truly had only wanted him to, as she'd said, teach her?

In that case, he told himself harshly, you should be damn glad. Because it'll make walking away a whole lot easier.

And after tonight, he knew that walk had to come even sooner than he'd planned.

"He quit?"

Hobie shrugged. "That's what he said. Reckon he's off to Whitey's or somewhere, to get himself good and drunk."

Tory sank down on the living room sofa. She'd heard Cole drive off before she'd even come in from the barn after settling Mac down and making sure Rocky hadn't inadvertently scratched the horse. She'd been startled by his tire-spinning departure, and had come quickly out of the barn in time to watch his truck pull out onto the main road. She'd found Hobie coming out of the office after shutting off the light.

Inanely, all she could think of to say was "It's nearly midnight."

"Closin' time's two. A man can get a powerful lot of drinking done in two hours."

"But...why?"

Hobie looked at her consideringly. "I thought you might be able to answer that."

Tory's eyes widened. Had Hobie guessed what had happened tonight? "What do you mean?"

"I got the feeling it was something to do with you."

Tory felt a sudden chill. "Are you saying he went out to get drunk because of me?"

"Honey, all I know is he's been as edgy as a green-broke stud ever since he got here. Why, the Cole I used to know was so laid back you'd think an earthquake couldn't budge him, until he uncoiled on you so fast it made your head spin. But now..."

He ended with another shrug. Then he yawned. "He's a big boy. He'll get home all right. I'm going back to bed."

She gave her uncle a hug, and watched him walk off to his room, but her mind was racing in what seemed like a hundred directions. And she wasn't liking what she found in any of them.

Why had he looked so grim, even after they'd found out what had caused the disturbance in the barn? Why had he left so abruptly? Why, after what had happened between them, had he felt the sudden need to escape? Why the apparent need to obliterate the memory? Had it been so distasteful to him?

It certainly hadn't seemed that way, not when he had cried out her name as he'd arched into her in those final seconds. Was he afraid she would now expect something from him? Hadn't she made it clear enough that she'd gone into this with her eyes open, knowing she would get nothing more than he'd promised her that day by the spring?

Or was that it? Had it been more for him, too, as it had for her, much more than just raw, out-of-control sex? Was that why he'd run? Because it *had* been more, and that scared him?

Dream on, girl, Tory chided herself, knowing she was being foolish.

She kept pacing, thinking, wondering, until she felt like she was about to spin off in all the different directions her thoughts were taking. The square of moonlight streaming in the front window that marked the halfway point of her circuit, gradually shifted shape and size, until it finally disappeared, continuing its arc behind the house. It was the absence of the silvery light that at last made her look at her watch. Nearly four. Whitey's had closed over an hour and a half ago. She came to a halt.

This was too ridiculous. Here she was, pacing the floor like some worried woman waiting for her wayward man to stagger home. It was such a trite picture it made her laugh. And then it made her angry. She wasn't going to be that kind of woman. She couldn't be.

She walked to the door of Hobie's room and listened. He was breathing easily; there was little trace of the rasp left. Reassured, she went upstairs to her room to change her clothes.

She felt her breath catch when she saw the patch of pale-blue cotton lying on her bed. And she remembered Hobie going into the office to shut off the light. He couldn't have missed the discarded pair of panties, if they'd been there. But they hadn't.

Cole. Cole had done this for her, so she wouldn't be embarrassed in front of her uncle. There could be no other reason. She felt like she'd been tossed from a horse and had the wind knocked out of her. She sat on the edge of the bed, fingering the blue cotton that matched her dress, trying not to think of how eager she'd been, how urgent he'd been, when he'd practically torn them from her.

When she finally left the house, clad now in her usual jeans, she wasn't sure any more if she was angry or worried. She drove carefully, searching the roadsides, and peering at the infrequent oncoming cars, looking for Cole's truck. She'd been concentrating so hard that when finally she did see a dark, squared off shape beneath the patch of scrub oak the main road had obligingly been curved around, it took her a moment to realize it was really him.

She pulled off onto the shoulder, her headlights bathing the back of the pickup in light. The cab appeared empty. It seemed awfully close to the trees, and for a moment she was afraid he'd hit them. She braked to a halt, threw the Jeep into Park and scrambled out.

"Hey, kill the lights, will ya?"

Cole's voice came from somewhere in front of the truck. She flipped off the headlights and hurried that way, deciding that if he was doing something embarrassing, it would serve him right.

He was sitting under a tree, his back propped up against the rough-barked trunk, his battered strawhat tilted forward over his eyes. The moment she got within a yard of him, she could smell the whiskey—or was it bourbon? She never had been able to tell.

"You *are* drunk."

"You bet."

"Well, at least you're not driving," she muttered.

He pushed the brim of his hat back with an unsteady finger. "Course not. I'm too drunk to drive," he said rather righteously. Then he grimaced, gesturing over his shoulder to some thick brush a few yards away. "Besides, I had to stop and get sick. I'm not used to this anymore."

"Charming," Tory said, gingerly crouching down beside him. But illuminating, she added silently. This obviously wasn't typical behavior for him. And oddly, although his voice was thick, his words weren't slurred. In fact, he was enunciating each one with great care, as if to compensate for an uncooperative tongue.

"Hey," he said, as if he'd only now remembered where he was, and that this was an unlikely place for her to be, "what are you doing here?"

"Never mind. It would take too long to explain, and you wouldn't understand right now anyway. Come on, I'll take you home." Home. Her mouth quirked wryly at the instinctively chosen word.

"Home?" he echoed, sounding puzzled. Then, his voice suddenly taut, the alcoholic haze lifting a little, "God, it didn't happen, did it? Hobie? Is that why you're here?"

"What didn't happen?"

He was sitting up now, grasping her arm so tightly it hurt. "He's alive isn't he? God, Tory, tell me he's all right!"

"Hobie?" She was utterly confused now. "Of course he is. Why wouldn't he be?"

"Because I came. Shouldn't have. They always die when I try to help."

There was something so bleak in his drunken voice that she couldn't help the shiver that raced up her spine. "Who always dies?"

"The ones they love."

The shiver came again at the starkly simple words, even though she didn't understand them. She tried again. "Who?"

He sagged back against the tree. There was very little light, since the moon had nearly set. All she had to go by was the tone of his voice. And it was appallingly grim when, after she'd thought he wouldn't, he went on. His voice was clearer, as if the horror had chased away some of the whiskey's effects.

"Gil. Neal. Little Timmy. All of them. Because the women who loved them asked me to help."

"Cole—"

"Ever been to a kid's funeral, Tory?"

"No," she answered, knowing she didn't want to hear this. But she didn't dare stop him, not the way the words were coming from him in slow, agonized stops and starts. This had clearly been building in him for a long time.

"It's the casket that gets to you," he said. "It's so damn small. And they're always white. Ever notice that? 'Cause the kid's an innocent, you know? Never had a chance to be anything else."

Tory felt her hands curl into fists, her nails digging into her palms.

"They told me the kidnapper killed him early, that he'd probably meant to do it from the beginning. But he was alive when I started looking. I know he was. I could feel it. Hell, he was my blood. I knew he was alive."

Oh, God, Tory thought.

"He was . . . family?"

"His mother was a . . . a second cousin, I guess. Closest relative I've got, anyway."

His head lolled back against the tree. His hat, nudged by the movement, slipped to one side and tumbled to the ground. He didn't reach for it.

"One little boy, and I couldn't find him. If I'd been better, or faster...or something..."

"Cole, stop—"

"You know what the worst part was? Lisa, Timmy's mom. She just looked at me, all sad, saying she knew I did my best. And then she asked if I'd come to the service." He groaned, low and harsh. "Me. She wanted me, the guy who didn't find her son in time, to be at the funeral. What kind of sense does that make?"

"Maybe she knew it wasn't your fault," Tory said, feeling far out of her depth, but knowing she couldn't let this kind of pain cry out unanswered. "Things like that happen, Cole. They're awful, but they happen."

"Yeah," he said. "They do. Especially around me." His voice caught. "Timmy was...the last straw. I knew I couldn't risk it again. He was just a baby, barely five, and..."

There was so much bitterness in his voice as it trailed she wondered that the acid of it hadn't hollowed him out inside. Or maybe it had. Maybe that was the answer she'd started out to find tonight.

"What did you mean, they happen...around you?" she said, feeling her way carefully.

He lifted his head then, and she knew he was looking at her, even in the darkness.

"Don't you see? That's why I didn't want to come here. You and Hobie. Me. That's the combination."

"The combination?"

"Gil and Sherry. The Carltons. Timmy and his mom. Them and me. And now you and Hobie. And me. It always happens."

"Cole," she said softly, coaxingly. Even though she already knew she didn't want to hear any of this, she also knew it was tearing him up inside and it needed to come out. "What always happens?"

"Told you. They die." His head fell back against the tree's trunk. "Gil. Neal. Timmy. And now Hobie, if I don't get the hell out of here."

The ones they love. That's why I didn't want to come here. You and Hobie. Me. That's the combination. They die. And now Hobie.

The combination.

Tory turned it over in her mind, trying to make sense out of his disjointed explanation. She was only able to come to one conclusion.

"Are you saying that... if a woman comes to you because someone she loves is in trouble..."

Cole said it simply, as if it were the most self-evident, incontrovertible of facts.

"He dies."

Chapter 14

Tory sat back on her heels, a little stunned. Surely Cole couldn't really believe he was...what, some kind of jinx? But the string of names he'd reeled off shook her. Three times, it had happened to him that way?

"Gil," she said, remembering the first name.

"My best friend, back in the army. We were in special forces together." She heard him swallow, as if his throat were painfully tight. "Made it through that. When we got out, he got a little crazy. Hooked up with some guy who was going to make him rich, fast, some kind of land deal. When Gil found out it was a scam, he went after the guy. Sherry came to me to try and stop him."

"But you were too late?" she asked softly.

He made a sound, a short, expressive intake of breath. "I wish I had been. Maybe he'd still be alive. All the guy wanted was to get out of the country with the half-million he'd looted. But when I got there...he panicked. And Gil was dead."

"That wasn't your fault, either," she began.

"That's what I told myself. Then, after I started with Sanders, it was the Carltons. Neal, and Jennifer. Poor Jenny. And I still didn't get it. The combination, I mean. There were other cases, where things went fine." He stopped, letting out a low, stifled groan. "God, why am I telling you all this?"

"Because you need to tell someone," she said softly.

And he needed to do it like this, she thought with a certainty she didn't question—in the darkness, where he wouldn't have to watch her face as he laid out his crimes for her. Cole Bannister had already judged and convicted himself, but he'd bottled up his own self-condemnation for so long it had come to this, a gut-wrenching confession that he couldn't seem to stop.

"What happened to Jennifer Carlton?"

A biting, humorless chuckle escaped him. "Nothing. Except that she buried her husband. Or what was left of him."

Tory's breath caught. "What?"

"Car bomb."

"My God." *And my looks sure as hell didn't stop that bomb.* She had her answer now. "Why?"

"Neal ran a little newspaper that stepped on some toes. Including some gang members who didn't like the way he kept asking for a truce on the streets."

Tory's eyes widened. She'd heard about that, hadn't she? Right after she'd come west to Hobie. She had a vague memory of news reports, of pictures of mangled wreckage sitting in front of a small office front. And something else. About the man who'd tried to save Neal Carlton.

"Your back," she whispered. "That's what happened, isn't it?"

He didn't answer. But she remembered, in the indelible way you remembered the gruesome scenes of a tragedy. She remembered that one of the others badly injured in the same blast that had killed the newspaperman had been the man who'd tried to save him.

"He wouldn't listen." It came out in a rush. "He just ignored the threats and kept on doing what he'd been doing. He couldn't believe anybody would really try to kill him for asking for peace."

"But his wife believed it," Tory said, understanding at last. "And she came to you to protect him."

"And a damn fine job I did, too. Just like Gil." He swore, low and harsh. "I told him to always let me check the car before he got into it, but he just went ahead. Jenny was worried because they'd found another threat painted on the front door. I stopped to . . . try and reassure her." He let out a compressed breath. "I woke up in a hospital bed a week later."

"God, Cole!" It burst from her involuntarily. "What were you supposed to do if he wouldn't listen?"

"My job," he said flatly. "I should have made him wait. I shouldn't have stopped to talk to her."

"But if she was so frightened, how could you not try to reassure her?"

"*She* wasn't my job. *He* was. And because I let myself get distracted, he died."

"But you can't think—"

"I did nothing *but* think, once I came to. For weeks, while I was lying in that damned hospital. And it always came up the same. She trusted me, and he died."

"And you nearly died, too, didn't you?" A week of unconsciousness and more weeks in the hospital was enough to tell her that. "Isn't that enough penance for something that wasn't even your fault?"

For a long time he said nothing. Then, quietly, "He had three kids. All under six."

"That makes an awful thing even worse," she said. "But it still doesn't make it your fault."

"If I hadn't stopped, I could have caught up with him—"

"You would have died, too. And he'd still be dead."

He let out a long, drawn out breath. "I've told myself that. I've even learned to believe it, some of the time. I can believe it about each time... by itself. But... "

Not three times, Tory finished silently for him. God, no wonder he was convinced he was some kind of jinx.

"You said there were other cases..."

Another long breath. "Lots of them, in four years. Men, women, young, old. It didn't matter. Everything was fine. Great in fact. Never lost a case or a client... as long it wasn't a woman trying to save her man. Or her son."

The combination.

"And you think because... I asked you for Hobie's sake... it will happen again?" She shivered involuntarily. "That's why you quit, isn't it?"

He didn't say anything. She supposed there wasn't much left to say. Three times. An innocent child. A father to three more innocent children. And his best friend. She couldn't begin to imagine the toll that would take. Or the haunting memories he must carry.

Just a big, strong facade, without a damned thing behind it.

His words came back to her, along with the pure conviction that had rung in his voice when he'd said them. It *was* a facade, that cool, uncaring front. But she'd been wrong about what it was covering up. She'd thought he was warning her off, telling her that he was the kind of man she'd thought he was when she'd seen him with Cindy Crain draped around him, that to him, one willing woman as good as the next.

But it hadn't been that at all. She had remembered when she'd thought about hollowness. It wasn't far from there to the understanding that this was what he'd been talking about when he'd told her not to trust him. That what he was covering was not the shallowness of a womanizer, but the pain of a man who felt utterly empty inside.

What had he said about Kyra? *I'm not her style... she knows better?* Is that how he'd felt, that women like Kyra—and perhaps like herself—wouldn't have anything to do with him if they knew what was behind the illusion, that image of tall, broad, impossibly handsome strength? That only women like Cindy would? Women who cared for little other than the image?

She suddenly remembered a horse she'd seen once, a big, gutsy bay stallion who'd been in a horse transport that had been hit by another rig. The animal had been hurt so badly he was obviously dying, but he kept struggling to get to his feet, trying to keep going. She'd been horrified at his pain, and had cried at his courage. She was feeling an echo of that combination right now, along with a fierce tightness in her throat. Several silent minutes passed before she could speak.

"I don't know what to say," she said huskily. "Except that none of it was your fault. But . . . I can understand why you might feel like it is, somehow."

Even in the nighttime shadows beneath the tree she could see him go very still.

"Nobody ever understood before," he said, in a voice so tightly controlled she wondered if he was as close to snapping as he sounded. "But I've never . . . spilled my guts like this to anybody, either."

"Sometimes it has to come out, Cole. If you don't talk about it, it will come out some other way. And those ways are usually worse."

He made a wry sound that was almost a chuckle. "Were you a bartender in another life?"

"No. I just know how much better I felt after you listened to me about my father."

There was a pause and then, quietly, "Is that what this is? A payback?"

"If that's what you need it to be."

And you don't need to know how much more it is to me, Tory thought sadly. You wouldn't want to know. She was only beginning to know, herself. In a peculiar sort of way, she'd been relieved to think of him as a casual, hit-and-run kind of lover, a love-'em-and-leave-'em type like her father, whom she doubted had ever experienced a sincere emotion in his life. It had made it easier for her to think she could keep her heart intact, knowing that there would be nothing beyond the physical in a relationship with a man like that.

But now she knew that Cole wasn't that kind of man at all. She knew that he was a man who, if anything, felt too deeply—too deeply to easily accept the assessment that none of the tragic deaths he'd been so close to were his fault. Too deeply to walk away and go on with his life untouched. Too deeply not to question what he might have done to save the people who now haunted him. And so deeply that he changed his life because of them.

So where did that leave her? How was she now to keep the distance between them? How was she supposed to protect her heart, when everything she'd heard made her want to hold this man close and try to heal him any way she could?

For a very long time they sat in silence. Tory might have thought he'd passed out or gone to sleep except for the faint gleam that told her his eyes were open. He was staring upward, at the leafy canopy of the old scrub oak.

It came quietly out of the dark. "Tory?"

"What?"

"Why are you here?"

It was a much more sober version of that first question asked, what seemed like hours ago. She stifled a sigh.

"Looking for you," she answered finally.

"In the middle of the night?"

"Closer to morning," she corrected, only now realizing it was literally true. The sky was growing lighter in the east.

"Why?" he repeated.

Fine time for him to sober up enough so that she couldn't divert him. Although the harrowing story he'd told her would be enough to sober anyone.

"I was . . . worried. And angry."

"Oh."

"And if you're going to ask why, don't. I haven't even figured that out completely myself."

"Oh."

His noncommittal response jabbed at her. "Would you like to define what the heck 'oh' means?"

She saw his mouth twist wryly in the slowly gathering light of dawn. "It means I don't know what else to say."

She hadn't expected that simple, honest answer. "Oh."

He looked startled. Then, slowly, the wry set of his lips became a half smile. As if played back in her head, she heard the absurdity of that last exchange, and couldn't help nearly smiling, too. But both expressions faded quickly. There had been too much pain, too much powerful emotion dragged out here to let it go easily. She felt exhausted; she could only imagine how he felt.

"We both need some sleep," she said, starting to rise. "Are you okay to drive home now, or do you want to come back for your truck later?"

As she said the word "home," she saw him stiffen. "I'll drive back. To pick up my things."

Tory sank back down, staring at him. "To what?"

"I told you. I've got to get out of here."

"But—"

"I'll find someone else to help you here."

"You're . . . leaving?"

He came up on his knees, a bare two feet away from her. In the new light she could see the rough texture of the beard stubbling his jaw, and the red-rimmed fatigue in his eyes.

"I have to, Tory. If you'd really walked into trouble tonight, you could have been hurt—or worse. Because I wasn't fast enough."

"Fast enough? You were right behind me!"

"Not fast enough," he repeated. "Once I would have been there first. But I don't have that edge anymore. And every second is critical. It has to be . . . instant, Tory. You could have died while I was . . . remembering."

And he couldn't take another funeral.

He hadn't spoken the words, but she heard them as if he had. And she had the awful feeling that, even if she were to pour every bit of her heart and hope and caring into it, she could never heal this man. Only he could do that, and he was carrying around far too much guilt to even let the process begin.

She wondered if she was going to be any better at healing than he was.

Numbly, she got to her feet. He rose as well, for the moment steadier on his feet than she was. She felt as if she were the one who'd tried to find oblivion in a bottle. Maybe she'd try it yet.

"You can explain to Hobie," she said, her voice sounding as weary as she felt. "I'm far too tired."

"Tory—"

She turned her back on him. She was afraid she was going to cry, and she didn't want him to see her. She'd made a promise to him, that she wanted nothing more than he was willing to give. She walked toward the Jeep, telling herself every step of the way that because she'd been kidding herself was no excuse for adding to his sense of guilt.

And she knew now that he would feel that way. That all his warnings to her, all his harsh words about himself and the way it would be, had been not solely to protect her, but himself, as well. Because if he knew, if he even thought she'd fallen as hard as she now knew she had, he'd take on that load, too.

Her hands were shaking as she opened the Jeep's door and climbed in. She'd judged him on his looks alone, and deemed him like her father. But he wasn't anything like that callous, using man. Where the one felt nothing, Cole felt too much. And he paid the price for it, as her father never had.

She glanced toward him, standing beneath the solid oak, looking nearly as solid himself. But much more alone. She'd never seen anyone who seemed so alone.

She had to blink rapidly as she pulled back out onto the road and turned the Jeep toward home.

Cole stood staring down the road until the square, white shape of the Jeep had disappeared. His head was beginning to ache, and although he tried to put it down to the excess influx of sour mash, he had a feeling it was just as much due to that unexpected outpouring of the grim details of his miserable life.

Another good reason for not drinking, he thought, rubbing his forehead. It loosens the hinges on your jaw far too much. He couldn't believe what he'd done. Poured it all out for her like Whitey had kept pouring that Wild Turkey.

He'd even told her about Timmy. No one knew about Timmy.

He'd been on vacation from Sanders when Lisa had come to him. That had been the last vacation he'd ever taken, until now. And despite his efforts, the toddler had been found dead. When he had returned to the Sanders offices, three days after that appalling funeral, there had been comments on his taciturnity, and shock when he'd accepted the transfer to Research which Sanders had offered when he'd told him he was quitting. But when he'd made it clear the subject wasn't open for discussion, they'd left him alone. And, thanks to the cooperation of a friend at the sheriff's office who kept it quiet, no one at Sanders knew that the little boy who'd so sadly been in the news was connected to him.

And now he'd not only discussed it, but poured his soul out to the one person he knew was most dangerous to his hard-won equanimity. The one person who had shaken his resolve to never let down his guard. The one person who had made him question the course he'd chosen, and the life he led.

The one person who would never, ever forgive him if he stayed and it happened again. It was just too much to risk. He couldn't bear to add Hobie's name to that list, for the sake of trying to disprove whatever hex fate seemed to have dropped on him.

He walked slowly—and carefully—back to his truck. His legs were apparently feeling the aftereffects of the unaccustomed binge. And the rest of him wasn't too happy, either. He felt exhausted, far more tired than a night without sleep should have made him.

Figures, he thought. It was his mind that he'd been trying to numb, and it was the only thing still working just fine.

He sat down in the driver's seat, propping his elbows on the steering wheel and cradling his head in his hands. And he admitted reluctantly that it wasn't just renewing his acquaintance with whiskey that had him so drained. It was renewing his acquaintance with a lot of old memories he'd kept buried, and buried deep, for a long, long time.

And the strung-out, wire-tight emotions that came with them. He'd had a lot of practice denying he even had such feelings. Five years ago, he'd walked away before they'd lowered that tiny white casket into the ground, and had sworn that caring and feeling were for fools. He'd sworn he'd never get close enough to anybody ever again to have to go to their funeral.

And he'd tried to make it stick. There were people he liked, people he respected, but he guarded his heart like a wary wolf guarded its cubs. And he'd got along fine, for years.

Then Kyra had come along. And she'd been even warier than he. When he'd realized she was afraid of him because of his looks, it had shaken him. He hadn't liked it, and had, at least temporarily, set himself to actually try to get close to someone. It had taken a very long time, and he'd learned a great deal from her about self-protection in the process. He'd also learned, eventually, that she had good reason for her reaction. And by the time she was comfortable enough with him to talk about it, he realized he'd done a very foolish thing; he'd fallen in love with Kyra Austin. Even knowing she could never love him back.

Or maybe because of that fact, he admitted at last for the first time.

He lifted his head to stare out into the pink light of dawn. She was Kyra Riordan now, madly in love with the husband who adored her, pregnant and happier than Cole had ever seen her. And he was happy for her, he told himself, as he'd always told himself when he thought of her.

And then, with a little shock of realization, it hit him. He *was* happy for her. And the happiness, for the first time, wasn't tinged with regret for what he'd...not lost, but never had.

He wasn't sure what the absence of that regret meant, but it made him uneasy.

As did thinking of Kyra and Cash, for a completely different reason. Because of Cole's expertise on terrorists, Bill Sanders, the head of Sanders Protection, had wanted to send him in to help Kyra when things had really got ugly at the end of that case, when the threats on Cash's life had been coming closer and closer. But he'd known it would be inviting tragedy, because by then it was obvious to him that Kyra had come to care for the surprisingly modest, unassuming star she'd been sent to protect. And throwing Cole Bannister into a case to help a woman—and a man she cared about—was like inviting disaster to strike. So he'd refused. And Cash was still alive. Proof in reverse, he supposed.

Proof that he needed to get the hell out of here.

He started the truck and pulled carefully out onto the road. It was getting brighter out, and his eyes—gritty from lack of sleep and hurting from too much alcohol—protested. He reached into the glove box and tugged out the wire-framed, aviator-style sunglasses he hadn't worn since he'd got here, relying on his hat for shade. He put them on, grimly acknowledging the ludicrousness of needing them when it was barely after dawn.

He drove toward the ranch, wishing he could put a halt to the mad racing of his mind. It was as if he'd stirred it up so with that rush of memories that now it wouldn't settle down. It was a good thing this road was deserted at this hour, because he wasn't concentrating on driving very well. He was too busy wondering what he was going to tell Hobie. And how the hell he was going to walk away from Tory.

But on some instinctive level his mind must be working, he realized, because he'd already slowed down before the dust cloud rising off to the right registered on his conscious mind. It was far down the road Tory had told him about, the road that came up on the far side of the hills. Whoever it was had already reached the end of the paved portion and was into the dust, kicking up the cloud he'd seen.

The fact that it was the road her trespasser had probably taken was enough to make Cole suspicious. He had checked it the day after she'd told him about it, and found what could have been recent tire tracks, and a few smudged footprints in the dust, but nothing else.

He turned off the main road and braked the truck to a stop. He reached once more into the glove box and took out the small binoculars he was now grateful he'd brought. The dusty windshield of the truck interfered, and he stepped to the ground to bring the binoculars up to his sunglasses.

The cloud seemed fainter, already dissipating in the morning sun, with no sign of the vehicle that had made it. Then he realized he was looking too far ahead. This was a second—or rather, first—cloud. The one he'd originally seen was farther back, apparently stirred up by a second vehicle following the first. He moved his head and the field glasses and focused again. And he felt his stomach knot when he saw the familiar, blocky white shape.

It was Tory.

Chapter 15

Cole lowered the binoculars, vaguely aware that he was gripping them so tightly his knuckles where white.

She must have seen the dust cloud raised by the passing vehicle just as he had. And had, with the kind of recklessness he'd seen too often lead to tragedy, gone charging after the intruder who might be the man responsible for the death of her beloved horses. It was useless hoping she'd realize her folly and turn back. When it came to a threat to her own, Tory Flynn would never back down. Images of the possible results that such a confrontation brought made his stomach clench nauseatingly. He fought it down.

There was no way, unless the trespasser was utterly oblivious, that he couldn't know she was behind him. That second rising cloud of dry California dust was a marker that would be hard to miss.

God, Tory.

"Move it, Bannister," he muttered. You freeze up now and you'll have another damned funeral to go to. Hers. And this time you might not be able to resist the urge to throw yourself into that grave, too.

He floored it until he ran out of pavement. And he didn't try for secrecy as he hit the dirt, in fact, he purposely swerved every few hundred yards to make sure the quarry knew Tory wouldn't be alone for long. The worn out shocks made it a rough ride, but he never slowed. He'd wasted enough time already, once more battling the memories that robbed him of those precious seconds that could make the difference between getting there in time and not. The old Cole Bannister would have been there by now, would have moved the instant he'd realized it was Tory following this unknown—and possibly lethal—intruder. He didn't know who this Cole Bannister was, anymore.

The truck hit a rut and veered sharply to the right. He wrestled it back and slammed down on the accelerator once more. He had no business being here, he thought, damning himself for not having sent somebody who could function like he once had. But right now he was all she had.

He swore as he had to slow for a sharp turn around a large boulder. Those seconds he'd wasted before loomed larger and larger. If he didn't—

He jammed on the brakes just in time to avoid Tory's Jeep. It was stopped just around the boulder. And just behind a large, gray four-wheel-drive wagon.

And then he saw her. She was next to the Jeep's still open door. The other driver was beside her, a short but very muscular man with neatly trimmed blond hair. She was saying something to him, and she was obviously angry. And as Cole's truck skidded to a halt, the man reached out and grabbed her shoulders.

Fury shot through him like a lightning strike. He didn't even remember moving, but the next thing he knew he had the man up against the side of the Jeep, his forearm across his throat. The man twisted and kicked. Cole dodged him easily. The man's hands came up and clawed at the arm that was cutting off his air. Failing to budge him, the man pelted him with fisted blows that made him wince, but Cole didn't let go. Fear began to dawn in the man's eyes, but Cole held him fast. Until, at last, through the haze of anger, he heard Tory.

"—stop! Cole, don't, you're choking him!"

"Did he hurt you?"

"No, that's what I'm trying to tell you. Let, go, Cole. He's not who we thought he was."

Cole's eyes flicked to her. "He's not your trespasser?"

"No. I mean, yes he is, he's the one I saw, but he's not a trespasser. Not that way."

Cole eased up slightly. The man gulped in air. Color began to return to his face. But Cole didn't let him loose.

"Then who the hell are you?" he snapped at the man. "And what are you doing here?"

The man made a rasping sound. He obviously hadn't regained enough breath to answer. His eyes, the fear ebbing now, shifted as he glanced at Tory.

Tory sighed. "He's an investigator." Cole looked at her. She shrugged. "For the insurance company that covered John's Prize."

Cole turned his gaze back on the man he still held pinned to the side of the Jeep. "You got some proof of that?"

"In—" The man broke off, wheezing. "Inside jacket pocket," he finally said.

Cole reached up with his left hand, keeping his right arm in place across the man's throat. In a moment he'd pulled out a black wallet. He flipped it open, studied the plastic-encased card in the front slot that identified the man as an employee of Western Equine Associates, then, reluctantly, straightened up and let the man go.

"Damn cowboy," the man muttered.

Cole lifted a brow at him. "Better put a comma in that, or you'll be back where you were—" he glanced at the identification card again "—Whitfield."

"Sorry," Whitfield muttered, eying Cole much like a visitor might eye a zoo's tiger when they weren't sure the gate was locked.

Cole glanced at Tory. "He's the one you saw? Up on the hill?" She nodded.

Cole turned his attention back to the wary insurance man. "You're lucky, Whitfield."

"Lucky?" he said in astonishment, rubbing gingerly at his throat.

"If you'd hurt her—"

"I didn't!" the man yelped. "I was just trying to get her to listen to me."

"Next time keep your hands to yourself."

"Look, I'm just doing my job here—"

"Which reminds me," Cole interrupted, "why did you come back? For that matter, why were you spying in the first place?"

Whitfield's eyes narrowed as he looked at Cole. "Who are you? I haven't seen you around before."

"I'm just a hand who doesn't want to lose his new job because the Flying Clown goes under. I work here. You're the trespasser. Why?"

The man shrugged. "We had a lot of money to pay out on that horse of Lennox's. You don't pay off a policy that size without checking it out. Especially when there's a string of dead horses."

Cole couldn't refute that. "Which leaves why you came back today."

Whitfield hesitated. He glanced at Tory, then looked back up at Cole. Cole leaned forward a little, figuring right now his size was his most effective weapon.

"You might as well tell me now. It'll be easier."

He said it casually, without a hint of threat, but Whitfield blanched anyway.

"My bosses aren't happy. Three dead horses makes them very suspicious. The other companies too, for that matter, from what I've heard from the Alliance and Worldwide guys. The whole thing is being left open for further investigation. This has gone past simple carelessness or bad luck." He looked at Tory pointedly. "And we won't stop until we find out who's involved."

His insinuation was clear, and Tory made a small sound of distress. Cole suppressed the urge to go to her, to put his arms around her and reassure her everything was going to be all right. There were too many reasons why he couldn't. He couldn't promise it was the truth. She probably wouldn't believe him. And he had no right to hold her, anyway. Not after he'd told her, within hours of their fierce, explosive lovemaking, that he was walking out on her and her problem.

He shook off the sudden swell of emotion that threatened to choke him.

"Just what were you expecting to find?"

Whitfield shrugged. "A pattern. A reason. Anything."

It sounded vague, but Cole knew that many times surveillances were exactly that, hours of ceaseless watching, just waiting for the one piece that didn't fit, the one thing out of synch that might give you the clue you needed. More than once he'd broken cases on little more than a feeling gained by seeing one small thing that didn't match the rest of the picture.

"It's not us," Tory said suddenly, her voice strained. "We would never... We have no reason to...to kill our horses."

"A kickback out of a million dollar payoff is enough reason—" Whitfield broke off, apparently realizing he'd been careless with his words. From his point of view, he'd just warned a possible suspect they were being watched.

"You've got a big mouth," Cole told him warningly.

Tory was shaking. As soon as Cole realized it, so did she. He saw her try to control it, clenching her hands into fists, savaging her lip with her teeth. He wanted to strike out at anything he could blame for doing this to her.

"Let's go, Tory," he said, his voice sounding nearly as strained as hers had.

Whitfield seemed surprised as they began to walk away. "That's it?"

Cole looked back over his shoulder at the investigator. "Believe it or not, we're after the same thing, Whitfield. The truth about what happened to those horses. If you can find that by sitting up in those damned rocks all day, have at it."

He walked Tory back toward the Jeep. Whitfield watched them go, then shook his head and climbed back into his four-wheel drive. By the time they reached the door she'd left open, he was driving off.

They came to a halt beside the Jeep. She had the shaking under control, but tiny shivers still rippled through her. Again he had to suppress the urge to hug her, to reassure her.

"What were you saying to him when I got here?" he asked, trying to divert her.

"I thought...he was the one. I told him if he'd hurt my horses, I'd kill him myself."

Cole groaned. "Damn it, Tory, what if he had been? Just what the hell did you expect him to do?"

"I don't know. I was just so angry. All I could think about was—" her voice began to waver, and she gulped in air before she went on "—the horses, and what if M-M-Mac was next..."

She was shaking again, misery clouding her eyes, already weary from a night spent listening to him cry in his beer. Or whiskey, he amended.

His internal joking didn't work. And this time the urge was beyond suppressing. He reached for her and pulled her tight against his chest.

She didn't protest, in fact clung to him for support, as if she'd only been waiting for him to offer. In moments, as he wrapped his arms around her, the tremors that shook her subsided. It made him feel guilty that he'd denied the urge until now. It seemed such a simple thing, to return what she'd given to him last night, to simply be there when she needed it.

At the same time it made him feel strangely satisfied that he was able to comfort her simply by being here, simply by holding her, no more. It was a novel sensation for him, and brought with it an edginess he didn't recognize. But he had the feeling that if he thought about it a little, he'd find it was somehow related to that uneasiness he'd felt when he'd realized he was genuinely happy for Kyra.

He stood there for a long time, just holding her. And tried to deal with the unexpected fact that he was taking as much comfort from it as she was.

"Insurance guy, huh?"

Cole nodded at Hobie as he chewed on a bit of the sandwich he'd fixed; it tasted like sawdust. He'd gone to bed feeling like he could sleep for a week, but he'd awakened after a few hours feeling as tired as when he'd lain down.

He'd told Hobie about Whitfield, omitting the details of the encounter, including Tory's reckless solo pursuit of the man. Tory herself hadn't reappeared since going to her room this morning after a brief greeting to her uncle.

"Hmm," Hobie said thoughtfully as he picked up the last of his own sandwich. "Well, I suppose it can't hurt havin' another pair of eyes on the place. As long as he don't go seeing what's not there."

"So far, it seems like there hasn't been a damned thing to see at all." Cole stifled a yawn.

"Rough night?" Hobie said, his tone a cross between amusement and commiseration.

"Sort of."

Cole felt a twinge of contriteness as he said it. He wondered what Hobie would say if he knew. What he would think of the idea of his supposed trusted friend taking his beloved niece in a frenzy, on a desk, too frantic to even give her the comfort of a bed?

"Figured as much, when I got up and neither of you were back yet, and then you both come draggin' in like a couple of tuckered out calves and head straight for bed."

Cole opened his mouth, realized he could think of nothing to say that wouldn't make that observation worse, and closed it again.

"Haven't seen you look this ragged since..."

"The last time I tried riding Stomper?" Cole suggested wryly when Hobie's words trailed off.

"I was thinking more of the night that big brindle bull tried to make me a permanent part of the arena."

A shiver swept Cole at the memory. He'd been aboard the big, mottled brown-and-black bull, had even made his ride, although it hadn't been a particularly artful eight seconds. He'd been halfway off the huge animal in a semicontrolled dismount, when the nightmare of every rider came true—his rigging didn't release. Hung up, caught by the hand and tossed like a toy despite his size—or, he'd finally realized, because of it—he'd been kicked, slammed against the bull's massive sides and had his nose broken by a fierce toss of the massive head before he got free. But even through the pain, he knew the only reason he wasn't dead was that the crazy guy in the baggy pants and the fright wig had kept the bull, aptly named Crusher, from succeeding in his usual habit of crushing hapless cowboys against the arena fence.

And after two other cowboys had helped him out of the dirt and out of the now-furious bull's path, only the shocked gasp that came from the throats of thousands of onlookers told him the bull hadn't given up, had merely changed his target. He'd caught and tossed Hobie Flynn's light weight easily, and the man in the silly outfit had gone down and been trampled repeatedly beneath the deadly hooves before his partner could lure the animal away.

"Thought I'd cashed in my chips for sure, that time."

Cole tried to smile. "They told us you were a goner. But you were too damned stubborn to die."

"You got that right," Hobie agreed easily. "Sometimes stubborn's all that gets you through." He gave Cole a thoughtful look. "Don't know as I ever thanked you for all the time you spent sittin' with me while I was laid up."

Cole shrugged. "It was the least I could do. If you hadn't distracted that damned bull long enough, I would have been the one laid up or dead."

"That was my job."

"That," Cole said flatly, "was over and above."

Hobie grinned. "Taught you that duty stuff in the army, did they?"

"Tried to."

Hobie had done that for him, too. In those days, when he'd been alone and headed down the wildest path he could find—his parents dead for years, his grandparents, who'd raised him, recently dead within six months of each other—it had been Hobie who'd suggested the army. Cole had laughed at him. He was making a living—barely—rodeoing, and that was all he wanted.

"They'll teach you things you need to know. And put you through school, boy," Hobie had said. "And don't you ever think an education's not the most important thing in life."

Cole had laughed again, but his heart hadn't been in it that time. He'd once nurtured a dream of going to college, but there was so little money left after his grandparents had died, he'd thought it impossible. When he'd starting rodeoing, he'd hoped to somehow amass enough money to at least try, but he'd had a couple of bad years—when he'd been hurt more than he'd been well—and he'd finally, as Hobie had the year before, seen the sense in hanging it up. And, feeling utterly at loose ends with the world, he'd at last taken Hobie's advice. He'd never regretted it. He owed this man for more than just saving his life nearly at the cost of his own that day.

"You want to talk about it?"

Cole was snapped out of his reverie by Hobie's quiet words.

"Talk about what?" he asked warily.

"Whatever it is that's got you looking like you've been rode hard and put away wet."

Normally the familiar words would have made Cole smile. But he wasn't in the mood now. Not when he was trying to think of a way to tell this man he owed so much that he was walking out on him at the very time when he needed help the most.

"Hobie, listen, I—"

He broke off as a familiar car pulled up in front of the house. Kurt and Eric, arriving for their afternoon of work.

"Good," he muttered. "I've been wanting to talk to them."

He got up, conceded when Hobie waved him away from the dirty dishes he'd been about to pick up, and headed for the door.

The two boys looked wary when he hailed them, and appeared more than a little nervous as he approached. They'd been acting that way every time he encountered them, and it was past time he found out why. He didn't think it was just caution around a stranger; they acted oddly around Tory and Hobie, too. His every instinct told him they were hiding something, and it was time to find out what.

They looked doubly nervous when he ushered them into the tack room. He didn't blame them. He'd picked the place because it had only one door, and he didn't want either of them getting past him until he got some answers.

"Okay, boys," he drawled as he leaned against the doorjamb, well aware that he blocked the doorway quite effectively. "You want to tell me what the problem is, or are you going to make things difficult?"

Eric pushed his hair back from his eyes. "What problem?"

"Yeah," Kurt agreed, tugging on the gold cross dangling from his left ear, "what problem?"

"The one that has you two jumping like the mice Rocky's been chasing. The one that has you looking over your shoulder all the time."

They both voiced an instant denial, but they did it looking first at each other, then at the floor.

"Okay," Cole said, in a voice that was quiet, yet held a warning that made them both shift uneasily on their feet, "then how about whatever you did that means you can't look anybody in the eye? Let's talk about that."

Eric continued to stare at the floor. Kurt swallowed, his Adam's apple appearing to bounce up and down his thin neck. Bull's-eye, Cole thought. These two had been—or were now—up to something.

"You hiding drugs out here or something?" he asked.

Their heads came up swiftly. "No!" they exclaimed simultaneously.

He hadn't thought so, but he'd succeeded in rattling them, which was what he'd wanted.

"What, then?"

They looked away again. Cole sighed audibly.

"I can see this is going to be a long morning. Can't you just tell me what you did, and get it over with?"

"We didn't do anything," Eric protested.

"Nope, not nothing," Kurt agreed.

Cole lifted a brow. "A triple negative? That's protesting a bit much, don't you think? Come on, out with it."

Both boys glanced longingly over his shoulder at the sunlight, then returned to staring at the floor. Again Cole sighed. He straightened up. Both boys backed up a step, and for the first time began to look frightened. Cole wasn't above cashing in on that fear. He wanted some answers.

"Now, listen, guys, I didn't get any sleep last night, and right now I'm feeling a bit cranky. Don't go aggravating me. Let's not do this the hard way."

Both boys swallowed, and looked at each other again.

"Damn," Cole muttered, then reached behind him and slammed the tack room door shut. Both boys jumped. Cole took one long stride toward them.

"All right, all right," Eric yelped.

"Shut up," Kurt said.

"We gotta tell him," Eric insisted. "Besides, it was an accident."

Cole felt a little spurt of satisfaction. He'd been right, they did know something. "What was an accident?"

"That horse," Eric said. "The spotted one. We didn't mean to hurt him."

Arthur. The water-phobe Tory had told him about. He remembered the pain in her eyes, and wanted to pick up these two and bang their heads together.

"What happened?" he repeated, his voice like ice.

"We were just kiddin' around, with the little tractor. Racing around. You know, like they do on TV with those trucks? But stupid, here—" he gestured at Kurt, who raised a finger in obscene suggestion "—he clipped the water-line."

"It wasn't my fault! The thing skidded!"

"Go on," Cole said, his voice tight.

"We got scared. We were afraid we'd have to pay for it. So we just quick put the tractor away and took off."

"You just left the leak going?"

"We didn't know what would happen!" Kurt exclaimed.

"And I swear," Eric added urgently, "that horse was okay when we left. We saw him. He musta slipped, just like they said."

"And now he's dead."

Both boys stared at the floor. After a long, tensely silent moment, Eric asked in very subdued tones. "What are you going to do?"

"You're going to tell me exactly what happened that day, start to finish. Every detail. And then, if you convince me you've told me everything, I'll give you a head start before I tell the Flynns what you did. What they do then is up to them."

He leaned back against a saddle rack and crossed his arms over his chest. The two teenagers gulped, swallowed and at last began to talk.

She'd sworn she wasn't going to do it, but when she woke up late that afternoon from a restless sleep that had done little to relieve her weariness, Tory glanced out her bedroom window. When she saw Cole's truck still there, she wasn't sure if she felt better or worse. Better because he was still here, or worse, because it hurt so just to look at him and know that she'd already had all she would ever have of him. That it was no doubt all he had to give didn't make her feel any better, it only made her ache for him as much as for herself.

She went downstairs, wondering what she would say when she saw him. She found him stretched out on the living room sofa with his back propped up at one end by the cushions, his boots pulled off, legs crossed at the ankle. Even sitting up, he took up a lot of the sofa's length. There were files and papers scattered all around him, and he was holding one folder, studying its contents intently,

A movement, close to the floor, caught her attention. Rocky, half-hidden at the end of the couch, was crouched in an attack posture, his gaze fixed steadily on Cole's hapless boots. She started to smile despite herself, and in that instant the cat pounced.

Or tried to. Without even looking down, Cole's right arm came down in a smooth, unerring motion and swept the cat up off the floor. He lifted the startled animal, who made a growl of protest, and deposited him on the back of the sofa, where, Tory saw now, her old bandanna lay crumpled. Rocky glared at Cole, then settled down atop the now grubby red cotton square as if this had been his intent all along.

Cole had done it all without ever looking away from the folder he was holding with his other hand. But he had done it, despite his tough talk about the "damn cat", with exquisite care. Tory felt an odd little ache inside as she looked at them. That pang distracted her just enough, and the first words that came out of her mouth were the last ones she'd wanted to say.

"I thought you were leaving."

He sat up, the file folder in one hand, and what looked like the geological survey in the other. "Not yet. Something came up."

She looked at the chaos that surrounded him. She gestured at the piles. "Something to do with this?"

He nodded. "Would you...sit down for a minute? I need to talk to you."

There was something very odd about the way he sounded. Slowly, a nervous little knot of anticipation tightening in her stomach, she sat on the edge of the chair closest to the sofa.

"Talk to me about what?"

"I need you to answer a question, Tory. Honestly, and without getting mad at me for asking."

She felt like getting mad at him for saying that. But she reined in her instant reaction; she knew she was tired. But he was being so...careful? Gentle? Was it something so awful?

"What?" she finally prompted, unable to bear waiting any longer.

"Is there *any* chance, any chance at all, that somehow you could have gotten some bad feed that didn't get noticed?"

He was right. She was mad at him for asking. She opened her mouth to snap at him, then stopped. *Something came up*, he'd said.

"Why are you asking this?" She managed to say it evenly enough.

"I just need to know if there's any chance, Tory."

"Why? What came up? What happened?"

He let out a long breath, and his eyes closed for a long moment. Then, sounding resigned, as if he'd hoped but not expected her to just simply answer him, he told her.

"Eric and Kurt?" she exclaimed when he'd finished. "They broke that waterline?" She blinked back tears as she thought of the sweet-natured Appaloosa, and how he'd died.

"They were stupid. And they ran out rather than face the music. But I believe they didn't mean any harm."

Tory bit her lip, but the tears spilled over, anyway. "He was such a clown, such a personality. And he had such talent, once we found out where it was. Poor Arthur." She swiped at her eyes. "Why didn't they tell me?"

Rocky meowed plaintively, as if her tears had disturbed him. It was an odd sound to come from the rough-and-tumble cat, and it somehow helped her control herself. When she looked up again, Cole was looking as if he felt like Rocky sounded.

"They were afraid to tell you," he said. "Especially after Arthur had to be put down, and they knew it was partly their fault. And they kept coming back because they thought if they didn't, you'd guess it had been them. Among other reasons."

She looked up. "Other reasons?"

"They also said they felt bad. And that they like you, and Hobie." Cole's mouth twisted wryly at one corner. "Maybe I'm gullible, but I believe them. They're just a couple of not-too-bright kids whose fooling around ended up with them in trouble and someone else—Arthur—hurt. It's not the first time that's happened."

She sat quietly, trying to take it in. It was a long time before she finally thought to ask what she should have thought of right away.

"What does that have to do with what you asked me?"

He fiddled with the file he was holding. He opened it, stuffed in the geological survey, and closed it again. He glanced at Rocky, who was watching him with every appearance of intent interest.

"Cole?"

He looked up at her. "What it means," he said at last, "is that if Arthur was really an accident, it raises another possibility here."

"What do you mean? What possibility?"

His lips compressed for a moment, and Tory knew that he didn't want to say this, whatever it was.

"What possibility, Cole? Do you mean about what's going on here?"

He let out a short breath. He leaned forward, resting his elbows on his knees. He looked at his hands, then laced his fingers together. At last he looked at her.

"I mean the possibility that *nothing*'s going on here."

Chapter 16

Cole watched Tory pale as all the implications of what he'd
said raced through her mind almost visibly.

"What are you saying?" she whispered at last. "That it
is our fault?"

"Tory, listen—"

She whirled away from him and walked toward the window. She came to a halt, to stand silently staring outside.
Rocky yowled and stood up on the sofa back, arching his
back as if they were getting thoroughly on his nerves. Cole
couldn't blame him; after the past eighteen hours, his own
nerves were just about shot.

"Let me get this right," Tory said, her voice slightly
higher and much tighter. "Arthur was an accident. And
Firefly and John's Prize were simply colic induced by bad
feed we gave them. Is that it?"

"I didn't say that. I just need to know—"

She spun back, glaring at him. "You need to know if
we're the kind of people who are careless enough to let a
horse be given moldy hay, or spoiled feed?"

Cole let out a compressed breath. He'd known this would be unpleasant, had known she wouldn't take well to any aspersion cast upon their care of their horses—the thing her entire life revolved around. But he'd had to ask. Hadn't he?

Tory's eyes narrowed then. "No, that's not it, is it? You know Hobie, you know he would never let something like that happen. So you must think it's me."

"Tory, stop. I know you wouldn't—"

"Do you?" Her arms came up to wrap around herself, as if she suddenly felt chilled. Or very alone. "What do you know about me, really? That I'm Hobie's niece? Is that enough? Don't forget, I'm my father's daughter, too. And he doesn't care about anyone but himself."

She began pacing, still with her arms wrapped around herself, only now Cole couldn't help thinking it was as if she needed to hold herself together with her own hands. He knew the feeling, that sensation that you were about to shatter into a million pieces and only with a concentrated effort could you hang on.

Suddenly she stopped, and turned to face him again. "Tell me something, Cole."

Uh-oh. The moment she uttered those telltale words, the back of his neck began to tingle.

"Why did you . . . make love to me last night?"

He wasn't about to answer that. He wasn't even sure he knew the answer, beyond the obvious one that he'd been so hot for her he'd been about to climb the walls. He'd finally admitted it was more, much more than that. He'd had to admit it, so powerful were the memories of that encounter. But he hadn't quite let himself decide exactly what it was. Not yet. Because he had that same sense of racing headlong toward some inevitable end, and he was afraid it was going to be a pain he didn't want to face. Whether he'd carry that pain or cause it, he didn't know.

"Is it some kind of male thing?" she asked, the distress in her eyes digging at him. "How could you . . . want someone you think could be so negligent?"

"I don't think—"

She laughed, harshly, cutting him off. "Don't think? I've heard that about men and their hormones before. I didn't believe it. I guess I should have. Why else would you have—"

"Stop it!"

Cole stood up, dropping the folder he'd been holding and not caring. Rocky hissed in disgust, caught up his precious bandanna, and scrambled out of sight behind the sofa. His eyes fastened on Tory, Cole crossed the space between them in one stride. She watched him come, but didn't move. Oddly, it was then that it hit him that she had never backed away from him, never been afraid of him in a physical way, despite the difference in their sizes. The trust that implied, that no matter how angry he got, he wouldn't use his size or strength against her, staggered him a little. And when he reached out to take her hands in his, he was more aware than ever of how easily he could hurt her.

But when his eyes met hers, and he saw the raw uncertainty there, he realized he had already hurt her a great deal. The kind of wounds that would be very slow to heal, if they ever did. The knowledge ripped words out of him that he'd never expected to say to her.

"You're an incredible woman, Tory. You've got more nerve and brains and heart than anyone I've ever known. You're beautiful, on the outside far more than you realize, and inside in a way that will never fade away. How could I..." He stopped, drawing in a deep, shuddering breath. "I couldn't say no to you. Even though I knew I should. Even though I knew I didn't...deserve what you were giving me. I wanted it too much to be noble about it."

She lowered her eyes then, to stare at their hands. He didn't know if he'd made things better or worse. He was in unfamiliar territory, but every instinct he had was clamoring about very thin ice. He tried for safer ground.

"Tory, listen to me. I never thought you were careless, or negligent or at fault here in any way. But I know how hard you've been working, with Hobie being laid up. Too much work, and too little time. No matter how thorough you are, or how careful, something *could* have slipped through. You just can't do it all, not by yourself."

She continued staring at their hands for a long, silent moment. When at last she looked up at him, the distress in her eyes had been replaced by an expression he couldn't name.

"I've had to compromise," she admitted, quietly, obviously calmer now. "Things have had to wait, and the house isn't what it could be, and we've been eating whatever's fast and easy...but I would never compromise the horses, Cole. They come first. They always have."

He looked down at her, at first absorbing not her words, but that look in her eyes. But it wasn't until he put it together with the words that he understood. She was telling him, openly and honestly, the truth. She wanted him to believe her, but she wouldn't beg him to. And it wasn't simply pride, either. She wouldn't beg him, because if he believed what he'd said about her, she shouldn't have to. Hell, he thought, after what had happened between them, she shouldn't have to, no matter what he'd said about it being nothing more than sex.

And when it came right down to it, she really didn't have to beg. He believed her. Whatever had happened to those horses, it wasn't out of carelessness or neglect or being shorthanded or even exhausted. Tory might neglect her home, her car, even herself—probably herself first, he amended silently—but she would never, ever shortchange her horses.

She was as honest in this as she was in everything. As honest as she had been last night, when she'd given him a fierce, open, genuine response unlike anything he'd ever known. A response that had made him wish he had something to give her besides the raw, hot sex he'd promised. A response that had the power to heat him up now, at just the memory.

Abruptly he released her hands. Touching her while memories of last night swirled in his mind was making it far too difficult for him to concentrate. He backed up, and sat down on the sofa once more, amid all the information that seemed to complicate rather than clarify things.

"I know," he said on a long exhalation. "I'm sorry, Tory. It's just that I keep going through all this—" he nodded toward the scatter of papers "—and I can't make it work. It's like there's a piece missing."

Tory sank down on the edge of the chair. "So now what?"

"For starters, I think we can eliminate the kids." Tory sighed, but nodded. "After that, I can come up with half-a-dozen suspects, and every one of them has a motive. Sort of. But enough of a motive to justify this?"

"Sort of a motive?"

"Crain's got a ranch under a hell of a debt load, but he's making it. The insurance money made things easier, but he wasn't desperate for it, unless he was determined to buy you out. But it wasn't really enough to do that, so even if he'd succeeded in driving you out of business..." He ended with a shrug. Then he gave her a sideways look before he admitted, "Same with John Lennox. My people say he's strapped tight, but he's not going under."

It was the perfect opportunity for an "I told you so," but she didn't take it. She merely nodded for him to go on. After a moment, he did.

"Charlie Lee would like your land added to his, but he's not in a rush to lay out the money for it, not enough to try and drive you out, either."

"What about those men who threatened Hobie?"

He blinked in surprise. "He told you about that?"

Her mouth quirked. "Somehow I knew you wouldn't have told me, either," she said wryly.

"I just...knew he wouldn't want to worry you."

"I've *been* worried," she reminded him needlessly. "But no, he didn't voluntarily tell me. Last year one of them left an ugly message on the answering machine, about his father being killed. When I asked Hobie about it, he thought I meant the man who'd been hurt himself. So I knew there'd been two."

"Yeah. But when I checked with the office, they'd found out George Wheeler hasn't left Topeka in a year. Bart Brock has, but he just got married. That's not a likely thing for a man nursing a lethal grudge."

Tory sighed. "I always thought they were just striking out, anyway. How could they really blame Hobie?"

"That's what I meant by a 'sort of' motive. None of them are really strong enough." His mouth twisted in disgust. "Now if I could just combine a couple of these so-called motives, we might have something."

"And I suppose finding out that insurance man was the trespasser lets out my gold mine theory," she said glumly. "I guess it was silly, anyway."

"Still worth checking out." With his foot, he nudged the folder he'd dropped that held the geological survey. "But the satellite scan only shows a few alteration zones, and they're so small and scattered it wouldn't be practical to try and get anything out."

"Alteration zones?"

"Sorry," he said wryly. "I've been reading this stuff too long. That's an area where the original rock has decayed into clay. It shows up on an infrared band in the satellite scanner. They generally mean a mineral deposit of some kind."

"Oh. No gold mine, then."

"Afraid not, honey."

Her gaze shot to his face, and only then did he realize what he'd said. It had slipped out so easily, although it was an endearment he couldn't ever remember using before. He averted his eyes, and hastily began to pick up the papers he had begun separating into some kind of order, and had given up on in annoyance when it became clear they weren't any help. The silence drew out, and he began to feel silly, fussing with a stack of papers just to avoid looking at her.

"Don't worry, Cole," she said softly, "I won't hold you to it."

He froze. His eyes closed as something knotted up inside him, some searing bundle of nerves that had only come to life since Tory Flynn had walked into his ordered little world.

"Believe me," she added, in those same soft, unaccusing tones. "You hold yourself responsible for enough already. You don't need me adding to it."

His gaze shot to her face then. There wasn't a trace of mockery or sarcasm or even hurt there, just a gentle understanding that made him feel an absurd urge to drop everything, grab her and hold on for as long as he could. The thought of that, of night after night in her arms, of chasing away the demons with the sweet, purifying fire he'd felt last night, made him shiver inside.

And then, in a voice that told him worlds about how much she'd learned since last night, she said huskily, "Don't look at me like that if you don't mean it."

His breath lodged in his throat. His body surged in response to the breathy sound of her voice. He tried to fight it down, but it was swift and fierce, and would not be denied. "And if I did mean it?" he finally managed to say.

She shook her head slowly. "You don't. I can't heal you, Cole. You have to do that yourself."

She was so uncannily close to his thoughts that it shook him. "I wasn't looking to be healed."

"I know. You're not even willing to let it start. You can't do that until you think you deserve to heal."

"When did you become an armchair psychologist?" he snapped, telling himself he was on edge because his body wasn't listening to his mind, not because she was hitting too close to home.

She smiled, a sad little smile that made him wish he could pull back the sharp words. He stood up suddenly, lifting a hand to plow his fingers through his hair. She didn't move or speak, and finally he turned to her.

"I'm sorry."

She shrugged. "Me, too. I'm sure the last thing you want or need from me is advice."

His mouth twisted. "Let's not start talking about what I want from you."

If she noticed his omission of the word "need" she didn't react. "Why not?"

A harsh, compressed breath escaped him. He turned away from her, standing as she had, staring out the window. "For your own good."

He sensed rather than saw her get up. "Why don't you let me worry about what's good for me?"

He whirled around on her then, stalking over to tower over her. And again she didn't move, didn't back away. Which only, he thought angrily, proved his point.

"Because you don't, damn it! You charge ahead without a second thought. Last night in the barn, and again this morning, following that car alone—"

"But I thought he was the one who killed—"

"Exactly! You thought he'd already killed three horses, but you took off after him anyway! What if you'd been right and he'd decided to kill you to keep you quiet? How do you think Hobie would feel?"

"Hobie would have gone after him, too," she protested, although it sounded a little halfhearted.

"Fine," Cole growled out. "You're both certifiable."

She looked at him a moment before she said quietly, "You came after me."

He reached out and grabbed her shoulders. "Because I didn't want to go to another funeral, especially yours! I—" He broke off, realizing he was practically shouting. His jaw clenched in his effort to control his voice. "Damn it, Tory, I couldn't take that. Anything else, but not that."

She stared up at him, her eyes wide and still glistening from her earlier tears. Or new ones. Cole couldn't tell. She lifted a hand to slowly, with a feather-light touch, caress his cheek. Cole closed his eyes as a shiver of heated sensation rippled through him. He tried to stop, but couldn't help himself. He turned his head to press his lips against her palm. She didn't pull away. And he felt that sensation of heat again, only this time it caught, swiftly, as the fire he'd tamped down earlier flared up anew at her touch.

"Where's Hobie?"

He was already nearly lost in the haze that seemed to overtake him every time they touched, and her soft question startled him. "What?"

"Hobie. Where is he?"

"I . . ." He shook his head to clear it, but she kept touching him, and it only worked marginally well. "He. . .he said he was feeling better, so he took Buck out for a ride." Cole's brow furrowed as he added, "Said he knew when to make himself scarce, but he'd be back by dark."

"Oh, he does know." She smiled, a soft, age-old, womanly smile. Her hand slid around to the back of his neck, and her fingers tangled in the thick hair at his nape. "And dark is a couple of hours from now," she whispered.

"I know." The import of that smile—and Hobie's odd words—hit him at the same time his body surged to attention once more at the feel of her fingers in his hair. "Tory. . . ?"

"Could we try someplace more comfortable this time?"

Cole shuddered first at her words, and again as her fingers began to trace fiery little circles over the sensitive skin at his nape, sending a burst of heat racing down his spine. He grabbed her hand to stop the touch that had his already-far-too-ready body beginning to pulse with need.

"You're charging in without thinking again," he warned, his voice hoarse. "You'll be sorry."

"I took the biggest risk of my life with you last night," she said simply. "I'm not sorry. Even if you walk away tomorrow, I won't ever be sorry."

She was offering him exactly what he wanted, with no strings attached. So why, Cole wondered, was he so damned ambivalent about it? Why did he want to shake her, and tell her she was a fool for settling for what little he had in him to give? Why the hell did he keep wishing there was more? He'd never cared before, had resigned himself to being alone with his haunted dreams. Kyra had, unintentionally, made him even more certain of it. He wasn't fit for anyone, but especially not someone like Tory.

But then she lifted herself up on tiptoe to press her lips softly to his. And in that instant, when the fire only she had ever roused in him flared anew, he learned something else about himself: no matter how wrong he knew it was, he didn't have the strength to say no to this woman. With the barest of touches, the softest of kisses, she owned him.

He was halfway up the stairs with Tory cradled in his arms before he even realized the decision had been made. He barely had the presence of mind to remember the box of condoms in his room before he carried her into hers. The way she looked at him as she took out one of the foil packets made him remember what she'd said about putting it on him, and he groaned, low and harsh with anticipation.

He wanted it to be different this time, to make up to her for his haste, his frenzy, for taking her on a damn desk with little thought for her comfort. But need was surging through him, nearly doubling him over with its power, and he felt as if his entire body was clenching, trembling, already so close to explosion that he seriously doubted his ability to hold back at all.

His hands shook as he undressed her, and the way she shyly let him only added to his fervor. He couldn't help staring; she was so beautiful, her body rounded and feminine, yet taut and fit from simple hard work. Naked, she sat on the bed and scooted back to make room for him, her eyes never leaving his face despite the color rising in her cheeks. That combination of modesty and eagerness made him stifle another groan, and he stripped off his own clothes hastily.

He felt her gaze on him, and for the first time in his life he had doubts. He'd never taken credit for the way women responded to him. The structure of his body and features were a gift—or curse—of birth, nothing more. He knew that Tory knew that, in the same way she knew the most beautiful of horses sometimes lacked the heart to be great. And he realized he was scared to death that she'd look at him and see that he lacked that same kind of heart.

Then she reached out, her arm raised in an invitation he could no more have denied than he could have stopped breathing. He went down into her embrace with the knowledge that his legs wouldn't have held him much longer anyway.

"God, you're beautiful," he whispered to her, and proceeded to indulge himself in a leisurely exploration of her body, stroking, caressing, first with his hands, then his mouth. He teased her nipples to rigid sensitivity, then suckled her until she cried out. He parted the sandy curls between her thighs and stroked gently until she moaned and her hips began to move. Then he trailed his mouth over her belly to that same place, savoring her cry at the first touch of his lips and tongue.

He lingered, loving the taste of her, and the way she gasped every time his tongue flicked over that tiny knot of nerve endings. He stayed until he knew from her tiny little moans and the slick readiness of her flesh that she was as close as he had been. Only then did he stop and slide off her to lie on his side next to her. He lay still for a moment, not daring to touch her again, painfully aroused by her fiery response to his touch and trying to rein himself in once more.

After a moment Tory raised herself up on one elbow. "Cole?" she asked, in a tiny, confused voice.

"You didn't have much choice about what happened last night, or how," he said. "I was too..." He had to swallow tightly before he could go on. "I was just taking. Now the choice is all yours."

Her eyes widened, and her breath seemed to catch as she looked at him. Her gaze slid down his body, and color crept once more into her cheeks as she realized what he meant.

"I ... I don't ..."

I'm not a virgin ... not physically, anyway.

Her words that day by the spring came back to him now, and he only now realized what she had meant. Whatever her experience had been, it obviously hadn't included much in the way of her own choice in matters. He became even more determined that this time would be different. This much, at least, he could do for her. At least he thought he could; when she lifted her gaze, still wide-eyed and wondering, he wasn't so sure.

"Whatever you want, Tory," he whispered. "This time is for you."

The moment she moved, the moment she began to do as he had done, to run her hands over every inch of him, he knew he'd overestimated his powers of restraint. She touched, she explored, she stroked, rousing sensations that made him wonder if his heart was going to hammer its way out of his chest. She traced a path from the line of his jaw, down the cords of his neck, over his chest—flicking his nipples in a way that made him jump—then down over his belly until the deep muscles there rippled involuntarily.

Her hand slid around his side to delicately trace the web of intersecting ridges of tissue left on his lower back by shards of glass and bits of metal that had been propelled into him like shrapnel. She followed the caress with a slow, soft trail of kisses that made him forget the haunting memory that had risen up when she'd first touched the scars.

Every time she paused, every time she moved to some part of him that shouldn't have been—never had been—so sensitive, her caress made him shiver, until his hands were knotting the quilt beneath him in his effort not to grab her and drive into her with every bit of his barely leashed urgency.

When her lips brushed over his distended flesh he choked back a shout, but was unable to stop the convulsive buck of his hips. She paused, as if uncertain, then did it again, and then tasted him with a loving curiosity and sweet gentleness that this time ripped that throttled shout from him.

When at last she opened the foil envelope and fulfilled her promise, she made it one of the most arousing things he'd ever had done to him, extending her caresses far beyond the simply donning of protection. At last he had to stop her, reaching down and dragging her hands away.

"In about another ten seconds," he growled, "that's going to be academic."

She blushed, and the color deepened when he grasped her around the waist and lifted her over him. But when she felt the first probing touch of him, her expression changed, changed to a look so ardent that he nearly lost it right there. He let go suddenly. He raised his arms above his head on the bed, and locked his hands around the headboard's crossbar. Tory's gaze flew to his face.

"Take me," he grated, every muscle in his body thrumming with the building pressure. "Like I took you last night."

He meant it. And the fact astounded him. He wanted her to do it, to be as wild—as out of control—as he had been. He needed to know she was, that it wasn't just him, and he didn't care what the significance of that was, not now, not while she was hovering over him, naked and flushed and beautiful, not when he could see the rigid thrust of her nipples, still wet from his mouth, not when the tip of his aching shaft was nearly inside her, already throbbing from the sheer heat of her. Not when—

She moved then, suddenly, taking him in with one swift lunge of her hips. Her name burst from his lips as she suddenly enveloped him in her hot, caressing flesh, and he bucked violently upward, driving himself into her to the hilt. She cried out, not in pain but in sheer, wondering pleasure, and the sound ripped through him, tearing away walls he'd spent years building.

She rode him, hard and fierce and joyously. It was all there in her face, along with something else Cole couldn't deny and knew he should have known long ago. She loved him. She would never tell him, knowing he didn't want to hear it, but in these moments of intimate power, all masks were down.

In the instant he realized it, her body arched atop him, her head went back and she cried out his name. He felt the sudden clenching of her inner muscles, tightening around him, drawing him up into the fire with her. He let go, his hands grabbing her hips to grind her harder against him. She writhed atop him, and he thrust upward again and again, no longer caring that he was again out of control.

And then he rose up off the bed to clutch at her as he felt the explosion begin, searing him so deeply all he could do was hold on and ride it out, groaning her name with every boiling pulse of his body.

Moments later, still locked together, they fell back on the bed, Cole at last surrendering to the urge he'd been fighting so long, to just take Tory in his arms and hold on. She clung to him, as if welcoming even this tiny sign of need from him.

If you only knew, he thought, at last admitting that this was far more than he'd ever meant it to be, far deeper, far stronger, and he knew he'd hit that crossroads he'd been fearing. And he didn't know what he was going to do about it.

But for now, this was enough. Just to hold her, just to feel her nestled against him so sweetly as she drifted into the sleep they both needed. And if he couldn't stop from wishing for an endless string of times like this, he had only himself to blame. And only himself to blame for being such a fool that he went to sleep thinking it might be possible.

It was much later, when darkness had descended on the ranch, that the gunshot woke him.

Cole jerked upright in Tory's bed. Small caliber. Probably a .22. Rifle. Firing a long rifle round, judging by the slightly muffled popping sound. Hobie's, he thought.

Cole's mind absorbed and cataloged the information in the first two seconds, in the same time span he registered that it was full dark and he must have slept for at least a couple of hours.

And then the realization came that wiped all the rest from his mind: he was alone. Tory was gone.

Chapter 17

Panic seized him, knotting his stomach. He didn't have time for it, or for the realization it brought to him about his feelings for her. So, for the first time in five years, he didn't fight it, he acknowledged it. Admitted he was afraid. Afraid of what could happen, afraid that he wouldn't be good enough, or fast enough to stop it. And then he ignored it. Detached himself from it. He would deal with it later. Right now only one thing mattered. Tory.

He made himself move, yanking on his jeans and boots. He started down the stairs at a run, gave up halfway and went over the railing, landing in the living room with an impact he felt from ankles to hips. He ignored it and kept going.

The shot had come from outside, toward the barn. He resisted the urge to head straight toward it, and quartered around from the west, toward the foothills, where he wouldn't stand out against the night sky. He ran, hunkered over, but still moving as fast as he could. His heart was slamming against his ribs, and he knew it had nothing to do with exertion. If anything happened to Tory...

He nearly tripped over Rocky, who was crouching near the closed barn door, tail twitching furiously as he stared at the wood as if he could see through it, and didn't like what he was seeing. Cole swore silently as he recovered his balance, and crept a few feet farther on to where Mac's run jutted out from his stall, through the barn wall. The outer stall door was still closed, sealing the horse outside in the summer warmth, but there was a small opening in the upper half, and he'd be able to see into the barn.

He went up and over the pipe railing in one step and a leap, sacrificing a bit of speed for silence. Mac nickered softly, and Cole froze, waiting. He could hear voices, but couldn't make out what they were saying. But one of the voices was female. Again that nauseating fear rose up inside him. Again he didn't try to fight it down. He let it rise, and simply ignored it.

Slowly he crept forward, and slowly rose to peer through the opening.

It was a scene from his nightmares. Worse, because this time it was Tory, her face bruised, a brawny arm across her throat as a dark-haired, stocky man he'd never seen before held her helpless. And had a small automatic pistol jammed against her temple.

Not the gun he'd heard, Cole knew instantly. The blue-steel little gun looked more like a .380, not much for stopping power at any distance, but that would hardly matter to Tory if he fired it now. So the rifle was somewhere else. Had Tory had it, and dropped it or had it taken away when she'd found the intruder? Or had Hobie had it? And where was he?

He waited for the panic as the old deadly formula seemed to have been fulfilled. It didn't come. The detachment held. Only then did he realize he was reacting automatically, as if at the sight of Tory in such danger everything except what he needed to function had shut down. The sweat, the hammering of his heart, even the fear didn't even register now; all that mattered was Tory.

Rocky yowled softly from near his feet. It was a measur
of the cat's upset that he took a rare swipe at Cole's boot
now, while he was in them. Cole wanted to hush the ani
mal, but was afraid of being heard. Mac wasn't so careful
he snorted at the cat, laying his ears back. The man holdin
Tory looked up.

He had to move now. The man was getting nervous. Col
could see it in his eyes, in the sheen of sweat on his face. An
nervous men did stupid things.

Swiftly he went back over the top rail and around to th
tack room. Rocky, cutting under the pipe fence, was ther
before him, almost tangling with his feet again. Dodging th
persistent cat, he grabbed a heavy rasp and jammed it into
his back pocket. He spotted the shearling jacket he'd throw
in the corner, grabbed it and put it on. He swiftly stuffed
sharp leather awl in one pocket, and a sawtooth curry blade
bent double and fastened, into the other. He didn't like th
idea of having to get close enough to use any of his make
shift weapons, not when the man had a gun on Tory, bu
they were all he had. Then he went back to the barn door.

And again Rocky was there ahead of him, nearly trip
ping him.

Damn cat, Cole swore again silently. He moved to swee
Rocky away with his foot. The cat spat, and took anothe
swipe at Cole's boots.

Cole froze. An idea glimmered in his mind. He woul
have preferred a .45, or better yet, Kyra's preferred seven
teen-shot, .40 caliber Glock, but he didn't have either. A
he had was himself. Himself and a cat more used to fight
ing than purring.

It was crazy, but it just might work. It might give him th
split second he needed. Shaking his head once sharply at th
sheer insanity of it, he bent down and scooped Rocky up i
his left hand.

The cat made a startled little sound, almost a yelp. Col
pulled the jacket closer over his bare chest and arrange
Rocky in the crook of his left arm, tickling his ragged ear a
Tory always did.

"Be useful for a change," he muttered. Rocky looked at him with those pale-blue eyes. And then, surprisingly, he settled down as if Cole made a habit of carrying him around like a pampered lap cat. But he looked back with a pained expression as Cole began to whistle, casually, a light, cheerful off-key melody, as if he hadn't a care in the world.

Tory heard the unexpected sound a moment before the man holding her whirled, yanking her with him as he turned toward the barn door. Cole, she thought, listening to the cheerful sound of his whistling. God, he was about to walk in on this crazy man, and he didn't know he had a gun. She sucked in a breath as the barn door began to slide open.

"Don't even think about yelling, sweetie, or you're dead," the man hissed in her ear as he dragged her back into the darkness below the hayloft. "And so's the old man."

Tory's eyes flicked to where Hobie lay so dreadfully still against a stack of hay bales, his small rifle lying a few feet from his outflung hands, where it had fallen when the man holding her had hit him with a rake handle. *Please, be alive,* she prayed silently. She turned her head to stare back at the opening door, as if she could warn Cole simply by wishing hard enough.

Cole strolled in casually, still whistling that absurdly carefree tune. Incredibly, Rocky was nestled in the crook of his arm, and Cole was petting the cat as if he were a beloved pet instead of a barely tolerated nuisance. And more amazingly, Rocky was accepting it. In fact, Tory realized with a shock that for an instant made her forget her precarious position, Rocky was purring.

The man holding her tensed as they stood there in the shadows. Cole kept coming. He never looked up. He just sauntered into the barn, his attention on the cat, as if oblivious. Still whistling.

Cole was never oblivious.

It came to her then that he knew exactly what was going on. She could only hope he knew what he was doing.

"Hey!" Cole stopped at Hobie's feet, blinking as if coming out of a daze. "You al' right, ol' buddy?"

If she hadn't heard him when he'd been drunk, she would have thought he was now. But Cole drunk didn't slur his words. They came out slowly, carefully, exactly, if not perfectly sensible. She didn't understand, until the man holding her relaxed slightly. He obviously thought he was dealing with a drunk who wouldn't be hard to handle despite his size. And maybe he was hoping Cole was so drunk he wouldn't even notice them, and would stagger on outside without ever knowing they'd been there, hidden in the shadows. And she knew then that that was exactly what Cole wanted him to think.

Cole staggered comically around to look at Hobie from the other side. This put him a bare six feet away from where they stood in the shadows of the hayloft.

He was practically on top of Hobie's rifle.

Even as she thought it, Cole moved. He flung Rocky into the shadows where they stood. The cat let out a small roar. He clawed madly, catching her captor's pant leg. The man jumped, startled, loosening his grip on her. Tory jerked away as hard as she could. She heard a tearing sound as her shirt gave way at the shoulder seam. Her captor swore. Rocky yowled, digging through cloth and into the man's leg and boots with needlelike claws.

And then Cole was there, Hobie's rifle in one hand, the other reaching to pull Tory behind him. The man suddenly realized he was in trouble. He tried to bring the gun around. Cole grabbed the heavy horseshoer's rasp and swung it hard and fast. He caught the man's hand and wrist in a blow sharp enough to numb fingers. The gun flew off to disappear into Mac's stall.

The man turned to run, but Rocky dug in again and the man yelped.

"I think you'd better stop right there," Cole said, leveling the rifle at the man. It looked like a toy in his big hands. "And put your hands on top of your head. This thing may only be a twenty-two, but it's semiautomatic, and I could put enough rounds in you fast enough to mess you up pretty good."

The man looked at him, as if gauging his seriousness.

"Believe me," Cole suggested, his voice taking on a deadly quiet tone that made even Tory shiver. But his left arm, around her shoulders now, steadied her. "There isn't a court in the world that would convict me, not after you tried to kill two people."

"I didn't try to kill anyone!" he squealed as he put his hands atop his head. His voice was absurdly high for such a stocky, muscular man. Or maybe he was just nervous, Tory thought, looking down the barrel of Hobie's rifle. Hobie. She turned, but Cole held her fast.

"That old guy, he just snuck up on me," the man protested while he tried to kick Rocky loose. The cat hung on. "I didn't hit him that hard."

"Hobie," Tory repeated, still trying to pull away. Cole hesitated, looked over at Hobie's sprawled form, then let her go. She ran to where Hobie lay. She knelt beside her uncle. When she touched him, the older man groaned.

"Thank God," she whispered.

"You'd better be thanking God," Cole told the man. "If he's alive, maybe I won't kill you after all."

The man paled then. He took a step back. Rocky let out a little yowl, and Cole glanced down at the man's feet. "Eelskin boots," he said in satisfaction. "Close enough." He lifted the rifle to his shoulder.

The man gaped at him. "You can't just—"

"Can't I? You're a trespasser, a burglar and armed. Like I said, I'd never even look at charges for taking you out. Especially if mine's the only story that gets told. And I put that little gun of yours back in your hand."

Tory's gaze flicked to Cole. He looked deadly serious. She wasn't sure that he wasn't. And moreover, she wasn't sure she cared. She supposed that made her unforgivingly vengeful, but she wasn't sure she cared about that, either. The man had been in Mac's stall.

"He was carrying a bag when I found him," she said. "It's over there." She pointed at a small canvas bag that lay a couple of feet away.

"Oh?" Cole said with obvious interest. He stepped forward and ran his hands over the man in a quick search. Then he swiveled around, keeping the rifle trained on the man while he put himself between him and the bag. He turned toward Tory, but she'd already read his intent and scrambled over to pick up the bag.

It was open, and she could see an odd arrangement of what appeared to be an industrial-weight extension cord and a length of wire with two large alligator clips on it. She held it up, puzzled, then looked at Cole. His face had gone rigid; he obviously knew what the contraption was. He turned back to the man. Tory set the bag down with distaste, even though not knowing what it was.

"What do people call you, besides stupid?"

The man twitched slightly, but his eyes never left the rifle or Cole's finger, which rested inside the trigger guard threateningly. He'd got smart enough to hold still, and Rocky, with a low snarling sound and a final claw at the man's boots, let go. He sidled over to Tory as if to check on her, then strutted back to sit at Cole's feet, as if quite proud of a part well played.

"Al," the man muttered at last.

"Okay, Al," Cole said in a voice like chips of ice, "give me one good reason why I should let you walk out of here alive."

The man's eyes widened again. "I didn't do anything to die over!"

"Neither did those horses."

Tory quivered at the sound of Cole's voice. The cool, barely controlled fury of it was also the voice for her rage, and in that instant she felt as close to him as she had in their most intimate moments.

The man didn't answer. His eyes were wide with fear, but he didn't speak. After a moment, Cole shrugged and lifted the rifle.

"Wait!" Al blurted.

Cole lifted a brow at the man. "The way I look at it, one of two things can happen here. You tell me who put you up to it, and maybe I go take it out of his hide instead of yours. Or you don't, and I take it out of yours, then go after your boss, anyway. I'll find him either way, it just may take me a little longer. And, of course, you'll be dead."

Al's eyes flicked from Cole to Tory, incredibly, as if he were looking for help. Tory thought of John's Prize, being carted away like so much dead meat. She thought of Firefly, stiff and cold in her stall. And Mac. She thought of Mac, and how close he'd come to being next.

"If he doesn't do it," she said, "I will."

"You won't have to, girl. *I* will."

It came from Hobie, propped up on one elbow, rubbing the back of his head with the other hand. The words were shaky, but blessedly rational. Cole shot them both a look, relief clear on his face. Then he looked back at the severely stressed Al.

"No, that's going to be my pleasure," he said mildly.

Al swore again, a profanity particularly appropriate to the barn they were in.

"What do you say, Al? You're in more trouble than you ever dreamed of. You gonna go down alone?"

Al swore, that same short word again. Tory helped Hobie get to his feet, then stayed close so he could lean on her. Cole glanced at them, gave Hobie a nod, then turned his attention back to Al.

"It's up to you, man. The deck's stacked, and it ain't your way."

Finally, Al broke. "I don't know who he is."

"Nice try." Cole lifted the rifle to his shoulder.

"No, man, I swear! I never saw him, never heard his name. It was all on the phone, you know? Somebody gave him my number. He called, we set up the hit. I called him back, told him where to send the money."

"Hit? Just one?"

"Yeah, at first. Just the big brown horse, with the white nose."

Cole glanced at Tory. "John's Prize," she whispered. "Then what?"

"Guy called again. Wasn't happy about it this time. Wanted a second horse hit."

"And he told you which one?"

"He just said the one in the next stall."

Firefly, Tory thought. And then she realized what that meant. Whoever was giving this man his orders knew what horses were in what stalls. Her gaze flew to Cole's, and she saw the same knowledge there.

"What about Arthur?" she asked. "The Appaloosa?"

"The spotted one? Yeah, that was the third call. He said it didn't really matter, just to clear with him which one I was gonna go after before I did it."

That made no sense, Tory thought, fighting that sick feeling again. "But why like that? Why his leg?"

Al shrugged. "Seemed better. I saw that puddle there, and figured it'd be a good cover. Anybody'd believe a slip and fall in that muck."

"Anyone except someone who knew the horse hated water," Cole said softly.

"Huh?" Al was clearly puzzled.

"Never mind," Cole said. "What did you mean, when you said he wasn't happy?"

"He just sounded like he didn't like any of this. I got the feeling he wanted to quit after the first one."

"Why?"

"How the hell do I know? I don't ask questions, long's I get paid."

"I'll bet," Cole said acidly. "Who gave him your name?"

Fear flared in the man's muddy brown eyes. "Oh, no. I give him up, I'm as good as dead."

"You're as good as dead, anyway," Cole reminded him bluntly.

Al stubbornly shook his head. "I'd rather be shot."

There was no denying that whoever the connection was, Al was more frightened of him than of dying right here. Even Tory could see he wouldn't talk. "Maybe you can still save your life," Cole offered after a moment. "What was the number you called this guy at?"

Al hesitated. Cole sighed, as if he were getting mightily tired of this.

"How about this, then, Al, old buddy. You don't tell me a thing, and I let you walk out of here."

Al blinked.

"And then," Cole elaborated easily, "we just let the papers know that you rolled over like a big dog, on the guy who hired you, and the guy who gave him your name."

Al paled.

"Yeah," Cole mused. "By the time he finds out you didn't squeal, you'll already be dead, won't you?"

Al spat out an obscene phrase that made Cole's mouth twist sourly. "No thanks. You're not my type. The number, Al. Now."

In disgust, he rattled off a number. Tory felt her breath catch.

"Good boy, Al." Cole glanced at Tory. "I'll just have my people trace—"

He broke off, and Tory knew what must be showing in her face. "Don't bother," she said dully. "I know the number."

Cole's eyes narrowed. "Tory?" he prompted when she didn't go on.

She sighed. "It's John's. His private line."

Lennox glared at Cole as he burst past a protesting secretary into his inner office, but his angry expression faltered when Tory came in right behind him.

"Tory? What's this about?"

"It's about," she said coldly as she slammed the bag holding the electrical wire down on Lennox's desk, "this."

Lennox stared at the bag and its contents. When he looked up, there was no doubting that his perplexity was genuine.

"You don't even know, do you, Lennox?"

Lennox rose to his feet at Cole's tone. "I don't know who you think you are—"

"You want to know what this is, Lennox? It's a murder weapon, that's what it is. Real slick. Take one friendly, trusting horse. Clip these on him—" he held up one of the large alligator clips "—in two different places far enough apart. Plug it all in. Zzzzt. One dead horse."

Lennox paled.

"That's what he used on your horse, to make sure. The bad feed was too much of a gamble, by itself. So he electrocuted him. No telltale signs, and with the bad feed in the horse's belly anyway..." Cole shrugged, then laughed harshly at Lennox's ashen face. "What's wrong? You don't mind ordering it done, but don't bother you with the ugly details?"

Lennox looked at Cole, then at the door behind him.

"Don't even think about it," Cole advised. "Even if you made it, Hobie's already talking to the cops. You're history, pal. Insurance fraud is damn near a hanging offense these days."

Lennox sank back down into his chair, obviously shaken.

"Why, John?" Tory implored him, anguish seeping into her voice. "Did you really need money so badly?"

The man seemed to collapse like a popped balloon, all his charm and style vanishing. "I'm going to be sued," he said tiredly. "Or rather my new software company is. By some little shoestring operation who says the core of our new commercial publishing program was lifted from a program they copyrighted a year ago."

"Was it?" Cole asked, merely curious.

Lennox glared at him, not answering. Which, he supposed, was an answer in itself.

"So," Cole said, "it's going to take a lot of money and a battalion of lawyers to save your butt. And a million plus in insurance will pay for a lot of billable hours, eh, Johnny?"

"How could you?" Tory cried. "Why couldn't you just sell him if you needed money?"

"There wasn't time to find a buyer willing to pay what I needed," Lennox said, avoiding looking at her.

Cole wished there was a way he could cushion this, but he knew there wasn't.

"And why the others?" Tory asked, sounding strained. "Just to cover your tracks? Arthur, and Firefly...they weren't even yours. And God, Mac, how could you—"

"That wasn't my idea!"

Cole lifted a brow at him. "Now there's a defense for you," he said acidly.

"It wasn't! None of the others were. I wanted to quit after the first one. I had enough money to buy me time until I could raise some more."

"Buy you time?" Tory said furiously. "With an innocent animal's life?"

For the first time Lennox looked at her. "There are more important things than your precious horses!" he snapped. "But you never could see that."

"Bruised your ego, did she, Lennox?" Cole's voice was coolly taunting.

"Let's just say her taste is questionable," he said pointedly, giving Cole a furious look.

"Because I didn't want to play your game?" Tory asked. "You know you only wanted me because I turned you down."

Lennox leaned back in his chair. The charm had vanished now, and the cold, calculating schemer was out in the open.

"Not exactly," he said.

Tory looked suddenly thoughtful. Cole didn't know what was going through her mind, but her expression made him uneasy. So did Lennox's.

"Was all your flirting to keep me...what, occupied? So I wouldn't ask any questions? Is that why you were so kind after Firefly died, even more than when John's Prize died? So you could head me off if I started getting too close?"

"I wasn't flirting," Lennox said. "I was dead serious. And if you weren't such a little fool, you would have realized that. You missed a hell of a chance, Tory. We could have really made it big, together."

Her brow furrowed. "Big? You're already big."

"Not as big as I want to be. You were going to do that for me."

"How? Don't tell me you want the Flying Clown, too?"

Lennox laughed. "That little place? Hardly. I had my eye on much bigger game. Much, much bigger, my dear."

Tory looked utterly perplexed now. But Cole felt a sudden sinking in his gut that had little to do with what they'd learned, and everything to do with what he was very much afraid was about to land on them.

"Bigger? I don't understand."

"That's because you're hopelessly naive and can't see past those damned nags of yours."

"Tory," Cole interrupted, "I think that's enough. It's over. Let's get out of here."

Lennox looked at him with interest. "Well, well, cowboy. Are you guessing, or are you smarter than I gave you credit for?"

"Let's just say I know about that little trip you took three months ago."

Lennox's gaze flicked to Tory. "And you haven't... shared that information?"

"There's no point to this, Lennox."

"Oh, yes, there is. I'm not taking the fall for this alone."

"Fine. But not now."

"Protecting her? How gallant. But she's going to find out, anyway."

Tory looked from Lennox to Cole and back. "What are you talking about?"

"I suggest," Lennox drawled, "that you ask your father."

Chapter 18

"You didn't have to come."

Cole gave her a sideways look. "Would you rather I hadn't?"

Tory turned her gaze back to the bank of buttons on the elevator-control panel. Her fingers tightened on the file folder she held. "I didn't say that."

"It was me or Hobie."

"Concussion or not, Hobie would have killed him."

"What makes you think I won't?" he asked wryly.

"Because," she retorted in the same tone when the doors slid open, "I may do it first." She started out the doors, then turned back to look at him. She held up the folder. "Thank you for this."

He shrugged. "It didn't take long, once they knew what to look for." He gave her a crooked smile. "Besides, you already thanked me."

Yes, she had. Fervently. Physically. Last night. And she had done it knowing that if things went as planned today, it would be the last time.

She couldn't think about that, couldn't deal with the idea of Cole walking out of her life, not now. The doors began to slide closed, and she reached out to stop them. She walked out of the elevator and turned right.

"You sure you don't want me to go in with you?"

"Afraid I really will kill him?"

"No. But I'm afraid you'll want to, and that's not a pleasant feeling."

"I just want him out of my life. Forever. And I need to face him alone." She stopped walking. He came to a halt beside her. She looked at him. "But thank you."

He shrugged, as if it were nothing. And perhaps, to him, it was, she thought sadly. She started walking again. She was still feeling sticky. In five years she'd gotten used to the dry heat of California. The sweltering humidity of Houston's summer made her feel like she was trying to breathe underwater.

Yes, it had been years, but she remembered as if it were yesterday. The walls were still an elegantly muted gray, the carpet a matching gray trimmed with a pale mauve. A strip of dark-oak baseboard, trimmed with brass ran along every wall. And an elegant brass plate proclaimed this as Flynn Financial Associates.

"Nice," Cole muttered.

"My father knows the value of the perfect facade."

Cole gave her another sideways look. "Speaking of facades, does all this—" he gestured at the perfectly appointed offices "—have anything to do with the way we're dressed?"

"Everything," she said, not even caring that he'd seen through her decision to wear her most faded jeans and T-shirt, her work boots, and one of her old baseball caps with her hair pulled up through the back. She looked like she'd just walked off the ranch instead of an airplane. So did Cole, having obligingly followed her lead. He hadn't shaved, and he'd worn his battered straw hat, pulled down low over his eyes. "I gave up playing my father's game years ago."

She pushed open the double-glass doors of her father's reception area.

"Yes, may I help—Miss Flynn? Is that you?"

"Don't bother to announce me, Gladys. I'll just go in."

"But—"

Tory walked past the polished, normally poised woman who now wore an expression of amazement.

"I wouldn't try to stop her just now," Cole advised the woman.

Tory smothered a wry laugh as her father's imperturbable secretary gaped at Cole. Dress clothes or tight jeans, the man had the impact of a racing train. She shoved open the doors marked Private with the inevitable brass plaque.

The man behind the desk was talking on the phone, and leaning back in a large, expensive-looking chair that matched the tone of the rest of the office. Everything was rich, deep-toned and reeked of success. When the door slammed shut behind her, he spun the chair around in annoyance.

"Gladys, I told—" He broke off, staring. "I'll get back to you," her father said into the phone, then stood up.

He was still drop-dead attractive, the gray at his temples only accenting his looks. His face was chiseled and tanned, and still looked as if he should be charming millions on a movie screen. Instead, she thought grimly, he charmed thousands in person, into doing just about anything.

"Victoria! What a surprise." He looked like he meant it.

"It shouldn't be."

She saw the change come over him, saw the practiced facade slide into place, hiding his surprise at her sudden appearance with a veneer of charm.

"Well, then." Jack Flynn smiled that charming smile. "To what do I owe the pleasure?"

"It's not a pleasure visit."

"Now, look, baby," he said soothingly, "I know we said some things we didn't mean when we spoke last, but—"

"It's over, *Daddy.*"

"Why, Victoria, darlin', what are you talking about?"

"I know why you wanted me home so badly."

He managed to look hurt. "You're my little girl. Of course I wanted you home, where you belong."

"You've never wanted anything that didn't directly benefit you."

"Now, that's no way to talk—"

"If you'll drop the act, Daddy, we'll get this over a lot sooner."

"I don't know what you mean."

"John Lennox."

For the first time, her father faltered. But he recovered quickly. "I don't know—"

"Don't you? You don't remember meeting him that day you came to the ranch to try and coerce me into coming home?"

"Now, baby, I wasn't coercing—"

"And you don't recall him flying here to Houston three months ago, to present his little plan that would help both of you?"

For the first time in her life, she saw her father look nervous. And she knew Cole had been right that day, when he'd said that if they could only combine a couple of those motives, they'd have one strong enough.

"Now, Tory," he began, and then she knew how nervous he was. He never used that name.

"He gets his insurance money, and what he thinks is a foot in the door here. In return for you bankrolling the murder of my horses, he promises . . . what?"

"Baby, you know I would never—"

"Could it have something to do with this?" She tossed the file folder down on his desk. "It's a copy of mother's will. Funny how I never knew what was in it."

Her father stared at the folder on the desk as if he thought she was bluffing. She had to give him credit; he took it smoothly.

"I only wanted to spare you pain, baby. Besides, you got all her things."

"Yes, I did, didn't I? Including her interest in this firm. Odd how I never knew about it."

"You were so upset when she died, baby. It went into a trust, anyway—"

"Until I was of legal age," she said flatly. "And you administered it, didn't you? You and some lawyer you had in your pocket. So how is it that I never knew that I've had the right to vote with those shares since I was eighteen?"

"It's business, baby. I knew you weren't interested—"

"Maybe not. But don't you think I would have been interested to know mother had left me enough that you can't make a move without it?"

"Your mother—"

"It was really *her* business, wasn't it? It was her father's, he built it, and when he died he left it to her. Is that why you married her, Daddy? For the business? How long did it take you to charm her into putting you in charge? About as long as it took for you to put your name on it?"

"You don't understand, baby. I—"

"I understand that she didn't give you a controlling interest. She held enough back so you couldn't do anything alone, even though she went along with you on everything. But then she left it to me."

"You have it all wrong, Victoria."

"Do I? Maybe you should know I had a long talk with John Lennox. You're birds of a feather, aren't you? He was looking at me like you must have looked at mother. What did he promise you? To deliver my real proxy? My signature on a permanent power of attorney for those shares? By romancing your naive little girl?"

"This is—"

"The truth, Daddy. For once. I know about the merger with Bowman and Carter. Afraid they'll look too closely? Afraid they'll find out what you've been up to all this time, voting shares you had no right to? Afraid I'd find out about those papers that I never signed? The ones you forged when I turned eighteen?"

Flynn sat down abruptly.

"Did you really think I'd come back? Even if you'd succeeded in putting us out of business, did you really think I'd come back and just be your little girl again, doing everything you told me? Maybe sign over my shares to you without thinking twice?"

Her father's expression was so openly calculating she wondered that she had ever been fooled by him. He looked like a little boy trying to judge exactly how much he could get away with. And in that moment, she knew Cole had also been right in the guess he'd made after he'd read all the information his staff had compiled in the past three days.

"I'd say," Cole had told her, "that in five years, he's realized you're not the girl who left him, and never will be again. That you aren't ever coming back. So he had to try something else. Something he knew would get to you. So he hit you where he knew it would hurt the most. The horses."

Just thinking of Cole now, as she stood here facing her father, the difference between them was so clear to Tory she shook her head at her own blindness. Next to her father, Cole stood out like a thoroughbred beside a flashy show horse without a trace of heart.

"So that was it," Tory said. "You figured if Hobie and I got in enough financial trouble, I'd come to you for help. And you'd... what? Magnanimously offer to buy my shares? Or were you even going to be that honest? Maybe you'd just offer me a loan, only it wouldn't be loan papers I'd be signing?"

Something in her father's eyes flickered, and she knew he'd even considered that, an outright fraud perpetrated on his only daughter. Pain flared within her, but not for herself. She'd been numb to her father's maneuverings for a long time.

"They were just horses, Daddy," she said. "Just innocent, dumb animals. Not very important compared to all this." She gestured at his opulent office. "I guess that makes it all right. The means to an end."

Maybe she wasn't as immune as she thought, because her next words escaped against her will.

"Why, Daddy? Why didn't you just ask me to sign everything over to you?"

"Ask?" he said, in astonished tones. "Nobody signs over a fortune like that just for the asking."

"That's where you're wrong, Daddy. Where you've always been wrong. I would have given it to you. I already have all I ever wanted."

The intercom on his desk squawked. "Mr. Flynn? There's a Detective Munoz here to see you."

"Detective?"

Tory took some small amount of satisfaction in the look on her father's face.

"Yes," she said. "He's very interested in the connection between you and one Al Patterson. And I think you'll find some investigators from assorted insurance companies hot on his heels."

Flynn sank back in his chair looking thoroughly deflated. The door to the luxurious office swung open and three men stepped inside. When they started toward her father, Tory turned her back on the man at the desk and started walking away. Cole would be outside, she told herself. In seconds she would be with him, and he would hold her, at least for now, letting her lean on his strength. She needed it; she felt utterly drained.

"Victoria!"

She stopped.

"It's all a misunderstanding, you know. You'll see. Everything will be fine. After all, no one really got hurt."

No one really got hurt.

She thought of Hobie, still woozy from a blow that could easily have killed him. She thought of her own moments of terror, when she'd been certain the man she'd interrupted was going to kill her. She thought of Cole, fighting his own demons to try and keep her father from succeeding. Then she thought of John's Prize. Firefly. Arthur. And even Mac.

She kept on walking, never looking back.

* * *

"You're going to be a wealthy young lady, with your share from the sale of the company," Hobie said as he sipped at his morning coffee. They'd taken to having it outside on the porch, savoring the coolness before the summer heat set in for the day.

"All I want is enough to buy Mac." Tory meant it. She wanted nothing to do with whatever money came out of the sale of Flynn Financial, except for whatever it took to make the liver chestnut—who had so narrowly escaped death—hers. "If you want it, you're welcome to it."

"Well," Hobie drawled, "I might think on takin' enough to pay Cole. Now that we can, I mean."

It was the first time Cole's name had been mentioned since the day two weeks ago when he'd loaded up his truck and driven out. He'd said very little after the confrontation with her father, to anyone. He'd been there for her, he'd propped her up and brought her home. But then he'd disappeared, and it had been Tory who had been left to explain the extent of her father's perfidy to Hobie. And only when she'd gone to investigate Rocky's unusually loud yowling, did she find that Cole had been packing to leave.

"I have some things I have to take care of" was all he'd said. "Things that have waited too long already."

She'd watched him, wondering if he'd even meant to say goodbye, or had he just planned to slide out when she wasn't looking. What did you expect? she had chided herself. A change of heart, a declaration of love? Don't be more of a fool than you've already been.

In the end, she'd said the only thing she could.

"I hope someday you find what you need to heal, Cole."

Hobie's voice drew her out of the painful memory. "What do you think, Tory? He did this on his own time, you know."

Yes, she did know. Now. The first vacation time he'd taken in five years. Since little Timmy's funeral.

"Fine," she said. "Send him a check as soon as the money comes in."

She was proud of the steadiness of her tone. She wasn't so proud of the ineffectiveness of her efforts to keep her heart intact. She'd told him she couldn't heal him. She hadn't realized she was going to be wishing for the talent to heal herself.

"I'm sorry about your dad, honey."

Honey. Instantly she was back to that day Cole had called her that, and the look on his face that had told her he hadn't meant to say it at all. It had given her so much hope, that slip of tongue. Hope that had obviously been unfounded.

"He was your brother, too," she said, pushing away the memory.

Hobie chuckled ruefully. "That's something I tried to forget a long time ago."

There was a long silence. Tory set the porch swing moving again; she seemed to have a need lately for the comforting monotony of the movement.

"You know," Hobie said at last, in that tone that told her his words were going to seem simple, but really wouldn't be at all, "It's hard, losing your trust in somebody. But it's harder to lose your trust in yourself. It takes a man time to put that right."

She lifted her eyes, not to Hobie's face, but to the spot on the porch railing where Rocky had always been. She even missed the raggedy-eared cat. She'd never found her bandanna. She wondered idly if Rocky still had it.

"I told him he'd never lost his nerve. Just his way."

Her gaze shot to Hobie's face. It was unlike him to be so direct, and this obvious reference to Cole startled her. When she saw the warm concern, and the touch of sadness there, she knew she hadn't hidden a thing from him.

"I guess it was only to be expected," she said ruefully. "Silly little country girl, and the big, high, wide and handsome cowboy. Like mother like—"

"Stop it, Tory. You're not like that. You know you're not. And Cole isn't like your father."

"No. No, he's not. I'm just not sure what he is." She set down her cup. "I'm going to go check on that steer that got caught in the wire last week. That cut may need some attention.''

As she rode out, she tried to concentrate on the good things. Hobie was healthy again, nearly back to full strength. She had the small, sad comfort of knowing that John's Prize and Firefly hadn't really suffered through a deadly bout of agonizing colic, but had gone quickly, with little pain. They still had the ranch, and the news about what had really happened had, fortunately, traveled almost as quickly as the bad news had. She still had Mac, and soon he would be hers for keeps.

And she would probably never see Cole again in her life.

She wasn't quite sure how that could be a good thing, except that perhaps it would make it easier to get over him. And since it was her own fault that she was in this mess, she supposed she should count herself lucky. It wasn't as if he'd lied to her. He'd always said he'd be leaving. He'd never made her any promises. Except one—he'd promised her raw, hot, out-of-control sex. And he'd certainly delivered on that one, she thought ruefully. Beyond her wildest dreams, he'd delivered.

For a few minutes, finding the steer she was looking for was a distraction. The rangy brindle was one of her favorites, because he never seemed to tire of the game of training new horses, and could always be counted on to give a good lesson or two to the horse who'd never had a live one at the end of the rope before. After a day spent in a corral with that steer on the line, the rope around the animal's belly instead of his horns, a horse learned real quick how to pivot, and to keep his legs braced and the rope taut, or he spent a lot of time flopping in the dirt.

She found the small herd, as she'd expected, by the spring. She steeled herself against the flood of memories that assailed her, and singled out the brindle steer. Mac obligingly and efficiently cut him out of the group, instinctively dodging to left or right in the instant before the steer went that way in his efforts to get back to the group. Noth-

ing distracted Mac, not even the buzz of a small plane flying overhead.

Tory felt a small glow of eagerness that had been sadly
missing from her life in the past two weeks, they hadn't really begun arena work, but Mac already had the knack. He
got her close enough to where she could see that the wire cut
the steer had acquired was healing cleanly enough. She
pulled up and let the steer scamper back to the herd.

"Pretty soon, boy," she told Mac, patting his dark, sleek
neck. "Pretty soon we're going to start working these guys
hard. You're going to be the best cutter to come along in a
long, long time. You'll be—"

She broke off as the small plane she'd heard before cir-
cled back, so low that the cattle scattered in fright at the
noise. She glared up at the neat, red-and-white, twin engine
craft, looking for the registration number. The local air-
strip was only a mile away. She'd call as soon as she got back
to the house and find out who this idiot was who thought
playing buzz the bovines was a fun way to pass the time.

With this in mind, a half hour later she rode up to the
house instead of the barn. She slid to the ground and loosened the cinch a little. Mac was fairly cool, since they'd
walked most of the way back, so he could stand ground tied
in the shade in front of the house while she made the call.
Then, she thought as she rounded the corner of the house,
she'd give him a bath and—

She saw the red flag of her bandanna first. Then Rocky.
He was perched in his usual spot on the porch railing, ban-
dit-marked face turned to the sun. As if he'd known the
moment she saw him, those eerie blue eyes opened. And
then, incredibly, he winked. The cat actually winked, one
eye distinctly closing.

And sprawled on the steps, long legs out in front of him,
battered strawhat pulled low over his eyes, was Cole.

"I figured that flyover would bring you back here," he
drawled.

Tory's brows shot upward, anger overcoming her shock
at his sudden appearance. "That was you? Are you crazy?"

"In a manner of speaking. It's a long hike from that landing strip in this heat, and in boots. Especially with a cat who's so lazy he wants to be carried all the way."

"You walked?" she said, her anger dissipating at the thought. That *was* a long, hot hike on unforgiving asphalt.

"Every toasty inch of the way. Not much traffic around here on a Tuesday morning or I would have hitched a ride."

He pulled off his hat and ran a hand through his hair. She studied him for a long moment, afraid to read anything into his unexpected return. But why on earth would he bring Rocky? And why the plane?

That, she decided, was a safe enough question. "Why the plane?"

"I was testing the commute."

"The . . . what?"

He got up then, crossed the distance between them in a stride, and took her hands in his.

"I didn't mean to be gone so long, but I . . . had some things to take care of," he began.

"So you said. In fact, that was about all you said."

He winced. "I know. I didn't mean to . . . hurt you. I just had to . . . work through some things." He lowered his gaze. "I went to see Lisa."

Timmy's mother? Tory's breath caught. "You did?"

"And Sherry. And Jennifer. The kids, too. I had to . . . put it to rest. You were right, Tory. I couldn't even start to put this behind me when I didn't think I deserved it. I had to face them, to talk to them . . ."

"To get permission?" she asked softly.

He let out a long breath. "Yeah. I guess." His mouth twisted. "They didn't blame me. They never had." He swallowed then, as if his throat were tight. "I may never get back that edge. I may never be what I was. But it doesn't matter, anymore. I can live with who I am, now. Thanks to you."

"Oh, Cole . . ."

He looked at her then. Intently. "Did you mean what you said?"

Caution rose up in her. "What I said?"

"That you ... hoped I'd find what I needed to heal."

"Yes," she said quietly. "I meant it."

He let out a compressed breath. "I prayed every mile of the way here that you meant it. Really meant it. Because I did find it, Tory. I found it here. With you."

She bit back her instinctive cry of joy. She'd been a fool before over him, she wasn't going to let go again without being certain she knew exactly what he meant.

"For the first time since ... Timmy, something mattered to me enough to ... to get past the memories. That night, when I knew you were in danger ... I knew I couldn't let it stop me. That no matter how scared I was that it would happen again, that no matter how sick the memories made me, I couldn't let them stop me. Because nothing was as important as the possibility of you being hurt. Nothing."

"'You never lost your nerve, only your way,'" she quoted softly.

Cole's gaze moved to her face as she repeated Hobie's words. "You showed me the way back. And you made me want to come back." He took a deep, quick breath. "I love you, Tory."

Her chest and throat tightened unbearably at the sound of words she'd never, ever thought to hear. "Oh, Cole ..." She swallowed and tried again. "I ... I love you, too."

"I know," he said softly.

Her eyes widened. She'd never said it, she knew she hadn't, she'd been far too aware that he wouldn't have welcomed it, then.

"I knew it that last night. I should have known long before." He smiled ruefully. "But I was too busy trying to convince myself I didn't love you."

She hugged him then, fiercely, full of joy at the knowledge that this man who had so much strength on the outside had at last rediscovered it on the inside. He held her close, so tight it was hard to breathe, but she didn't care. She only cared that it was Cole, that he'd come back, and he was beginning to heal. And he would regain the trust in himself Hobie had spoken of, too. She would see to that.

It wasn't until he tilted her head back with a finger under her chin that she realized tears were spilling down her cheeks. He brushed them away with his hands, those big, strong hands that could be so gentle it took her breath away.

And when she looked up at him, she thought she saw the sheen of moisture in his own eyes.

"So," he said, in a tight voice that told her she'd been right, "do you think you can stand to take us on?" He nodded toward Rocky, who was sunning himself unconcernedly on the porch railing. "I'm afraid it's a package deal. I can't seem to get rid of him."

"Don't even try." Tory laughed through her tears of joy. "He's a wizard, haven't you noticed?"

"A wizard in a cat suit?" Cole shook his head. "No, he's just a pest. He's been moping around for two weeks now. Refusing to eat. Dragging that old bandanna of yours everywhere. Giving me dirty looks. Tearing up the house. Clawing up my boots again. With me in them."

She smiled up at him. "Maybe he was trying to tell you something."

This time Cole smiled back. It was a soft, loving smile she'd never thought to see from him. "Maybe he was. Maybe he has been all along, and I was just too stupid to see it."

"No." She reached up to touch his face. "You're many things, Cole Bannister, but stupid isn't one of them."

"Does that mean...yes?"

Tory tilted her head to give him a sideways look as she realized she wasn't really sure what he was asking for an answer to. What had he meant by "take us on"? She'd been so elated that he'd come back at all, she hadn't cared until this moment. But now she found she did care.

"I don't know," she said. "What exactly was the question?"

He looked suddenly sheepish, as if he realized he'd been a little vague. Then, urgently, he said, "Marry me, Tory. Soon. Please." He stopped, running a hand through his hair. "Sorry. That wasn't very romantic, was it?" He let out a little breath. "I've . . . never done this before."

"It was fine," Tory said, hugging him. "Believe me, it was fine."

He went very still. "Then . . . that is a yes?"

She leaned back again to look up at him. "Only if Rocky comes with you," she said solemnly.

He looked at her as if he wasn't sure she was teasing. Then he chuckled, as if he'd decided it didn't matter. "If that's what it takes. I'll even feed the pest."

No more damn cat, Tory noticed, but wisely didn't comment. "Good" was all she said. "It will be good practice."

Cole blinked. "Practice?"

She nodded. "Hobie wants grandnieces and nephews, you know."

Cole looked stunned. Then, slowly, like the dawn rising over the eastern hills, he smiled. Then grinned, a silly, sappy kind of grin she would have thought impossible for him when she'd first laid eyes on him.

"Yeah. This place needs some kids," he said, with a note of wonder in his voice that touched someplace very deep inside Tory. And it made her suddenly think very seriously about what had begun as teasing. And the thought of Cole's baby made her feel very odd indeed. Warm and shivery at the same time.

"Maybe," she said, feeling suddenly shy, "maybe we should practice that, too."

And as quickly as that, the heat was there in his eyes.

"Yes," he said, sweeping her up in his arms. "Maybe we should. A lot." He lowered his head to kiss her, with a gentleness that belied the fierce need that showed in his face. "And maybe, after about fifty years or so of practice, we'll have it right."

Tory smiled up at him, every bit of her love glowing in her face. Cole kissed her again.

Rocky watched them go inside, gave a little nod of his head that looked oddly like it was in satisfaction. Then he turned his face back to the sun.

*   *   *   *   *